IRELAND

THE CLADDAGH

Book One:
The Loyalty of the Leprechauns

THE CLADDAGH

Book One:
The Loyalty of the Leprechauns

M.R. Street

turtle cove press

Tallahassee and Ochlockonee Bay, Florida

This is a work of fiction. Names, characters, business, events, and incidents are the products of the author's imagination. Any resemblance to actual persons, living or dead, or actual events is purely coincidental. Places mentioned are either fictitious or used fictitiously. Do not try to find the Great Faerie Ring; you will not be successful.

ISBN 978-1947536333

Library of Congress Control Number: 2023940325

Printed in the United States of America

The text of this book was typeset in Palatino Linotype and Eagle Lake

Cover design by Allison Street

10 9 8 7 6 5 4 3 2 1   1 2 3 4 5 6 7 8 9 10

To everyone who is searching for their magic:
You will find it if you look within yourself

Contents

The parts of the Claddagh are three:
Friendship, Love, and Loyalty

Prologue: Captured

Across a long meadow, the walls of the Great Faerie Ring rose out of a forest of oaks. The fortress of ancient monolithic stones meant Sanctuary for Seamus Greenapple and his family—if they could reach it.

From his perch high in a willow tree, the only tree to be found in the broad, grassy expanse of pasture, Seamus gazed through his telescope and calculated the distance to the Faerie Ring, and how fast he and his family could get there.

His wife, Agnes, stood at the base of the tree; their two boys huddled close. Three pairs of owl-wide eyes stared up at Seamus. "Are ye sure we've been followed?" Agnes asked. "I've not seen nor heard anything unusual."

"Aye, dear. Two hunters. They've been on our trail since at least Ballyhaunis."

"How did they find us? We used the protective curtain that Marnie taught me. Did I na do it right?"

"You did it brilliantly, dear. But once we broke camp, the protective curtain fell. That's when the dogs picked up our scent."

"They've dogs?" A shiver shook Agnes's shoulders.

"Aye. A brace, by my reckoning." Seamus lithely leapt to the ground.

"Da?" the younger boy asked. "Will they turn us into gold?"

A groundswell of dread coursed down Seamus's spine. He would not let his family see his fear. "Nae, Lucas. We're Greenapples.

We'll not let that happen, will we?"

A whisper-thin breeze wafted through the willow's boughs, rippling the leaves and sending a wave shooshing through the slim tendrils. The breeze carried an unwelcome passenger: a low, baying howl.

Agnes clasped her hands in fists over her heart. "The hounds."

Seamus grabbed up Lucas in one arm. His telescope dropped to the ground.

The older boy bent to pick it up.

"Leave it, Ardeen," Seamus said. "We've no time."

Ardeen cast a worried look at his mother.

She read his silent question and responded with confidence, "I may not be a fancy-footed footballer like you, Ardeen, but I'll keep up."

"Let's go!" Seamus and his family fled across the meadow toward the safety of the Great Faerie Ring.

They were almost to the edge of the wood when a large man with a dark, bushy beard, a brown cheesecutter cap, and a grey tweed jacket stepped out from behind a massive oak tree and pointed a shotgun square at Seamus's chest.

Seamus slung Lucas off his hip and shoved the boy behind his back. Agnes pushed Ardeen next to his brother and stood shoulder-to-shoulder with her husband.

"Well, well," the hunter gloated, adjusting his cap with one hand while keeping his weapon trained on Seamus with the other. "What have we here?"

A second man, narrow as a stick, stumbled toward the family from behind, clutching the leashes of a pair of snarling Irish wolfhounds.

Seamus's shoulders fell. They were surrounded.

The stout man jabbed Seamus's chest with his gun barrel. "Do ye have the mark?"

2

Seamus clinched his jaw. "What mark do ye mean?"

"Dunna play dumb with me, eejit. I know Leprechauns have a tattoo that signifies your clan. Stupid of ye to brand yourselves. Anyone who knows of the practice can check for it. Roll up your sleeves."

"He thinks we give ourselves the tattoo," Lucas whispered to Ardeen.

Seamus shot the boy a warning glance, then rolled his sleeves up to his elbows. He extended his arms toward the hunter, showing first the wrist sides then the backs of his arms.

"I dunna see no mark, Mr. Lynch," the skinny hunter said, craning his neck to see around the boys.

Lucas pulled at Ardeen's coat sleeve. "He dinna see Da's tattoo!"

"It's on his shoulder, same as mine," Ardeen whispered back.

The man called Lynch glared over Agnes's shoulder. "You lads! What are you whispering about?"

Ardeen and Lucas jumped at the man's tone.

"Nothing, Sir," Ardeen said.

"Nu-, nu-, nothing," Lucas said.

"'Nu-, nu-, nothing,' eh?" Lynch's voice was full of ridicule. "Come out here where I can have a look at your arms."

Agnes stepped forward, her eyes glaring. "Keep away from my boys, ye overgrown playground bully."

"All right, then," Lynch said, poking the barrel of his gun at Seamus's breastbone again. "There's more than one way to skin a cat."

Both of the hounds started barking and growling. They jerked their heads around, looking for their favorite prey.

"Mr. Lynch, please dunna say 'c-a-t' in front of the dogs," the skinny man said.

"Finbar, ye culchie! Houl yer whist." Lynch smacked the thin man with his cap.

Finbar twisted the leashes around his wrist to gain better

control of his dogs. "Sit!"

The dogs obeyed, but continued snarling. The muscles in their massive haunches twitched as if ready to spring, either at the Greenapples or at any "c-a-t" that might be slinking about.

Lynch stepped closer to Seamus. He jabbed the barrel of his gun under Seamus's throat. His noxious breath blasted Seamus. "*Are you Leprechauns, like we was told?*"

"Who filled your heads with talk of Leprechauns?" Seamus scoffed. Beads of sweat dribbled down his cheeks from his brow to his chin.

"He's been talking about Leprechauns ever since that lad told us where we could find—"

"I said, shut your pie hole, Finbar!" Lynch reeled toward his hired man. The dogs immediately leapt to their feet and growled. Lynch waved the gun at them and growled back. The dogs tucked their tails and scooted closer to their master for comfort and protection.

Lynch re-trained his gun on Seamus. "I asked ye a question."

"No offense, but I think the sun must've gotten to ye," Seamus said with a chuckle. "Do we *look* like Leprechauns?"

Finbar scratched his wispy beard. "He's not little nor green. Nor has he pointy ears."

"An honest mistake," Seamus said. He held out his arms to herd his family to the side. "Ye'd best let us be on our way."

"I think he's right, Mr. Lynch." Finbar pulled the dogs back to give the Greenapples room to walk away.

Lynch ignored his fellow Leprechaun hunter. "Hold it! I know your laws," he barked at Seamus. "You canna lie to me. And dunna try to confuse me with your blarney. You think because ye can fool this eejit, you can fool me, but ye're sore mistaken, you are. Now, tell me afore I blow a hole in your chest, and the slug takes out the lad behind ye as well. *Are. Ye. Leprechauns?*"

Before Seamus could answer, Agnes swatted Lynch's gun toward the ground. "Aye, we are that. And by the looks of you, 'tis about time some luck came your way, even if you did have to hunt it down."

Lynch stepped toward her until he was breathing down on her head. She pushed her chin up in defiance.

"I could send you to meet your maker right now, you old cow."

"You'll do no such thing," Agnes replied. "For a dead Leprechaun will na bring you one red cent, much less the pot o' gold at the end of the rainbow."

"Lucky for you. And your family."

"Ha!" Finbar barked. "Lucky!"

Lynch glared at him, and he cleared his throat and cast his eyes down.

"What will happen to us now?" Lucas whispered.

"Mother Cass will find us," Ardeen whispered back.

"She's an old woman! She canna search for us."

"She'll send someone."

"What's all that jabbering? You'll all stay quiet and do as I say," Lynch ordered through clenched teeth. The dogs snarled as if reinforcing Lynch's words.

A rush of wings caused them all to look skyward as a flock of doves took wing from the branches of the oak trees behind Lynch.

Seamus gazed at the sentinel trees. Not forty meters into the wood, and they would have been safe within the walls of the Great Faery Ring.

The doves fluttered overhead, and before the last one flew away, it dropped a grey blob on Lynch's shoulder.

Seamus cupped his hands to his mouth. "Coo-coo! Cock-a-coo," he called to the birds as they disappeared into the distance. Hoping they understood his message, and knew who to deliver it to, he whispered, "Our lives ride on your wings."

5

Chapter 1: Dune's Journey Begins

The end of the line—again. In all the years Dune had trudged and traipsed the annual trek to Doolin for the Kelly Ceili, the view never changed. It consisted of the moonlit backs of his younger brothers, Gilroy and Travis—Travis with his ever-present fiddle case jutting out of his knapsack—and his little sister, Fionn. Ahead, the shadowy figures of his mother, Maureen, and his other sister, Ayne, toed the line. Always in the lead: Dune's father, Paddy.

Dune would much prefer to be at the head of the line as his family travelled along under the blanket of stars, rather than taking up the rear where his job was to keep his three youngest siblings in line. Why couldn't his mother or Ayne ride herd on the wains while he helped his father at the front of the line? Or even took his father's place? After all, Ayne was fourteen and, he had to admit, mature for her age. She could handle babysitting duty.

Paddy constantly harped that Dune needed to take on more responsibility, especially now that he was almost sixteen. Dune doubted he could show his father how responsible he was if he was always relegated to the back of the line, his one duty: Watching the wains.

Not that they were much trouble. At seven and ten years old, Gilroy and Travis mostly just picked at each other. As long as they were quiet about it, Dune let them have their fun.

Five-year-old Fionn, on the other hand, was a chatterbox, especially when she saw or thought about an animal of any kind.

Fionn thought about animals, and therefore talked about animals, incessantly. Dune repeatedly had to shush the ebullient little girl. Any sound that could alert Humans to their presence would spell disaster. Fionn knew this, as did they all. It had been drummed into them from the time they were wee wains as a matter of survival. But it was not in Fionn's nature to be quiet.

For now, all was calm, and the monotony of the night caused Dune's mind to wander. He thought about the Ceili, and what the annual family reunion held in store.

The Ceili was a time to catch up with cousins whom he hadn't seen all year. Then there were the sporting contests. He and his mates from Yulnear would win the Gaelic football championship yet again, no doubt.

The week would be filled with music and dancing, to be sure; it was, after all, a ceili. Although he enjoyed the music, Dune preferred to watch rather than participate in the dancing. His thoughts drifted to a girl he had seen at last year's Ceili. She was part of the Appalachian branch of the family, honorary members of the Clan, some of whom were descended from Mother Cass's goddaughter. The girl—really a teenager about his own age—had long hair like corn silk and eyes like the shimmering blue forget-me-nots that grew around Sraheens Bog. And how could he forget her? As she twirled and skipped and laughed, others in the dance called her name, "Kyna, dance with me!" and "Kyna, you're a natural at step dancin'!"

He shook thoughts of her out of his head and replaced them with eagerness for something he was more familiar with—football. No matter how many times he stepped onto the pitch, it always exhilarated him: The scent of the grass, the feel of the ball when he plucked it out of the air, the way his muscles moved for the save, almost before he commanded them to. His teammates—and even players on rival teams—said his skill was magic.

And this year held another event, the Presentation of the Clover, a ritual only held every twenty-five years. In a solemn ceremony, Mother Cass, the clan Matriarch, would announce a new Keeper of the Clover.

Paddy had held the title for twenty-five years. But like it or not, Paddy would soon have to pass the responsibility of Keeper over to someone else. Mother Cass, who had appointed Paddy Keeper of the Clover, would name his successor at this year's Ceili. The annual family reunion that brought together Kelly kin from all across Ireland—as well as members of the honorary branch of the family from American Appalachia—was always fun and exciting.

This year, Dune could feel his excitement build with anticipation. On whom would Mother Cass bestow the Clan's greatest honor? As Paddy's son, Dune hoped he would be next in line. That would show his father he could handle responsibility!

A covey of birds burst out of the grass to the left of the narrow lane, flapping and fluttering in front of him, bringing Dune out of his reverie. He ducked instinctively. "Blasted fool birds."

"Where be Fionn?" Dune's father asked, his voice muted but urgent.

Dune straightened up. "Right here, Da—"

But Dune's little sister was no longer in her place in line ahead of him.

Frantic, Dune backtracked down the path at a jog, scanning both the path and the grassy banks on either side, thankful for the light of the waxing gibbous moon.

"Fionn," he called, a strained whisper, as loud as he dared. "Answer me, Fionn!"

A tall patch of grass shook and seemed to giggle. Dune parted the curtain of grass and found a tiny, freckled face bordered by bright red braids and lit up by a wide grin.

"Look at this little ginger rabbit I've found," Dune said. "Dinna

I ken better, I would think you were my sister, Fionn. But of course, my sister Fionn would *never* cause her family such panic by leaving her place in line and hiding in the grasses."

Dune checked his surroundings for any movement, listening for sounds that would indicate the presence of intruders. Satisfied that no-one other than his own family was about, he picked Fionn up and hugged her tightly. She hugged him back, wrapping her arms around his neck and her knobby-kneed legs around his waist.

"You dinna panic," Fionn whispered. "You found me straightaway."

"But a Human could have found you first," Dune scolded. "And then our whole family would be in danger."

Fionn's grin disappeared. Her eyes grew wide and filled with tears. "I dinna mean to cause trouble! I was just so bored."

"Promise you'll na be trying a trick like that again, little rabbit."

"I promise, Dune." She gave her brother a hug. "Is Da mad?"

"As a hornet, but I will na let him sting you."

Dune carried Fionn back to where the family waited.

"Explain yourself," their father rumbled.

"Dunna be mad, Da. She promised not to run off again."

"Mad? At Fionn? She is but a wain and does na know better." Paddy's voice rumbled with anger, though he maintained a whisper. *"You* are the one who is almost a man, or so you are always telling me. *You* are the one supposed to watch out for the family. My job is to lead." He placed his fingertips against his chest. "That is why I am at the head of the line. I protect from the front. Your job is to make sure no-one—" Paddy jabbed Dune's shoulder with an index finger.

"Goes." Another jab.

"Astray." Another jab.

Paddy pulled Fionn from Dune and set her on the ground. "Is that so difficult?"

9

Dune looked at the toes of his dusty boots as he felt his cheeks grow hot. "No, sir."

"Then try to do a better job of it!"

"Yes, sir."

Dune knew his father was right. He had an important job and his family's safety depended on him doing it well. Yet resentment festered in his chest at the way Paddy treated him. He would be sixteen soon, and could very well be the next Keeper of the Kelly Clover. Maybe then his magic would manifest itself. Most Leprechauns had discovered their magic by around their thirteenth birthday. Dune was the only member of his football club who still hadn't found his special magical talent. He checked his arms and shoulders every morning, hoping to see the tattoo of a four-leaf clover—his clan's insignia—that would confirm the manifestation of his magic.

If those things came to pass—the arrival of his magic and being awarded Keeper of the Clover, his father would have to agree to some changes in the family hierarchy.

Not only would Dune adjust the line-up on these cross-country treks, he would insist on having his own room, even if he had to build it himself. Even if he had to move out of his family's enchanted underground tree and find a place of his own. Of course, he would remain in western Ireland. He would need to stay close-by to fulfill his role as protector of the whole clan.

As they trudged on in silence, Dune kept a close eye on the wains—Fionn, Gilroy, and Travis, all of whom behaved without further incident—until the sky pinked in the east and the breeze carried a new sound that caused the family to freeze in their tracks.

"Dogs," Paddy said.

"Puppies?" Fionn asked hopefully.

"Shh, lass." Dune scooped her up in his arms and whispered in her ear, "Hunting dogs."

"Everyone to the middle of the road," Dune's mother ordered. She pulled a small velvet pouch from the folds of her dress. "Dune, help me."

Dune handed Fionn to Ayne, but the little girl struggled to cling to him.

"I want to come with you," Fionn cried.

"Nae, you must stay with Ayne," Dune whispered. "You know how scared she is of dogs. You must keep her calm. Can you do that for me?"

Fionn nodded. Her lower lip trembled as she embraced her sister.

"Ayne! This way," Paddy gestured for his oldest daughter to join him where he stood with Travis and Gilroy, a point in the road that would be the center of the circle Dune and Maureen laid out.

Dune dashed to his mother's side. He scanned the road and the surrounding pastureland for any sign of the hunters and their dogs. If anyone—dog, human, or any other creature moving on two or four feet—were to approach through the pasture, he would see the tell-tale bending of the tall grasses marking their path. The road was fairly straight in both directions, and they were at the top of a small rise. This would allow him to see anyone coming up the road, but it also meant that they were fully exposed, and would be until his mother's magic rose like a concealing curtain around them.

Maureen selected a stone from her pouch, rubbed it in her fingers. "Take this," she said, placing a smooth grey stone, etched with a rune, in his hand.

Five more stones followed, each carved with a different rune. Dune cupped his hands together to hold them all.

"Hours of the clock," Maureen said. "Counter-clockwise from … here." She darted to the edge of the road, bent at the knees, and laid a rock on the ground at her feet.

Dune knew the spot marked three o'clock, and that twelve

would be to the north. He put his rocks at two, one, twelve, eleven, ten, and nine, while Maureen placed rocks at four, five, six, seven, and eight o'clock, creating a circle of stones around the family.

"One more." Maureen pulled a pink quartz rock from the velvet pouch, this one as flat and smooth as a skipping stone. No runes were etched into it, and there was nothing uncommon about it except for a perfectly round hole, carved straight through one end by eons of rushing water from the creek in which Maureen had found it. She placed the quartz under the three-o'clock stone.

Turning to face east, then south, west, north, and east again, Maureen whispered the protective words of her rune spell. Something inside him urged Dune to join his voice to his mother's, but he dared not. He knew the chant, but had not quite memorized it. If he misspoke the words, he could banjax the whole thing and leave his family exposed to danger. He didn't even want to think about how badly it could turn out. So he stood quietly, watching his mother as she carried out the ancient ritual, following along in his head.

> *Echo, echo, hear my call.*
> *Dim the lights and raise the wall.*
> *Dark-on-dark the curtain rise,*
> *Conceal us from unfriendly eyes.*

"Everyone, be sure you are inside the circle," Maureen cautioned. Ayne pulled the wains into the very center of the circle.

"Dune!" Paddy frantically pointed at Dune's feet. His toes were outside the circle.

Fionn yanked on his arm and he stumbled toward the center.

Barely had Dune come inside the protective circle when a snarling Irish wolfhound crashed through the tall grasses onto the road. Long-legged and so skinny Dune could see the washboard of its ribs under its coarse brown coat, the beast brushed its muzzle left and right along the road, chuffing with excitement.

Fionn grabbed Dune's pants leg and buried her face in the cloth. Dune slowly placed his hand on her head but otherwise made no motion.

The dog stood with its paws centimeters outside the circle, oblivious to the stones or the family huddling within Maureen's magical cloak. It raised its muzzle and sniffed the air. Its lips curled back and its teeth glinted in the early morning light. Dune felt its breath on the back of his hand. The dog growled, then sniffed the air again and bounded down the road. As quickly as it appeared, it was gone.

"That was close," Gil said.

"Shh!" Dune warned.

A moment later, two men emerged onto the road, both of them carrying shotguns and the thinner one gripping the lead of another scruffy-looking wolfhound. Streams of drool dripped from the dog's jowls. "Which way'd 'e go, Mr. Lynch?" the thinner man asked.

The larger man rubbed his bushy beard, took off his cheesecutter cap, and wiped sweat off his brow with the back of his wrist. "He's your dog, Finbar. You tell me."

Finbar knelt and looked at the road. "Tracks are muddled here."

"Well, that should na be a problem for ye. You *are* the expert tracker, are ye not? That's why I bring you and your stinkin' hounds along."

Finbar pointed up the road. "North. He went north."

"Then let us be headed north as well."

"Do you think the lad was right, Mr. Lynch? About more Leprechauns hereabouts?"

Dune and Paddy shared a worried glance.

"Hush with that talk, you gombeen," Lynch said. "You want someone to hear ya?"

Finbar looked all around. "Way out here in the middle of

nowhere? Who would hear?"

"Just get moving," Lynch growled.

Lynch trudged down the road, Finbar and his dog a couple paces behind. Suddenly, the dog whipped his head around and sniffed the air. Finbar looked over his shoulder, following his dog's gaze, directly at the spot where Dune and his family huddled.

The dog strained at the end of his leash, whining.

Finbar gave the leash a sharp tug. The dog yelped as the collar yanked roughly against his neck, and both he and his master loped down the road to rejoin Lynch.

None of Dune's family moved a hair until the hunters' shadowy figures had disappeared over a rise.

"Is it clear?" Maureen whispered.

Paddy straightened his shirt collar and tugged at the hem of his vest. A drop of sweat trickled down his cheek. "Aye, Marnie. 'Tis all clear. Travis, Gilroy, help your mother gather up the stones," Paddy ordered. "Quietly!"

"The stones saved us, dinna they, Da?" Travis asked.

"'Twas your Ma's magic saved us," Paddy replied. "Without her, the stones be but useless lumps of rock."

A shiver passed through Dune's shoulders. He had helped lay down the stones in the protective circle. Could he have inherited some of his mother's skills? His name, after all, meant *protector* in the Old Language.

He dismissed the thought quickly. His mother had touched each stone—she handed them to him immediately before he placed them on the ground. The magic—and credit for the family's safety—were all hers.

"Da?" Gil asked. "They said they're looking for *more* Leprechauns. What do you ken they mean?"

"They mean someone has bragged that they've found or even caught a Leprechaun." Paddy sneered. "Foolishness to listen to that rubbish. No-one who's found a Leprechaun is going to tell anyone about it, much less give them a map! And if someone actually caught a Leprechaun, telling about it would immediately break the bond. 'Tis the Code of Erin."

Maureen held up a palm. "Shh! Someone's coming!"

Chapter 2: Birdie's Alarm

The last of the rune stones just having been returned to Maureen's pouch, there was no time to rearrange them into the protective circle.

Dune realized the family's options were limited. "Compass points," he ordered. He, Paddy, Maureen, and Ayne took their positions: Paddy facing south, Maureen to his left facing east, Dune to her left facing north, and Ayne opposite Maureen, facing west. The four oldest members of the family now encircled the three youngest.

Dune began his mother's chant.

> Echo, echo, hear my call.
> Dim the lights and raise the wall.

Maureen joined in. Their voices blended together like a psalm.

> Dark-on-dark the curtain rise
> Conceal us from unfriendly eyes.

As Dune peered at the road ahead of him, a shadowy figure took shape, approaching rapidly. "Da, look north," Dune whispered.

Paddy craned his neck around. "I canna see! Change positions with me!"

"Nae, hold your position," Dune said. He had never spoken to his father with such authority, but he somehow found the courage to do so now. "All I see is one, but there may be more."

The figure suddenly thrust his arms out from his sides as if to prevent himself from going over a cliff, and skidded to a stop.

He had spotted them!

The rune had not worked!

Dune felt a rush of sheer panic, coupled with the belief—no, certainty—that the failure was all his own. He had somehow banjaxed the rune. The compass points were not strong enough to sew the veil. Because of him, his family stood in the middle of the road, completely unprotected, awaiting their fate.

Fionn burrowed her head into the side of Dune's leg. He unsheathed his athame with one hand and grabbed Fionn tight with the other so that at least she would be protected, shielded by his body. He clenched his teeth and his chin jutted out. *He'll have to kill me before he gets my family,* Dune swore to himself.

But the man in the road stood where he was.

After a long silence, at least a second or two, the man lifted a hand to his mouth and made a bird call "Coo-coo! Cock-a-coo!"

"Be ready," Dune said. "He's alerting his allies."

"I dunna think so," Maureen said. She took a hesitant step toward Dune, breaking the circle.

"Ma, get back!" Dune flailed one arm in his mother's direction.

"What are ye doing, woman?" Paddy hissed.

Maureen cupped her hands around her mouth and returned the bird call, note for note except for a tiny inflection on the last syllable.

At the sound of her voice, the man ran toward them once again with a hobbling gait, stopping in front of Maureen and bending over, hands on his knees, trying to catch his breath.

"Thank the stars, 'tis you, Marnie," he panted.

He was a fellow Leprechaun, Paddy's age or a little older, lanky and bony, with a short, scruffy beard. His plain brown jacket was threadbare, and his paddy cap, brown tweed with a blue jay feather stuck in its band, had, like the rest of his attire and the man himself, seen better days.

Fionn poked her head around from behind Dune's leg. "Who is he, Ma?" she asked in a trembly whisper. Dune and his other siblings gawked at the man.

"This is Mr. Donal MacBressal," Maureen answered.

"Aye," the visitor said, touching a finger to his hat brim and taking in huge gulps of air. "Birdie, if you please."

"Birdie, what is it?" Maureen asked. "Are you being chased?"

The man shook his head. "Nae. 'Tis Seamus Greenapple."

"What of Seamus?" Paddy asked, approaching Birdie.

"He and his family. They have been captured."

"What do you mean, 'captured?'" Paddy asked. "The man is constantly on high alert. I canna imagine anyone catching him unawares. Not to mention letting his entire family be captured."

Dune ducked his head, feeling his cheeks burn. If Birdie had been Human, Dune's carelessness could have led to the same fate for his own family.

"Seamus and his family were headed to the country to pick up Agnes's people," Birdie explained in a shaky voice. "They were all going together to the Ceili. Long about Brownsgrove, they realized they were being followed. They made a dash for the Faerie Ring, but were surrounded by hunters with hounds." Birdie took off his hat and twisted it in his fists. He looked at Maureen with woeful eyes. "Taken. The whole family."

"Beggin' your pardon, Mr. MacBressal," Dune interrupted. "But how do you ken this, if they were all captured?"

"I'll bat your noggin for your impudence, boy," Paddy growled.

Birdie held up a hand. "Nae, Paddy, the lad's sharp as a tack, he is. Come here, young man." He hooked his finger at Dune to draw him closer.

Dune leaned in.

"I'm a bird whisperer."

Dune stuck a finger in his ear and wiggled it around to loosen the wax that must have built up. "I dunna think I heard you right, sir. Are you saying the—birds—told you what happened?"

Birdie winked at Dune. "That is exactly what I'm sayin'."

Dune squinted his eyes. "Ye must've been in a faery ring, then."

The wiry little fellow snapped to attention and yanked on his bowtie to straighten it. "I dunna need a circle of mushrooms to hear what the birds have to say."

"Really, now," Dune said.

"Marnie here will back me up on it," Birdie said.

Dune looked to his mother, as did the others.

"Sure, 'tis Donal's special talent," Maureen scolded. "As 'twas his father's before him. We canna all be master trackers or rune casters, now can we?"

Dune snorted as if his mother were trying to pull a big joke.

"Laugh if you want," Maureen said, "but I've known Birdie since we were wains. The birds have always flocked to him, so they have."

"I've seen birds flock to all sorts of people if there's a crumb to be had," Dune countered. "But I've not heard of birds nor beasts talking to the Folk. Not outside a faerie ring."

"Then it proves you are never too old to learn something new," Maureen said. "With my own eyes, I've seen Birdie talk with the birds many times."

"Aye, Marnie," Birdie said with a quick nod. "I knew you'd understand."

Dune might have doubted the man's tale initially, but his mother's confirmation of Birdie's skill was irrefutable. And as unlikely as it seemed that Seamus Greenapple would be captured, Dune had to believe that it, too, was true. "Do you ken where the Greenapples are now?"

Birdie shook his head. "Nae, I've told ye all I ken."

"What do we do now?" Ayne asked.

Paddy scratched the back of his head. "The best thing we can do is get to Doolin. Mother Cass will know what to do. Ayne, find some water for Mr. MacBressal. Dune, make yourself useful. Scout ahead for a place to make camp. The sun is almost up."

Dune nodded to his father once, briskly, and jogged up the road.

***

The flat, open landscape offered little in the way of a hideaway, much less a protected space large enough to accommodate the whole family, which was now increased by one with the addition of Birdie. Acres of rolling grassland stretched out as far as Dune could see in all directions.

Above the sound of morning birds announcing the new day, Dune heard a rush of flowing water. He followed the sound to a clear, pebble-bottomed creek that twinkled in the sunrise. Dune filled his canteen, screwed the cap back on, and latched the canteen by a carabiner clip to a loop on his trousers. He scanned the area for signs of danger, simultaneously searching for a suitable shelter.

In the distance he saw a massive willow tree. It must have been hidden from view until he crested a gentle rise of the land.

I dunna ken, Dune thought as he approached the tree. *It does na look like much protection.* With a gnarly, knobby trunk at least two meters in diameter, the tree spread branches in a cascade of green that bent toward the ground like the spokes of an umbrella.

He circled the tree, looking up into the canopy, assessing the branches to determine if they might be strong enough, and concealing enough, to offer safety and shelter. They were bendy and flexible, not sturdy enough to hold much weight. One cracked and broke when he tugged on it, exposing tender green strands.

With his eye on the tree's crown, he stumbled on a root and fell to the ground. With the instincts of a goalkeeper, he spread his arms in front of him and rolled to break the fall. "Osh! I've made a complete haymess out of this," he grumbled. As he leaned against the tree to massage his foot through the toes of his hiking boot, he noticed an indentation in the tree trunk. Upon closer inspection, Dune found it to be an opening; the tree was hollow. "A cave in a tree," he mused, "just like home." He poked his head in and looked around. Although it was too dark inside the hollow tree to clearly judge its size, he could tell his family-plus-one would all fit. A bit of magic: The tree was bigger within than without. This did not surprise Dune. The Tuatha de Danann, an ancient people who were the ancestors of the Leprechauns, had had an affinity for trees, water, and stone. They were believed to have imbued many natural features across what is now Ireland with their spiritual essence and magic.

As the sun rose in the sky, Dune raced back to his family. "I've found shelter," he told Paddy.

He led his family to the giant willow. They went as fast as they could, Dune carrying Fionn piggy-back, but it was still a ten-minute hike in broadening daylight.

As they arrived at the tree, Dune knelt to let Fionn slide to the ground. "Will this do, Da?"

Dune's father eyed the low-hanging branches, tugged on one to test its strength as Dune had done, then surveyed the open, rolling pastureland all around. "Nearby to fresh water is helpful, but 'tis wholly exposed and unprotected."

"We'll not be in the branches, Da. Look on this side. 'Tis a cave, right in the side of the tree. Like our home in Yulnear."

"Our home is a tree in a cave, not a cave in a tree," Paddy

groused.

"Our home is a cave in a tree in a cave," Dune countered.

Maureen gently laid her hand on her husband's shoulder. "Paddy, dear. Dune has done a fine job of locating shelter. And we *are* Kellys, after all. We know how to protect ourselves."

"Then set out your stones, Woman," Paddy grumbled. "We'll camp here till nightfall."

"I'm hungry," Fionn wailed.

"I shall fix us some tuck," Ayne said. She ducked inside the tree-cave and Dune could hear her humming, a sure sign that she, at least, approved of the accommodations. Paddy and the wains followed her inside. Dune ducked his head to follow too, but his mother called to him.

"Dune, will you help me?"

Dune came to her side.

Maureen opened her knapsack and removed the pouch that held the rune stones. She paced three steps out from the side of the tree. "You were a big help back on the road," Maureen said, pouring a few stones from the bag into her palm. "I could na have completed the circle in time without you."

"If I had done it wrong, the whole family—"

"Did you think at the time to do it right? Or to do it wrong? Or just to do it?"

"I suppose I was na thinking at all."

Maureen looked up from her handful of stones and gave him a smile. "*That* is the key. Hold out your hands." She placed two rocks in his open palms, furrowed her brows, took one stone back. She rubbed her thumb across its polished surface. "No, that one is not quite right." She returned it to the pouch and replaced it with a different stone.

Dune noticed that she was being more particular with the selection of stones than a few hours ago, when they needed to put their protection in place quickly, before the hunters saw them. Her instructions for the ritual were more complicated as well. "Put this one at the East and the other one at the South. First the East, then the South. I will fill in behind you."

"I want to help, too," Gil said, reappearing from inside the tree.

Maureen handed two more stones to Dune. "Give these to your brother."

"Ma?" Dune cast his mother a worried look. He was still not convinced of his own ability to participate, much less Gil's.

"Do you feel the warmth of the stones?" Maureen asked, cupping Dune's hands in her own so the stones were pressed snugly in his palms.

"Aye?"

She reached up and put her hands on his cheeks. "And do you feel the warmth of my hands?"

Dune felt slightly awkward, clasping his hands around the stones while his mother's hands embraced his face. "Aye."

"'Tis the same warmth."

Still a bit unsure of the process—why did his mother not give the stones directly to Gil?—Dune did as his mother instructed.

Gil cupped his hands to receive the stones. Dune placed four stones in his brother's hands, then wrapped his own hands around Gil's and gave them a squeeze. *How small his hands are,* Dune thought. *The stones barely fit.*

Dune stepped away, and Maureen took his place in front of Gil. She bent her knees so she could look at him eye-to-eye and placed her hands around his, the way Dune had.

Dune realized that Gil's hands were bigger than their mother's.

"Listen carefully, Gilroy," Maureen said. "Dune will place a stone, then I'll place one behind his, then you place one right behind mine, about yea far apart." Maureen released her youngest son's hands and spread her arms to indicate roughly a meter's length.

23

"Aye, Mum." Gil opened his hands to look at the rune stones. He shifted his hands up and down, measuring the weight of the stones. "All these rocks must be heavy to be carryin' around the countryside, Ma. Glad I'm not totin' your pack!" Gil held his hands up to the rising sun. The smooth grey-black surfaces of the stones shone as if they were wet. "They sure are pretty, though."

"If you want to help, you must be quiet and follow instructions," Dune said.

Gil gave his brother a quick nod. "Aye, Dune. I shall."

Dune placed the first stone at the East. "Just put the stones in place, like Ma told you. Quietly."

When all twelve stones were placed on the ground, Maureen handed Dune one final stone, the flat, shiny piece of rose quartz. Dune knew what to do with this one. After all, had he not watched his mother conduct the protection ritual ever since he was a wee wain? He lifted the first stone, the one marking East, and tucked the quartz underneath.

Maureen chanted the rune. Dune closed his eyes and let the words form pictures in his mind. His lips moved along with the words, but he dared not even whisper them for fear of banjaxing the ritual.

> *Echo, echo, hear my call.*
> *Dim the lights and raise the wall.*
> *Light on light, the curtains rise*
> *Conceal us from unfriendly eyes.*

When she finished, Gil rushed into her arms for a tight hug. "I was good, right Ma?"

Maureen cupped his chin in her hand. "You were a big help." She smiled at Dune. "Ye both were. Now let's go inside and have some tuck."

Chapter 3: The Pooka

Maureen bent slightly to enter the tree; Gil followed, hopping with one arm stretched up as far as possible to rap the top of the hollow with his fingertips as he passed through the entryway.

Dune took one last circuit around the protective border, pausing to adjust one stone that was placed slightly akilter. Satisfied, he ducked his head and entered the tree.

Lit by a single candle, the inside of the tree glowed.

"Tis a wonderful shelter you've found us, Dune," Maureen said, rubbing her arms through her thin shawl.

"Ma, where is your coat?" Dune asked.

"I've given it to Fionn. She's lost hers."

Probably when she was hiding in the grass, Dune thought. "Da, should I go back and look for it?"

"Nae, 'twould be too dangerous for you to be out there traipsin' about in broad daylight."

"I'm sorry, Da," Fionn said. Her lower lip quivered.

Paddy scowled but did not raise his voice to his youngest child. "'Tis a lesson for you, little one."

"Here, Ma." Dune shrugged out of his grey tweed coat and handed it to his mother. "I'm warm enough without it."

"Thank you, son," she said. She wrapped herself in the coat and sat against the wall of the tree next to her husband. Paddy put his arm around her and adjusted the coat so it wrapped around her more snugly. He pecked her fondly on the cheek.

Dune looked away. It wasn't that he was embarrassed by his parents' displays of affection. He just felt like he was intruding on a personal moment.

The woodsy smell of the inside of the tree reminded Dune of their home in the village of Yulnear. Built in a hollow tree that grew beneath the bare rocky surface of Achill Island, their underground home was remarkably intact for its age. It was said to be an ancient artifact from the days when Ireland was inhabited by the Tuatha Dé Danann. It had provided protection from treasure hunters and other invaders all those centuries ago and continued to be a safe shelter for Dune and his family.

Ayne offered Dune a cloth with a faded paisley pattern. He found a spot to sit cross-legged against the smooth interior surface of the tree and unwrapped his dinner—a wedge of hard cheese, a thick slab of oatmeal soda bread, and apple slices. He would have preferred a hot meal, but he knew better than to complain when his sister offered him food, especially when she had been toting enough for the whole family.

Birdie, on the other hand, polished off his dinner as if it were the grandest feast imaginable. He licked a finger and pressed it against the cloth square that served as his tablecloth, placemat, and napkin, not wanting to miss a single crumb. "Marnie, your daughter has a gift, to be sure."

Ayne lowered her head to hide her blushing cheeks. "Thank you, Mr. Birdie."

Gil sat beside Dune, crossing his legs in the same manner. "Tell me about Ma's rune stones," Gil said. "Why do they feel different from regular rocks?"

"You think they feel different?" Dune asked. "They feel like regular rocks to me, except for the etchings."

"Why could na the Humans see us? Or see the rocks themselves, even?"

"The pattern of the rocks is like a giant clock with each stone marking the hours," Dune said. "When the circle is complete, it makes us as safe inside it as if we were in the Great Faerie Ring itself."

"Faerie Ring," Travis said. "Pfft."

"Dinna you see how the magic protected us from those dogs and hunters?"

"Aye, but Da said that was Ma's magic. It had naught to do with the Great Faerie Ring."

"Ma's circle of stones symbolizes the Great Faerie Ring. That is why her magic is so powerful strong."

"What's the Great Faerie Ring?" Gil asked. "Is it like Ma's wedding ring?"

"No, 'tis far too big for your ma's finger." Dune tousled his brother's hair.

Gil swatted Dune's hand away. "A circle then, like stones around a fire pit?"

"You're thinking along the right lines now, but the Faerie Ring is bigger still. Like Beltany or the Seven Priestesses. But their magic pales next to that of the Great Faerie Ring."

"How do you ken about the Faerie Ring?" Travis asked. "How do you know 'tis not but a faerie *tale?*"

"I've read about it in *Rune Éire*. 'Tis a fact, or it would na be taught in *Rune Éire*."

"Why is it so magical?" Gil asked.

"'Tis an ancient altar of giant granite boulders set carefully in a ring by an early clan of Leprechaun ancestors," Dune explained. "With the help of some Druids."

"'Twas mostly the Leprechauns," Paddy added.

"Pfft," Travis said again. He licked his finger to collect the last of the crumbs on his cloth as Birdie had done, then gathered everyone's cloth napkins and returned them to Ayne.

Although Ayne had been helping their mother with preparing meals and cleaning up afterwards as long as he could remember, Dune could not recall a time when she had ever complained about the task. Even now, as tired as she must be, she collected the dirty cloths and shook them clean in a corner where she wouldn't disturb the rest of the family, before putting them back in her sack.

"I'll carry the tuck tomorrow," Dune offered.

"Oh, sure. Now that the load is lighter," Ayne replied with a wink. She laughed lightly, her voice tinkling like windchimes.

Travis found a spot opposite Dune and stretched out, his lanky legs sprawled into the middle of the room. He held his fiddle across his lap and rubbed it gently with his polishing rag. "Ma's magic needs no Faerie Ring, great or otherwise. Nor does Da's. Nor will mine when I am old enough to use it."

"I wonder what my magic will be," Gil asked. "Maybe I'll be a Runecaster like Ma. She said I helped today. I think I'd be a good Runecaster. The stones felt different to me. Even Dune could na feel it. *Your* magic will na be in runes, will it, Dune? I wonder what your magic will be. Should ye na already have it? Should ye na—"

"Go to sleep, Gil." Dune rubbed his eyes. His brother's non-stop chatter was wearing him out. He grabbed a blanket from his knapsack, then fluffed the pack to serve as a pillow. He closed his eyes and arranged the blanket, prepared to let his weariness float away.

Within moments, two small bodies snuggled against his sides. He knew without opening his eyes who it was, and he knew from experience that sleep would be delayed. Sure enough, his two youngest siblings started picking at each other, striking pinch-finger attacks across the battlefield of Dune's chest.

"Fionn! Gil! Dunna you ken I'm trying to sleep here?"

"Tell us a story," Fionn said. She pulled at the corner of Dune's blanket and tucked it under her chin.

Dune sighed. "I'm weary to the bone, little one. I'll tell you a story tomorrow, when we've reached Doolin."

"But I'll not be able to go to sleep without a story." Fionn walked her fingers across Dune's chest.

"All right, all right. If you keep still." He clapped his hand around Fionn's fingers, squeezing them gently. "What kind of story suits your fancy?"

"Ponies," Fionn demanded without hesitation.

"Pies," Gil said, poking Dune in the ribs. "I'm so hungry for a bite of pie."

"No, I want ponies!"

"Pies!"

"Ara be whist! To satisfy you both, I shall tell you a story about a pony that was made into a pie, and eaten up by a giant in one bite."

"Ewww, nae!" Gil scrunched up his face. "Disgusting."

"Poor pony," Fionn cried, tears springing from her eyes. "Please don't put the pony in a pie-eeee!"

"Dunna worry, little one." Dune wagged one of Fionn's braids. "Even I would not put a pony in a pie. Though it would be tempting."

Fionn snuffled and managed a half smile. "I still want a story about ponies."

"The only pony I know to tell a story of is … *The Pooka!*"

Fionn squealed in delight. "Yes, the Pooka!"

"Pooka. Pfft. No such thing," Travis said from across the room.

"But, Dune, 'tis a horse, not a pony."

"True, 'tis a horse. But not like any normal horse. The Pooka is a spirit-horse that loves to play tricks on mean people and to torment those who fear it."

"The Pooka is only mean to those who deserve it," Fionn said.

"Unlike ponies, who are vile and mean-natured to everyone,"

Dune replied.

"Ponies are only mean if they've reason to be."

"Just tell the story already," Paddy grumbled. "Some of us would like to sleep."

Dune propped himself up against the side of the tree, repositioning his knapsack. Gil mimicked the procedure, while Fionn claimed an even larger portion of the blanket.

"Mary McPhee had no joy in her life but a ginger cat," Dune began. "A ginger cat named … Gilroy."

"Did you hear that, Gil?" Fionn said with a giggle.

"Yeah, yeah. I heard. But on the back of the cat lives a flea named Fionn."

"Does not!"

"Does too!"

"Does not!" Then to Dune, "Gil feels about cats the way you feel about ponies, though both of you are wrong in the head. How could anyone not like two of the sweetest creatures—"

"Do you want to hear the story or not?" Dune interrupted.

"Yes, please," Fionn and Gil chimed in unison.

"Then no more interruptions. Now, where was I? Ah, yes." And with that, he began.

Mary McPhee had no joy in her life but her wee ginger cat. The old woman and the cat lived a meager existence on Achill Island, not far from our home, as a matter of fact.

Fionn narrowed her eyes at him. "Is that really in the story?"

"Nae, but 'tis true. Do you ken that tiny hut on the very edge of Keem Bay, the one that's all run down and falling right off the cliff?"

Fionn's eyes opened wide. Her eyebrows sprang up and disappeared beneath her bangs. "That was Mary McPhee's place?"

"Aye. But no more interrupting or I'll not continue."

Fionn used an invisible key to lock her lips, and Dune

continued.

One night, Mary McPhee was walking down the long, lonely path to her home when she stubbed her toe on a large black pot in the middle of the road. "What a strange place for someone to leave a pot," she said. "I'll take it home and find out who it belongs to in the morning."

But the pot was too heavy for her to lift, so she wrapped her shawl around it and began to drag it down the road. With each step she took, it seemed the pot grew heavier. When she stopped to rest, she saw the pot was now full of gold coins. "'Tis my lucky night," she exclaimed. "Maybe the owner will give me one or two coins as a reward."

Mary continued dragging the pot down the road until she had to stop and rest again. This time when she looked back, the pot of gold was a pot no more, much less full of gold. It was nothing but a lump of iron. Mary said, "My luck is even better, for do I not need a doorstop? And no-one is going to come 'round to claim a lump of iron."

When she got to her front door, the lump of iron began to shake and shudder. It grew legs and hooves and a tail and a long, arched neck and a head and body as black as a preacher's sin and eyes that shot blue sparks in the night.

"The Pooka!" Fionn cried.

"The very same!" Dune said.

It knelt down so Mary McPhee could climb upon its back. Mary was powerless to resist. As soon as she was on its back, the Pooka galloped so fast that its hooves left the ground. Mary held tight to the Pooka's neck as they flew across the island in the moonlight.

Finally, the Pooka returned to the ground and stopped before a luminous mansion. "I'd no idea there was a mansion away out here," Mary McPhee said in awe.

"Go inside," said the Pooka. "They are expecting you."

At this, a shiver ran up the old woman's spine. What folly had the Pooka in mind for her? The Pooka, sensing the old woman's fears, reassured her, "'Tis a party. Join them. Dance till dawn, then I shall take you home."

When Mary went inside, she was greeted by a beautiful sight: Ghostly men and ethereal women, waltzing around a glowing ballroom. The men were dressed in magnificent tuxedos, and the women wore shimmering ballgowns. An orchestra of spirits played hauntingly beautiful music that Mary recognized from her youth, a long, long lifetime ago.

Then out of the crowd of dancing couples, a ghostly figure emerged whom Mary knew well, though she had not seen him in almost seventy years. 'Twas her first and only love, a young sailor to whom she had been betrothed, but had been lost at sea the night before their wedding was to have taken place. He extended a hand to Mary and whisked her onto the dance floor. In an instant, she was young again, dressed in a flowing silver gown with a pink ribbon 'round her waist. She looked into the eyes of her true love and he looked back at her. For the first time in many, many years, she was completely happy.

"Aw, not a love story," Gil whined. "I thought the Pooka was a ghost story."

"Have you not been listening? This story is full of ghosts."

"Not scary ones, though."

"Not to worry, Gil." Dune leaned over and whispered in his brother's ear, "The Pooka will send the scary ones to visit you in your sleep."

"Enough, Dune," Maureen said.

Dune looked at his mother with surprise. "How did you even hear that?"

Her look told him not to backtalk.

"Yes, ma'am." He tousled Gil's hair. "I was only kidding, mate."

"Is that the end of the story, then?" Fionn asked. "What happened to Mary McPhee?"

"The Pooka returned and carried her back home, safe and sound," Dune said. "She lived out the rest of her days quietly and contentedly, knowing that her beau would be waiting for her when she left this world."

"Time for bed," Maureen said. She arched an eyebrow at Dune. "If either of those children wakes up with nightmares, you will be the one who has to see to them."

"Yes, Ma."

Paddy sighed. "Good night, family." He blew out the candle, plunging the tree-cave into darkness.

Tired as he was, Dune could not turn off his brain to let sleep envelop him. After trying unsuccessfully to find a comfortable position on the moss that carpeted the tree floor, he got up, rummaged in his sack, and slipped outside with a small leather pouch.

The early morning light cast long shadows of Dune and the tree. The meadow was alive with songbirds, flitting between patches of thick grass. They called cheerily to each other, either in greeting or announcing their territory.

Careful not to step outside the protective circle of stones, Dune sat back against the rough, knobby bark of the willow, facing north. He cupped the little pouch in his hand, felt its weight, and slid the drawstring wide with his fingers. The pouch and its contents were a gift from his mother—a set of wooden tiles etched with runes. He emptied a dozen small, square tiles into his hand, felt their coolness between his fingers, listened to their whispers as they clinked up against each other. This was really a child's set of runes, made of wood instead of stone. More for practice than for practical use.

Runes were his mother's specialty. Dune himself had no special skill for the craft, but every year Paddy insisted he enter the rune-casting contest at the Ceili. The highest he had placed was sixth out of six, a sore disappointment to Paddy. Gil could probably do better. The thought struck Dune that he should give Gil this set of Runestones for his birthday at the end of Summer.

But Paddy would probably squash that idea, preferring Dune to remain shackled to his misery.

Dune tipped his hand and the tiles tumbled back into the bag. He took a square of plain white cotton cloth out of his jacket pocket and spread it on the ground. He closed his eyes, drew in his breath, and as he exhaled, whispered an incantation, "Echo, echo."

Why had those words come to him? They were the opening to his mother's protection rune, but she had already protected their hiding place.

He quieted his thoughts and concentrated on the message the runes might give him. The tiles would tell him important aspects of his past and present, and possible outcomes in the near future, related to his question—if he chose the right question. He whispered, "What will the Ceili hold for me?"

Taking a deep breath, he pulled five tiles out of the leather pouch, one by one, and laid them on the cloth face down in the form of a cross, centered in front of him.

The horizontal row represented the past, present, and future. He turned over the middle tile—the present—to show its rune: Raido, the traveler's rune. Dune understood its significance related to his current travels, but he also remembered that Raido signified not only a physical journey but a spiritual quest—the journey of life.

Next, he overturned the rune to its left, the rune of the past, indicating what led him to his current position. Thurisaz, the rune of chaos and conflict.

Dune had heard Thurisaz referred to as the Devil's rune, but he didn't believe the Devil had anything to do with it. Chaos, conflict: These characteristics needed no supernatural explanation. Some folks were just weak-natured, easily tempted by greed, love, or power. The lust for wealth or power led some of them to wreak chaos on their clans, their countries, or the world.

And other folks, Dune believed, simply had a streak of evil in them. Humans, especially, were tempted by evil and greed to kidnap Leprechauns for their own enrichment. No matter that in doing so, they separated loving families and sometimes, Dune had heard, even committed murder by turning captured Leprechauns into solid gold statues which could be melted down into gold bars or coins. Dune shuddered at the thought. He didn't know any Leprechauns who had met this fate, but the Clan Matriarch, Mother Cass, had seen it. She rarely spoke of what she had seen, except to remind the members of the Kelly Clan why it was so important not to be discovered by Humans.

Dune pulled his thoughts back to his rune casting. What else did he know about Thurisaz? It warned of dangers in the path ahead, but also could be a catalyst for change. Maybe his perpetual conflicts with his father were finally coming to an end.

He turned over the third tile to reveal Ehwaz, the rune of teamwork, trust, and loyalty. Its position at the top of the cross meant these were forces that would help him through his journey. He immediately thought of his football teammates, how they were loyal to each other, and how they trusted him to keep the ball out of their goal. The rune was also associated with horses and marriage, but Dune dismissed those connotations as irrelevant.

The fourth rune, the one below the center rune, was Hagalaz, the rune of disruption. Its position on the five-rune-cross layout meant he was in for pain, loss, and suffering, and he would have to accept it. *Great,* Dune thought. *Just my luck.*

Dune turned over the fifth and final rune, the one placed at three o'clock, indicating the future and the final outcome of Dune's question. It was Ingwaz, the rune of love, harmony, and peace. It pointed at the possibility of a time without anxiety.

He closed his eyes as the image of a girl he had met last year drifted across the landscape of his mind. Her hair was the color of the harvest moon, her skin the shade of his favorite dessert, the coffee-and-vanilla-ice-cream treat known as a Moon o'er Erin.

After a moment, the picture in his mind faded like a cloud dispersed on the wind. Dune inhaled deeply, clearing his thoughts once again.

Echo, echo. The words floated into his mind again.

He couldn't help but read the runes to indicate he would be rewarded for overcoming his challenges. The Presentation of the Clover ceremony would be held on the final day of the Ceili. Dune would be dubbed the next Keeper of the Clover. He was suddenly sure of it. He would finally receive his father's approval.

If this child's playset of runes could be trusted to reveal truth.

And *if* he had properly cast the runes and accurately interpreted their meaning.

That, Dune's father would undoubtedly agree, was a big "if." And just as suddenly as the certainty of success had warmed him in a sunny glow, a cloud of pessimism settled over him.

Dune swept up the rune tiles and poured them back into their leather pouch. He folded and put away the cotton cloth and returned to his place inside the tree, careful not to step on his sleeping family.

The aroma of lavender, his sister Ayne's favorite fragrance, mingled with the tree's woodsy scent. She was forbidden to wear scents on the journey, for fear of giving away the family's presence, but apparently had brought a cachepot which she had uncapped.

Good. Maybe the calming aroma would help him sleep.

He punched his gunny sack into a pillow and got as much sleep as he could, considering how cold and hard the ground was despite the thin layer of moss. Having donated his coat to his mother, he plucked at the edge of his blanket, only to discover that Fionn had wrapped herself in it like a cocoon.

When he finally dozed off, dreams of a golden clover danced

through his mind, and he smiled in his sleep.

The family slept through the day and at dusk, packed their gear and carefully swept away any trace of their presence.

Maureen lifted her arms up to cover Dune's shoulders with his coat. "I stayed toasty warm, son. I hope you dinna suffer too much on the cold ground."

"Woman, don't coddle the boy," Paddy groused.

Dune buttoned his vest and shoved his arms roughly into his coat sleeves. "I was fine, Ma. I'm too tough to be bothered with chills and such as that."

"How much farther do ye think, Marnie?" Birdie asked. "I can tell ye how far as the crow flies, but I dunna think that will help us."

"We are almost to Doolin," Maureen replied. "We should be there by dawn."

"Everyone, try to keep up," Paddy said. "Dune, keep track of the little ones, and keep your eyes sharp for any danger approaching from behind."

Spoken like a "keeper," Dune thought. *But does Da realize that I am the one doing the keeping?*

Chapter 4: Cairdeen's Journey Begins

About 120 kilometers east of the enchanted lands of Achill Island, a bone-thin Connemara mare paced in circles, straining at the end of a short rope. Her sorrel hide had the dusty matte look of ancient brick, her ribs jutting just under the hide like washboard slats. Her long, flaxen mane and tail were matted and knotted, with twigs and burrs sticking out of the snarls here and there.

Keep walking, Cairdeen, the mare told herself. *You've naught to do but walk, so if you canna keep walking, you're naught.*

The rope, tied to a stake in the ground, was not long enough to allow Cairdeen to reach even a blade of grass, not that there was much grass to be had in the sandy field. With sweat lathering the pony's neck, the rope had rubbed raw patches like the mark of a hangman's noose.

The pony looked longingly at the scrap of shadow cast by a single scraggly pine tree, just outside her circle of motion. The sun's journey to the west had sent the long, thin line of shade reaching to the other side of the field. Soon it would be night, and she would feel some relief.

As she passed a rusted-out bucket, Cairdeen flared her nostrils, hoping to catch a whiff of water. But the Farmer had left the bucket there three days ago, and had not returned since. Between the rusty leaks, the relentless sun, and Cairdeen's thirst, the bucket was bone dry.

Why does he even keep me if I'm such a bother to him? Cairdeen often wondered. She sighed, fluttering her lips as she exhaled. She might never know the reason.

Cairdeen shuffled around and around at the end of her rope. Her hooves were cracked, dry, and overgrown. She had worn a shallow circular rut in the parched earth where she lumbered through the days and nights.

Keep walking.

The motion of walking round and around, straining to reach a bit of grass or shade, had loosened the stake in the ground. Each time the pony completed a circle, the stake pushed the dirt a little farther away, widening a cone-shaped hole.

The sun finally dipped behind the horizon, and a cool breeze blew across the field, fluttering through the pony's tangled mane. She lifted her muzzle to sniff the breeze. It smelled invitingly of juicy Irish grass; cool, fresh water; and other, unfamiliar but appealing aromas.

Ah, grass! What a wonderful fragrance, the little pony thought. *I almost dinna believe there was any grass left in the world.*

As the pony stretched her neck to the West, toward the setting sun and the wonderful wind with its enticing scents, the stake snapped out of the ground with a pop.

Cairdeen perked her ears and tossed her head.

She was free.

Dragging the rope and stake behind her, she left her rutted path and began her trek. Although she did not know where the alluring aroma would take her, she knew it would be away from the Farmer who had chained her in the field and seemingly forgotten all about her.

Not that she would prefer that he remember her. The rare times when he came out to the field, he threatened her repeatedly, and occasionally actually struck her with his knotty cane. An unpleasant shiver rippled the length of Cairdeen's back from wither to flank as she thought of him. She never learned the Farmer's name, and he either didn't know hers or didn't care; he just called her "Nag."

He blamed her for the destruction of the field, for he occasionally had to move her stake from one bleak area to another, resulting in several hoof-trodden rings that scarred the field. In the Farmer's mind, this was the pony's fault. If he had just let her roam freely, she would have grazed evenly and not worn ruts where he staked her.

"Don't let the crows carry you away, you old nag," he had growled the last time he re-staked her. "Or maybe 'twould be better if they did." He set the bucket down with a slosh, spilling half the water, which immediately soaked into the parched ground.

That's just what he'll think has happened, the pony thought as she plodded steadfastly toward the West. *That the crows have carried me clean away. He'll be happy to be rid of the nuisance I am to him.*

Cairdeen came to a barbed wire fence, three strands running the length of the field. She walked parallel to the fence line until she came to a place where a fence post had rotted and fallen over, bringing the stretch of wire with it.

Carefully, the pony stepped between the biting strands of wire. She nickered with joy and hunger as she headed toward a small patch of grass.

Suddenly, the rope around her neck went taut. The stake, trailing behind at the other end of the rope, had snagged on the barbed wire.

Cairdeen pulled with all her might, lowering her head to put the load on her shoulders. She veered left and then right, then once more to the left, and the stake slipped free of the wire.

Beyond the sandy field where she had been staked, Cairdeen discovered the world was lush and green. Without breaking stride, she dropped her head and grabbed a mouthful of grass. *Sweet delight,* she thought. *The world is a feast, waiting to be tasted.*

In every direction, she saw fields so green she thought she was dreaming or had stumbled into a faerie tale. *If 'tis but a dream, I dunna want to awake.*

Enticing as it was, the tasty grass was not what had lured Cairdeen farther and farther from her old life. She shook her head, feeling the ripple—a pleasant sensation this time—travel down her body. *I'm shaking out of that old life like a threadbare saddle blanket,* she thought. *And each step takes me closer to—I dunna ken exactly what, but closer to something, something ...* better.

As evening fell, the glimmering moon rose above the horizon and hung low and almost full behind Cairdeen. One by one, stars poked holes in the night sky, and fireflies danced in loops and spirals around her until Cairdeen was surrounded by a twinkling entourage as she walked briskly through the night.

Keep walking, she thought, following a two-rut dirt road that meandered through moonlit meadows. *Not because you dunna have anything else, but because walking will lead you to everything else.*

After several hours, she stopped to roll in the dewy grass. It felt soft and cool on her back. *If only I could lose this bothersome rope and stake,* she thought.

A rustling in the brush brought Cairdeen bolting to her feet. She shied to the other side of the road.

She snorted and bucked her head, alert to whatever had made the rustling noise. "Who goes there?" she said, incredulous at the sound of a voice speaking her words. She realized the voice, soft and a bit quivery, was her own.

As she peered into the brush on the edge of the road, she saw a shiny black nose and two small, shiny eyes. With more rustling, a black-and-white face slowly emerged from the brush, and she saw it was a badger. The badger tentatively took another step toward the skittish pony, then scampered across the road and sniffed at her hooves.

Cairdeen stood perfectly still except for bending her head down to sniff the badger in greeting. "Be you friend, then, Badger?"

"That I am," the badger said in a low and gravelly voice, "if a friend you be—wha'?" The badger was apparently as stunned as Cairdeen at the voices. Then he looked around at the luminous white mushrooms growing in a circle around where they stood. "Oh, that's the thing," the badger said. "A faerie ring."

"What? What is it? Do you ken why I'm hearing voices?"

"Oh, that I do," the badger said. He scratched his ear with his sharp claws. "'Tis the faerie ring. Er-hm—" He cleared his throat and then recited:

"When standing in a faerie ring, be you beast or bird,
In the moonlight soft, your voice, spoken will be heard."

Cairdeen looked around at the circle of mushrooms. "A faerie ring," she said. "Amazing." She looked down at the badger, whose stout black body and black-and-white mask shimmered in the moonlight. "Have you a name?"

"Canavan," he said. "They call me Canavan."

"How do you ken about the faerie ring, Canavan?"

"You sound as if you'd never seen a faerie ring in your life," Canavan sniffed haughtily.

"Nor much of anything else," replied the pony with a soft whicker.

"What's that 'round your neck?"

Cairdeen twisted her neck to one side, wincing at the rope's chafing. "'Tis the rope that kept me tied to the ground."

"You're not tied now."

"That I'm not. But this rope is a sore nuisance."

"I can see that," Canavan said. "'Tis rubbing your hide pure raw."

The badger raised up on his hind legs to peer more closely at the rope around Cairdeen's neck. "If you will let me try, I believe I can get rid of that for you."

Cairdeen nodded and bent her neck as low as she could.

Canavan strafed at the knot with his sharp claws, nicking Cairdeen.

She whinnied and jerked her neck.

"Sorry, Lass. The knot is too tight. I dunna want to injure you."

"Thank you for trying. I might not be free of the rope, but at least I'm free of the Farmer. I would carry this rope till the end of my days, knowing he is not on the other end of it."

"The Farmer?"

"Aye. Wicked cruel, that one is."

"What did he do to you?"

"He had a cane with him at all times, to help him stand and walk, you see. But he seemed to have no trouble standing when he hit me with that horrible stick."

"Oh, dear me," Canavan squeaked. "And did he bash your mate and cubs as well?"

The pony gasped. "Why, no, I have no mate nor cubs—er, foals."

"Nor have I—anymore," Canavan said softly. He lowered his nose to the ground and flicked at one ear with a paw. His shiny black eyes glistened in the moonlight.

Cairdeen was afraid to ask, but afraid not to know. "What happened to them?" she whispered. "If you dunna mind me asking."

"A pack of Humans descended on us and set fire to our burrow. We all ran out, me mate Aisling and I, and our three little wains. But the wains were too slow, too slow. I picked one up with my teeth, and Aisling did the same with another. But they were too heavy, and in their fear, they wriggled loose and ran in different directions. I could hear their terrified screams, crying for their ma they were, and screaming 'Dragons, dragons!' But when I turned around, I could see naught but swirling smoke, and glimpses of the Humans, swinging their clubs. Aisling was beside me, both of us looking on in terror. I told her to keep going, that I would go back for the wains. But before I could stop her, she rushed into the smoke to try to save them."

Canavan wiped his eye with the back side of his paw, his sharp claws curved away from his face. He sighed and closed his eyes tight shut. "Then there was a terrible fierce noise, like boulders crashing down a ravine, and all I could see was the smoke, swirling, billowing. I could do naught but hide in the wood and cover me eyes."

Cairdeen shivered at the thought of what Canavan had gone through. She knew he must be reliving those horrible moments. "You dunna have to go on."

Canavan shook his head. "'Tis good to tell someone. When the wind and noises ended, and all the smoke had dissipated, Aisling and the wains were gone. Me whole family, gone without a trace. Those men had destroyed everyone I loved in the world, and left nothing behind but me own worthless hide."

"How horrible," Cairdeen said softly, dropping her head and brushing her nose close to Canavan's face. "Why did they do it?"

"I dunna ken. Sport, I suppose. Pure sport." Canavan sniffed the air and brushed his paw against his cheek. "I've been wandering, and wondering, ever since, trying to make sense of it all. Why was I the one to survive? Why?"

Cairdeen brushed her muzzle against Canavan's cheek. "'Tis the eternal question, I suppose. Ye mightn't find the answer here on earth, but I hope you find peace."

The badger shook, first just shaking his head, then his whole body, down to the tip of his bushy tail. "Be careful! Not every face you meet will be a friendly one like mine. Fare thee well, Pony." Canavan turned and walked out of the faerie ring, back across the road and into the brush.

"Canavan! I have a name, too," the pony called after him. "'Tis Cairdeen."

Canavan poked his face out of the brush. His dark eyes twinkled in the moonlight as he lifted his snout and called out a reply, but he was beyond the faerie ring, so all Cairdeen heard was a friendly, wordless squeak.

As the badger disappeared into the brush, the pony whispered to herself, "Cairdeen." Charmed at the sound of her name, she said more loudly, "My name is Cairdeen!"

Chapter 5: Leprechaun Magic

As the sun set, Dune and his family continued on their journey. Birdie walked behind Maureen, bobbing his head and picking his feet up and setting them down in a toes-in way that reminded Dune of a pigeon's walk.

"You wains stay close," Paddy said. "No tellin' what kind of traps might be lyin' in wait for an unlucky Leprechaun."

"But, Da, I dinna ken Leprechauns were *un*lucky," Gil said.

"Sometimes our luck be the very thing that makes us unlucky to our own selves," Paddy said.

Travis nodded and stroked his chin as if he were a sage, bearded elder. "I ken 'tis true, Da," he said in a deep voice, full of invented maturity and wisdom.

Dune gazed at the backs of his brothers' noggins. They were nothing alike. Gilroy was dark-haired, willowy like their mother and with her sharp cheekbones. He was always asking questions. Travis, three years older than Gil, was stocky, like their father. Travis had untamed auburn curls, like Dune and their father. Also like Paddy, Travis made up his mind about things before you even talked to him, and was not easily dissuaded. Thank the stars Travis had not developed their father's temper along with his build and impulsiveness.

Dune was all too familiar with Paddy's temper. As the Keeper of the Clover, Paddy Kelly expected everyone to bow down to him. Everyone except Maureen, of course. Maureen and the Matriarch.

Dune had once again felt the burn of Paddy's temper one night shortly before they set out on the trip to Doolin. You would think, with Paddy's influence, he would be able to use his leverage on his son's behalf when it came time to choose the new Keeper. But when Dune had hinted to his father that he should speak to the Matriarch, Paddy had practically exploded.

"I canna just stroll up to Mother Cass and say, 'I've this son who'd like to be Keeper. He's not shown any magic or skill or any such talent that would make him deserve such an honor.'" Paddy's round cheeks got redder and redder as he paced around the main room in their underground tree home, flailing his arms to punctuate his words. "'But you never know. He could become a talented rune caster any day. Or show some other skill. *Something* to show he's a Kelly.' Is that what you'd like me to do?"

Dune should have dropped the subject. But his father knew how to push his buttons. "I've a skill. I'm the best keeper Yulnear's had in generations."

"A *goalkeeper?* You think *football* is a skill? Being a keeper in a stupid game doesn't make you fit to be Keeper of the Clover. It doesn't make you fit to carry the Kelly name!"

Dune had slammed out of the house, taking the stairs up to the cave entrance two at a time and bursting above ground in total disregard of the rule of caution. After thundering several meters across the rocky terrain, he had slumped to his knees, balled his fists, and pounded the rocky ground.

Dune had wondered, not for the first time, what Mother Cass had seen in Paddy that qualified him to be Keeper of the Clover. Yes, he was a skilled tracker, but not the only one in the Clan. Sure, he could mediate disagreements over a potluck dinner where the luck was in a pot of the stew Paddy was famous for. But somehow his father had never taken the time to teach Dune the secrets of tracking; had never treated Dune with the calm neutrality of a skilled mediator.

His anger spent, Dune had turned his attention to the night. The only sounds were those of the normal activities of his above-ground neighbors preparing their evening meals, muffled laughter coming from bungalows whose windows glowed with, Dune imagined, the love of the families within.

Dune had allowed himself a few moments to breathe in the salty air blowing across the cliffs from the Atlantic Ocean. Then he had stood up, brushed dirt off the knees of his trousers, and walked back toward his home and his family.

Thinking of it now, as he plodded along the path toward Doolin, Dune shook his head. It had been irresponsible to burst out of his house like that, without checking for danger. *I'll not let my temper endanger my family ever again,* he vowed.

Dune counted heads as he continued walking. The family crested a low hill, and the Milky Way glittered overhead in the vastness of the universe. Dune was a month away from his sixteenth birthday, getting closer step by step to the Ceili and the Presentation of the Clover Ceremony, and yet he was nowhere near knowing how to claim his magic.

Magic. Every Leprechaun has it. Some of Dune's cousins on his mother's side had practically been born casting runes. Paddy was a skilled tracker, seemingly able to create a path where none existed. But Dune suspected that Maureen's magic surpassed even Paddy's. She was a natural at casting and reading runes, and used them in powerful protective spells, like the curtain he helped her raise to hide from the hunters. She cast her rune stones with grace, and was always able to read them with precision.

Maybe that's why Paddy was so hell-bent on Dune taking up the mystical fortune-telling practice, even though Paddy himself constantly berated Dune for his lack of skills. His father was wrong, though, about Dune not having any skills. His skill *was* playing football. His teammates and even members of opposing teams said he was magical on the pitch.

But that wasn't *real* magic. Not the kind of magic that conjured the mystical tattoo identifying a Leprechaun's clan. Not the kind Paddy expected his son to display. Not only display, but excel at. Paddy, whose greatest claim to fame was that he was Keeper of the Clover. What had *he* done to deserve that honor? Why didn't Dune deserve the same honor? Dune could only surmise that, decades ago, the Clan had needed someone with Paddy's unique mixture of blarney and bravery.

As they trekked on through the night, Dune remembered to check on his siblings. Travis and Gil marched along with their heads down. Gil occasionally batted at the tall grass that encroached on the path. He yanked out one long stalk and set about tickling the back of Travis's neck with it. Travis swatted it away as if it were a fly pestering him. When he finally turned around and caught Gil in the act, Travis wrapped his arm around his little brother's neck and made him walk bent over until he promised to quit.

"Ara be whist, you two," Dune scolded. "You mustn't make so much noise."

They straightened up, and Ayne glanced over her shoulder at him with an approving smile. She quickly turned her attention back to the path. Her eyesight was not good at night, and she had to keep focused so as not to stumble. Ayne tried to walk and behave as gracefully as their mother, but whereas Maureen had the quiet grace of a doe, Ayne more closely resembled a gangly fawn, trying to grow into its too-long legs.

Dune felt certain that Ayne, a year younger than he, would be a healer like Mother Cass. Her impromptu culinary concoctions called forth the secrets of the ancient Tuatha Dé Danann and the knowledge of the Kelly family's forebearers. In fact, her skills were not strictly medicinal. Cooking—whether in the kitchen or over an open campfire—was a talent Ayne inherited from both their parents. Maureen had tutored her eldest daughter in all aspects of meal preparation, and whenever Paddy announced, "I shall be makin' a stew for dinner tonight," Ayne sprang to his side, eager to help.

Paddy's stews were legendary. Thinking about his father's famous cooking made Dune's stomach growl.

"Stop that," Fionn said, poking Dune's belly. "You're making me hungry."

Dune tapped his little sister on the top of her head. "I'm hungry too, lass. And mark ye well: I've got my eye on you from now on. So dunna be trying any more of your tricks, or I'll be nibbling on your fingers for a snack."

Fionn tugged on the tail of Dune's jacket. "Carry me?"

Dune picked her up and swung her onto his shoulders. But this did not quiet her complaints. "Da, is it time to stop?" she whined.

"Not until dawn," Paddy said. "We've got to make as much progress as we can if we're to make it to Doolin by daybreak."

"If I had a pony, I could be in Doolin already," Fionn said with a pout.

"Not unless that pony would hold both you and your brother Dune," Maureen said. "For a wee wain like you'll not be going anywhere by yourself, much less all the way to Doolin."

"And dunna count on *me* riding any smelly, cantankerous pony," Dune said.

"Ponies are na smelly. Or cankerous."

"Cankerous—ha! All ponies are smelly and can-*tank*-erous." Dune bounced as if he were trying to buck Fionn off his shoulders. "And I am as close as you're getting to a pony ride tonight."

"Whoa, pony! You are being too can—, cankankerous!" From her perch on Dune's shoulders, Fionn kicked him in the ribs.

"Oof!" Dune almost lost his balance. "If that's the thanks I get, you'll be walking the rest of the way to Doolin, Missy. And if you ever do get a pony, which I hope is never, you'll be a smelly, cantankerous pair, you will."

"Ma, he called me smelly! And that other thing."

Maureen wheeled and in one smooth motion, swept to the back of the line and plucked Fionn from Dune's shoulders. Holding her daughter nose-to-nose, she whispered, "Quiet, girl."

"Yes, ma'am," Fionn squeaked.

Dune put his hands on Fionn's shoulders. "She'll ride quietly now. And I'll be a quiet pony. Not a bit cantankerous."

Fionn climbed back onto Dune's back, and soon he felt her head snuggle on his shoulder as she fell asleep. The tower of Dun Guaire Castle, silhouetted against the moonlit bay, was the only witness to the family passing through.

***

Hours later, with the waxing moon hanging low and pale white on the western horizon, they crested a small grassy rise and were greeted by a cool, salty breeze. After walking inland and southward so long before finally turning back to the west, their journey was almost complete.

Below them, not more than an hour's walk farther, the sandy shore of Doolin Bay glimmered in the light of the setting moon. Lights twinkled on boats tied at the harbor, their moorings clinking like bells. More lights dotted the hillside. Dune knew even more would greet them as they entered the Hidden Harbor that Mother Cass had cloaked from view. The secret sanctuary within and above Doolin Harbor, concealed from Humans through her powerful magic, waited to welcome the weary family. No-one other than Leprechauns knew how to find it, and the loyalty of the Leprechauns, spelled out in the Code of Erin, forbade revealing such important Clan secrets to Humans.

Paddy took Fionn from Dune's aching back and settled her on his hip.

"I wanna be held, too," Gil whined. He tugged on his mother's skirts.

Maureen tweaked the little boy's chin. "You're far too big."

"Maybe for you, but Dune could carry me," the boy insisted.

"Dune's not much bigger than your ma," Paddy said.

"You have na noticed, Da," Dune replied. "I'm taller than you." Dune dropped his gunny sack and bent at his knees. "Come here, Gil, I'll carry you."

"But you've been carrying Fionn all this way," Maureen said. "Dunna you need a rest?"

"I'll be fine." Dune kneeled to let Gil scramble up on his back. He grunted under his brother's weight. "How old did you say you were?"

"Seven, but just barely."

"Are you na always sayin' you're seven and a half?" Ayne mentioned. "Now you're usin' your baby voice and wantin' to be carried like a wee wain."

"I am not a wain, I am just tired."

"You're fine, Gil." Dune laughed. He flipped his gunny sack into the air with the toe of his boot and grabbed the handle end of the stick to which it was tied.

"Travis, carry Gilroy's pack for him to lighten Dune's load," Maureen said.

"I've got it, Ma." Dune hoisted Gil—pack and all—to a more comfortable position on his back.

"Sure, you are a strong lad, Dune," Maureen said, "and such a good brother."

"Can we dispense with the chit-chat and get down this hill?" Paddy grumbled. He adjusted Fionn on his hip and stepped carefully down a path through an outcropping of flat-topped boulders that formed a steep, natural stairway.

Behind Paddy, Birdie held out his hand to help Maureen and Ayne down the first few steps before falling in line behind them. Dune took up the rear as usual, but this time with Gil on his back.

At the bottom of the embankment, a narrow, sandy footpath snaked through tall, reedy grass. Paddy set Fionn down on the path and touched his fingers to his lips. "No talkin', now," he whispered. "'Twill be light soon. We must be completely quiet the rest of the way to Hidden Harbor."

Fionn nodded wordlessly and placed a finger over her own lips.

Paddy looked from one member of the family to the next; they each nodded their understanding. Dune squatted so that Gil could slide off his back. The boy yawned and rubbed his eyes, but managed a nod when Paddy looked his way.

As they walked down the hillside, Dune's mind leapt ahead like a stag. He wondered what the morning would bring: Would the Ceili begin as scheduled? Or would Birdie's news about the Greenapples scramble the plans? Most likely, Mother Cass would organize a search party. Dune hoped that the Greenapples would be found safe but disoriented after taking a wrong turn somewhere. And they would all have even more to celebrate at the Ceili.

Dune tried to convince himself of this scenario, but the thought gave him a foreboding chill. Seamus Greenapple's legendary tracking skills were second only to Paddy's. And with Maureen's confirmation of Birdie's bird-talking skills, Dune couldn't discard Birdie's account of the Greenapples' capture as the rantings of a confused old man.

The decision about how to respond to Birdie's "information" would be up to the Matriarch. When they reached Doolin, Paddy and Birdie would find her and tell her what Birdie knew—or thought he knew—about the Greenapples.

While they handled that, Dune would help the family get

settled in one of the small bungalows along the cliff overlooking Hidden Harbor. It would be their home throughout the week-long Ceili. He'd finish his chores quickly, register for the competitive events, then relax on the beach with the menfolk and enjoy a pint of ice-cold cider while he waited for Mother Cass to let everyone know that the news about the Greenapples was all a big misunderstanding. He was sure she would tell them that Birdie had misinterpreted the message from the birds. That was far more plausible than Seamus Greenapple getting captured.

Dune's mind jumped back and forth. Birdie misinterpreted the message and the Greenapples were merely lost. No, Seamus would never lose his sense of direction; the family must have been captured. No, Seamus would never lead his family into a trap. Then a third possibility occurred to Dune: Maybe the Greenapples were already at the Ceili, and all this worry was for naught. When they arrived in Doolin, Mother Cass would assure them that the Greenapples were safe and, in fact, had already settled in to their favorite bungalow in Doolin.

The more he thought about it, the more Dune convinced himself that this scenario was much more likely than Seamus getting lost or captured.

The next day, Dune would join hundreds of relatives, from toddlers who could barely walk to the Matriarch herself, in the ritual round dance that gave its name—the Ceili—to the entire reunion.

That's what he told himself.

But he could not shake the feeling that Birdie was right.

***

They entered the town proper of Doolin just before daybreak, passing through the secret streets of Hidden Harbor. Even though the section of town along the beach was cloaked from the perception of Humans by the magic of the Folk, amplified by the powerful presence of Mother Cass, Paddy still insisted on complete quiet until they began to see other Leprechauns and he was sure the curtain of camouflage was engaged.

The village was crowded with dozens of Kelly kin from across Ireland with whom the small band shared happy greetings.

Paddy and a man passing the other way grasped each other's forearms. "Top of the morning to you, Cabe!"

"And the rest of the day to yourself, Paddy. Why, hello, Birdie. Why are you tagging along with Paddy's caravan?"

"'Tis the Greenapples," Birdie began.

"Nae, tis Paddy Kelly, to be sure," Cabe said. "Have ye nothing but feathers in your head?"

Before Birdie could explain, Cabe had spotted someone else to welcome, and skipped off down the cobblestone lane.

"We best not speak of the Greenapples until we've had a chance to notify Mother Cass," Paddy cautioned.

Birdie nodded. "Of course, Paddy. 'Twould na do to have word reach her piecemeal and her not know what to believe."

"Nor do we want to sow panic."

Dune was happy to see many relatives whom he had not seen since last year's Ceili. From first and second cousins to fourth cousins five times removed, they all greeted him warmly. But he was weary from walking all night, night after night for almost a week, and soon lost patience with the constant yak-yak-yak every time they turned a corner.

'Tis a true shame the no-talking rule no longer applies, now that we're in the village, he thought.

When they finally arrived at the bungalow that Dune and his family would call home for the week, Paddy and Birdie set off immediately to find Mother Cass.

As Maureen laid the circle of stones in the yard, encircling the bungalow with the protective curtain, Ayne tackled the kitchen, preparing for the family's first hot meal in a week that did not require a campfire, Dune quickly unpacked his gear and helped Fionn, Travis, and Gil unpack as well. "I'll be headed down to the shore," Dune announced when he finished.

"Nae, lad," Maureen said. "You'll be tucking in the wains for naps."

"Then can I go out?"

"Nae, Dune. You need a rest yourself." Maureen held up her hand to silence Dune's objection. "Sleep for a few hours, and then you can join your mates."

Dune made all the beds with fresh linens and tucked Fionn into her bed. After he assured himself that Fionn was asleep, he went to the room he would share with his brothers and lay down in his bed.

"What do you make of Mr. Birdie?" Gil asked.

"He says he talks with birds," Travis added.

Dune stretched and rubbed his eyes. "Aye. Ma says that's his magic."

"But what about what he said? About the Greenapples being captured?"

"He and Da will talk to the Matriarch." Dune yawned widely. "And she'll know what to do."

Dune was asleep as soon as he shut his eyes. When he woke, the light coming through the window told him he had slept more than a few hours. He slipped quietly out of the room to avoid waking his brothers, grabbed his jacket from a peg by the door, and headed to the beach.

Approaching the wide stretch of snowy sand, Dune felt the pleasant nip of the sea breeze on his ears and nose. The late afternoon was just cool enough to be invigorating. The beach was lit with dozens of torches whose flames flickered in the breeze, and by strings of lanterns that bobbed like buoys on a turbulent sea, soon to replace the glow of the setting sun.

Several people stood around a steel drum where a bonfire burned.

"Dune! How ya, head?" A bull of a fellow, his suspenders fairly bursting over his bare barrel chest, jogged over to where Dune stood. He gave Dune a bear hug that knocked his derby hat to the ground.

"Kane Kelly, my nemesis in the flesh," Dune said with a weak laugh after Kane released him and he was able to catch his breath.

"Sign up with Killarney and we'll be on the same team for a change," Kane said.

"Sure, it'd be my fortune to not worry about you comin' at me for a shot on goal." Dune collected his hat off the ground, swatted away the sand that clung to it, and shoved it on top of his thick auburn curls. "But I canna desert my mates from Yulnear."

Kane clapped Dune on the shoulder. Dune's attention was drawn to Kane's forearm, where a four-leaf clover tattoo was barely noticeable under the thick padding of hair. "You're a right fine keeper," Kane said. "I truly have to think when I'm facing you."

"That's hard for you, I ken."

"You old melter. What else will you be signing up for, other than the Gaelic football?"

"Lore Showdown, Rune Casting."

Kane's eyebrows raised. "I dinna ken you could tell runes."

"Ha! I've no talent with runes. My da makes me enter. He thinks I'll get the hang of it one day."

"It'll just mystically flow into you," Kane said, wiggling his sausage-shaped fingers at Dune.

"Yeah, no. He thinks I need to apply myself more."

"I'll tell you what you should be applying yourself to." Kane edged in close to Dune and spoke in a conspiratorial whisper. "Makin' money. That's the way to catch the eye of the ladies!" Kane laughed hard, bathing Dune's face with acrid breath.

Dune swiped at the stale air in front of his nose. "Ach, Kane, you could reap a vast fortune in the competitive onion-eatin' contest."

"Is that new? Did they replace watermelon seed spittin'?"

Dune grinned, watching as the realization spread across his friend's face.

"You melter," Kane said.

"Me, a melter? You're the one whose breath could peel paint."

"Serious, though." Kane draped his bear-like arm across Dune's shoulders. "Have you an eye for any o' the lasses?"

Dune scrunched his eyebrows together. "I may be stating the obvious, but 'tis the Kelly Ceili."

"Yeah?"

"'Tis a *family reunion*? We're all related."

Kane laughed and pushed Dune's shoulder with the butt of his hand. "Second cousins can marry, dunna ya ken. And besides, the Mountain Clan from America is here," he said. "They're not blood relatives, only honoraries. I've me eye on a certain lass. Her name is—"

Dune found himself silently wishing, *Please not Kyna. Please not Kyna.* He knew Kyna was from the Appalachian branch, and she wasn't a Kelly by birth. Not that any of that would matter. She was as beautiful as sunshine on water; way out of his league. Nonetheless, he didn't like the idea of Kane courting her.

"Dearbhorgaill," Kane sighed.

"Dear—? She sounds, er, lovely," Dune said, stifling a laugh. "Far too pretty to be interested in an ox like you."

"Shows what you know." Kane leaned back on his heels and slid his thumbs up and down behind his shiny black suspenders. He snapped them against his bare chest and winced. "She's already agreed to be my date at the dance."

"You're in me wick."

"Nae, she did. I know the language of women." Something in the way Kane licked his lips rankled Dune like the taste of spoilt milk.

"Do ye, now. And how do you say, 'Please, ma'am. Would you like to date a goon with onion breath?' in the language of women?"

"I just mention my friend Barney Dillions."

"Barney Dillions as in rhymes with millions? You offered her *money* to go out with you?" Dune shook his head. "Even you're not *that* smelly."

Kane playfully grabbed Dune's neck in the crook of his elbow. "I dinna offer her anything. I just let slip that I recently came into some money."

Dune tugged from Kane's grip and rubbed his neck. "Why, Kane Kelly. You must have gotten yourself a job!"

"You might say that."

"Where do you work? Wait, 'tis goldsmithing, isn't it?"

Kane's shoulders stiffened. "You know Mother Cass will na let us use our magic for our own enrichment. Lot of good my rightful talent of transmogrifying objects to gold does me."

"Then what kind of job is it?"

Kane's eyes darted left and right. "'Tis more of a … consulting position. Canna talk now. Gotta run."

Kane ran up the path toward the bungalows, leaving Dune scratching his head. "I wonder what he meant by that."

"Dune Kelly!" someone in the group around the fire called. "Come say hello!"

Dune shrugged off the weird sensation from his conversation with Kane and strode over to the men. They welcomed him to the group with smiles, handshakes, and pats on his back.

"Yulnear's sure to win the football championship," one man said, offering a mug of mead which Dune declined.

"Aye, with Dune here and Sligo down a man."

"Who is missing from Sligo?" Dune asked.

"Ardeen Greenapple. His family has na arrived, and they were due to get here early. Agnes was supposed to be chairing the seine-net weavers exhibition. Lady Beckta's in a fluster trying to fill in."

"They can't have gotten lost," another man chimed in. "Seamus could find the way to Doolin with a blindfold over his eyes."

"And his wife would never squelch on a commitment," another man said. "Something must have happened to delay them."

Dune cast his own eyes down at the embers, glowing and fading at the edge of the fire. He knew the men were right, that the absence of the Greenapples was not due to Seamus getting lost. Yet he couldn't reveal what he knew. It wasn't his place to be the bearer of such important news.

"Did ye hear what I said, mate?" One of the men shook Dune's shoulder gently.

"Sorry, what?"

"Ardeen Greenapple is Sligo's best player. If he's been delayed, that should make it easier for you boys from Yulnear."

Another man said, "But you still have to deal with Kane and his Killarney Killers."

"Kane, I can handle," Dune said.

The man with the mead took a sip from his mug and eyed Dune closely. "Do you know something, Dune?"

"I—I'm not sure. We ran into Birdie MacBressal on the way here. He seems to have heard something. He and my da are on their way to speak about it with the Matriarch."

One of the men said with a laugh, "Birdie? Where'd he hear it from, one of his coo-coo birds?"

"He's the one who's coo-coo!" another chimed in. "Right, Dune?"

Dune scrunched his shoulders. He had thought so, too, up until his mother vouched for her friend. But he hesitated to defend

Birdie. "I dunna ken."

"Whatever it is, Mother Cass will straighten it out directly, I'm sure," the man with the mead said.

"Aye, 'tis fortunate we are, to have her," another added. "She will know what, if anything, needs to be done."

The others nodded in agreement.

Dune took comfort that they were right about the Matriarch. Although she was as old as the Cliffs of Moher, her leadership was astute and her insights undeniable. She would straighten out the situation, and the Ceili would proceed as planned. He hoped.

One of the younger men asked, "Is it true Mother Cass once changed a rabbit into a cat?"

"I heard 'twas a badger, and she turned it into a rabbit," said another.

"Badger, cat, rhinoceros," a third man scoffed. "What would be the point of it? 'Tis just a rumor meant to distract us from the important matter at hand."

"And what matter might that be, Liam?"

"Why, that would be the little matter of who she will choose to succeed Paddy Kelly as Keeper of the Clover." Liam cocked an eyebrow at Dune. "Has your da given you any clue as to the Matriarch's favorites?"

"Dunna look at me," Dune said with a snort. "'Tis hard to say who is the bigger mystery, Mother Cass or my da."

The men laughed in friendly agreement, and the conversation turned to sports, a subject that Dune felt less reluctant to discuss, and more knowledgeable to speak about.

Chapter 6: The Competitions

Dune jogged down the sandy path, one hand on his derby hat to keep the sea breeze from blowing it off his head. Multi-colored flags snapped impatiently on poles that lined the path, directing Dune toward a group of canvas tents near the shore. A banner marked "Sports Registration" hung between two poles in front of the tent area, flapping like a sheet hung out to dry.

"Brilliant!" Dune rubbed his hands together against the chill breeze coming off the harbor. He headed toward the registration area.

More brightly colored pennants, pinned along the edges of the tents, announced the events. Dune read the banners as he meandered among the tents. "Ponies and Carts. I need more than a cart between me and a pony. Like the whole of Doolin Bay."

He walked farther, noting the different activities. "Goldsmithing. Too artistic." *Gil should probably enter, though,* Dune thought. *He has an eye for detail.*

Dune snorted in disdain as he read the next banner. "Partners Dancing? I dunna think so." He noticed the Irish Fiddle—Youth Division and Advanced Division sign-up area had quite a crowd. *Travis will have some competition!* Travis was mechanically minded. He had seen someone playing a fiddle when he was four or five, and within a few hours, he had worked out the mechanics of the instrument and built one himself out of their mother's small keepsake box and some twine. Dune chuckled as he remembered

Maureen's reaction. She vacillated between pride at Travis's ingenuity and frustration that he had taken her keepsake box without permission. She had finally resolved the situation by promising to get Travis a real fiddle if he, in turn, would promise to practice every day.

Finally Dune found the registration tent he'd been looking for. "Aah, here we go: Gaelic Football."

He joined the throng of teenagers gathered around the registration desk, shaking hands and bumping fists with old friends and cousins he hadn't seen since last year's family reunion.

Dune realized something was poking him in the arm, and that something was a long, pointy pencil in the hand of a small, pointy woman.

"Signing up for a football team, Dune?" the woman behind the registration desk asked.

"Yes, ma'am, Lady Beckta. I'll be playing with Yulnear."

"And your da has already made it clear you're to register for the Lore Showdown and Rune Casting." Lady Beckta pointed with her pencil toward a different area, where no-one was in queue to register. A classmate of Dune's staffed the otherwise abandoned table, rolling his pencil back and forth over a stack of registration forms that waited in vain for participants to sign in.

"Yes, ma'am." Dune sighed, knowing he'd have to sign up or bear the wrath of his father *and* Lady Beckta, who happened to be his high school principal.

"Do ye think your sister Ayne could be troubled to assist me with registration? Mrs. Greenapple has na arrived, which means I've no-one to organize the entries for the seine net exhibition."

"I'm sure she'd be happy to help."

"You know, Dune, were I a betting lass, I'd put a gold coin on your being chosen the next Keeper of the Clover, which even a blind man could see your da is thinking, too."

Dune absent-mindedly signed the contest registration forms she passed under his hand. "I suspect the blind man does na see as well as you give him credit for," Dune said. He held no illusions that his father had any such expectations.

"We shall see," Lady Beckta said with a wink. Placing his forms in a box, she handed him a timetable of his events.

"Thank you, Ma'am."

"Needle and thread to you, Dune," Lady Beckta said.

"Ma'am?"

"To sew up your good luck." She winked at Dune. "But mind, while the Ceili is a fun and joyful time, and you've a real talent at football, and of course, the presentation ceremony is important, still, as your principal, I trust you will not let your studies lapse over the summer. 'Tis quite important for a young man to hone his education as well as his aptitude in sports. Why, in my day—"

"Thanks, I'm sure." Dune shoved the next person in line toward the registration desk so he could escape what he and his mates called a "Beckta Lectcha." Lady Beckta was known for long and boring speeches.

Dune doffed his hat to Lady Beckta and darted away to the Lore and Runes registration area. "*Cad é an scéal*, Tim?" he greeted his friend who sat behind the Rune Casting registration desk.

"Gor, I'm bored to death." Tim scratched his head with the pencil he'd been rolling on the desk. "No-one wants to sign up for Rune Casting any more. It's such an old-fashioned pastime."

"I ken, I ken," Dune agreed. "But for sure, 'tis useful if you do it right. It can be the difference between life and death."

"Oh, right! I ken your mother's a right expert with runes. I dinna mean any disrespect. But not many of our lot are keen to learn it."

"Well, the fewer people who sign up, the better chance I have to win, eh? Although Gil will probably put me to shame!"

"Then, here's the form for Rune Casting. Lore Showdown, too?"

Dune nodded, and Tim grabbed another form from a stack on the ground next to his table.

"De ye ken where Yulnear's practicing?"

"Up toward the pony paddock, I believe."

"Right. See ya round." Dune shoved the completed entry forms across the desk and jogged farther up the shore, toward the pony paddock.

Although Dune didn't see his mates from his Gaelic football team, a small rise with a gentle slope provided a good vantage point to watch the crowd. Perhaps to spy a certain flaxen-haired lass. He leaned back with his elbows against the fence rail and crossed his legs at his ankles.

How's a mud-rumpled mate like me to impress a lass like Kyna? Dune thought. *I wonder if she studies ancient lore. Sure, she'll appreciate my ability to recite the family legends in the Lore Showdown. I know almost the entire* Rune Éire *by heart.*

Dune leaned back against the paddock fence, throwing his arms out and draping his elbows over the top rail.

Maybe he would amaze her with his skill as a keeper on the football team. He realized how little he knew about her. He didn't even know whether she liked sports.

Maybe she was more into the mystic traditions of the Leprechauns. Rune casting was one of his people's oldest talents, dating back to the days of the Viking explorers. It was his mother's forte, and even Gil could cast runes more convincingly than he could. Gil would easily win the children's category, and would probably be at the top of the upper age group competitions if allowed to enter them.

From where he stood, Dune could see the "Ponies and carts" and "Bareback pony races" pennants fluttering from the registration tent. "Trust my bad luck," Dune mumbled, "not to like the one thing girls always go for: ponies—Ouch!"

Dune yanked his arm off the rail and rubbed his elbow. A pair of teeth marks reddened the skin which was exposed by a newly frayed hole in Dune's sleeve.

On the other side of the fence, a shaggy, palomino pony with a wide white stripe on its face glared at him with beady eyes half-obscured by its long forelock. The pony pulled back its lips in what Dune knew in his heart was a malicious laugh at his expense. A scrap of green and black cloth was stuck between the pony's teeth.

"This is my best team jersey! Or it was, you infernal beast."

The pony blew a raspberry through its lips and trotted away, shaking its long, tangled mane.

"Dune, you old blackguard, are you ready to have a practice?"

Dune turned to see Brian Thomas, the Yulnear captain, and several others of his mates striding toward him. "Sure, I was born ready, Brian!"

The rowdy group of football players were all dressed in black, knee-length short pants and green-and-black plaid jerseys that matched Dune's—except none of his mates' jerseys had pony bites in their sleeves. As he joined his mates swarming across the pasture in a shortcut to the football pitch, Dune heard the harness bells tinkling on the ponies in the corral.

He hoped with his whole heart that Kyna liked Gaelic football better than she liked ponies.

Chapter 7: Mother Cass

After the practice, Dune returned to his family's bungalow.

Because of the timing of their arrival in Doolin, his longer-than-intended nap, and not wanting to waste any time before he got down to the registration area, he hadn't eaten since the night before. When he opened the door and was greeted by a chorus of sweet, tangy, and succulent aromas, he smacked his lips. "Mmm, Paddy Kelly's Award-Winning Vegetable Stew."

Dune's father looked up from the cauldron he was stirring in the hearth. "The same," he said with a wide grin. Paddy had given Dune his curly red hair and muscular build, but not his aptitude for cooking. "My reputation precedes me."

"That and your belly," Dune's mother said from the kitchen nook.

"Now Marnie, I canna help it if my cooking's so irresistible, even I have to partake of seconds."

Dune noticed Fionn sitting in an overstuffed armchair in front of the fire. She was reading—or pretending to read—*Rune Éire*. He took off his hat and, with a quick flick of his wrist, sent it flying. It landed on Fionn's head.

She peered out from under the brim and grinned. "I'm a turtle and this is my shell." She pulled her legs up to her chest, and wrapped her arms around them. She held the book between her knees. "It's hard to read when you're a turtle."

Dune retrieved the hat and placed it on the coatrack by the door.

"Did you and Birdie talk to Mother Cass?"

Paddy paused before he answered. "Aye."

A knife clattered in the kitchen sink. Dune turned to see his mother staring at him with wide eyes, her hands gripping the sink behind her back.

A shiver ran down Dune's spine. "And?" he asked, swallowing the lump in his throat.

"And nothin'. Birdie told her what he knew. She wanted Birdie to stay with her, in case he remembered anything else."

"That's all? Dinna she tell you what we should do?"

Paddy swirled the ladle in the stew again, then knocked the spoon's long metal handle against the cauldron and hung it on a peg in the mantel. "She's an old woman. She has strange ideas sometimes."

"Like what?"

"You'll find out soon enough," Paddy said, practically growling, "if she doesn't come to her senses first."

"Are you na going to tell him what she said?" Maureen asked.

"I prefer she tell him herself, if need be."

"What is it?" Dune asked. He stepped closer to his father. His heart fluttered like a flock of quail flushed from the heather. "Are the Greenapples ... are they ...?" He glanced at Fionn, who was paying close attention, and decided not to finish his question.

"'Tis not the time to discuss it," Paddy said.

Dune knew he would get no further information from his parents. Paddy had closed the subject. But whatever he had told Maureen about his conversation with Mother Cass had obviously unnerved her.

"Ma, do you need any help?" he asked.

"Nay, son. Not just now. Why dunna ye sit with Fionn and read for a bit until dinner's ready."

Dune lifted Fionn out of the chair and sat down with her in his lap. "How about I read out loud, Miss Turtle, and you can listen?"

Fionn handed him the book. "Turtles are good listeners."

Dune opened *Rune Éire* to the ribbon that bookmarked the chapter on Entrances and Extrances. He swiped at his bangs and turned to the page on the Great Faerie Ring and the Gatestone. He planned to recite the Gatestone Rune for the Lore Showdown. He had to get it perfectly. Not just the words, but the rhythms as well. The proper tone, a delicate mix of authority and humility. *Lady Beckta doesn't realize how much studying the Ceili requires*, he thought.

"'The Great Faerie Ring provides sanctuary to travelers and other Folk who need shelter,'" Dune read aloud.

"Is that the word *shelter?*" Fionn asked, pointing to the page Dune had been reading.

"Mm-hmm," Dune responded, but he was finding it hard to concentrate. Between Birdie's news about the Greenapples and Paddy's refusal to divulge details of their conversation with the Matriarch, Dune felt a huge weight of foreboding. Why could Paddy tell Maureen, but not tell Dune? Since Dune was friends with Ardeen Greenapple, maybe it was bad news about him, not the whole family. A sprained ankle or broken arm, something major enough to delay their arrival at the Ceili, but not as drastic as Birdie warned.

Dune was peripherally aware of his family bustling about. Travis practiced a squeaky rendition of *Greensleeves* on his fiddle. Gil and Travis were absorbed in a game of cat's cradle. Fionn's attention had drifted from *Rune Éire* and she was chattering about—of course—ponies. Only Paddy, Maureen, and Dune himself were silent. He was sure they were all thinking about the same thing.

"I like the ponies here," Fionn gushed. "There's a nice old pony who'll be Lucy's friend when she gets here."

Dune marked his place in *Rune Éire* with a slender blue ribbon and put the book on the little wood table next to the chair. "Who's Lucy?"

"She's my pony."

"The invisible one?"

Fionn frowned. "I dunna have an invisible pony."

"You dunna have a visible one, either."

"Poor thing has some sort of string or fabric stuck between his teeth," Fionn continued, unfazed.

"Your pony?"

"Nae, her friend. The one in the paddock. I call him Blaze because he has a white blaze on his face."

"Aw, not that one," Dune said, rolling his eyes. "That's the one that bit me. That fabric in his teeth is a souvenir from my jersey." He turned his arm to show Fionn the hole in his sleeve and the bruised elbow it revealed.

"Poor Blaze must be terribly hungry to try to eat your smelly shirt."

"Poor Blaze? What about me? Those are the beast's teeth marks on my elbow!"

"Don't worry, Dune." Fionn patted his arm. "One taste of you, and I'm sure Blaze will never bother you again."

"Luck be with me," Dune grumbled.

Just then, the door opened and Ayne came in. She unwrapped a long scarf and hung it on a peg by the door. "Whoo! I forgot how annoying Lady Beckta can be."

"Lecturing you about studying?" Dune asked.

"No, for once! But even *more* annoying. She was gushing about you and the football matches! And when she had exhausted her stockpile of synonyms for 'brilliant,' she started harping on about how rude Mrs. Greenapple was to neglect her duty."

"You dinna say anything, did you?" Maureen asked.

"No, ma'am. Has there been any news?"

"Nae!" Paddy shouted, drawing raised eyebrows from both Maureen and Ayne. Paddy never spoke harshly to his daughters. In a calmer voice, he said, "Wash up, now, and give me a hand with the stew. Please."

Maureen opened the cupboard doors above the kitchen counter. "Dune, will you help me reach the soup bowls?"

As Dune helped stacked the dinnerware in her hands, Maureen asked Ayne. "Are you prepared for your skills presentations tomorrow?"

"I've more sewing to do," Ayne said. "She crumbled some herbs over the stew pot. "I'm not satisfied with the hem."

"I'm sure you'll be able to finish after dinner. Travis, that note should have been a D, not a C."

"Aye, ma'am. I'll start over."

Dune brought down the seventh bowl and closed the cupboard doors.

"One more, if you please," Maureen asked.

"Will Birdie be joining us?" Dune asked.

"Nae." Maureen placed the bowls on the table. Without glancing toward the living room, she said, "Fionn, come out from behind that chair."

"How did you ken I was there?" Fionn asked.

"Ma has a wicked sense of knowing things that defy logic," Dune answered. "'Tis part of her magic."

"'Tis no more magic than you yourself possess, Dune," Maureen said.

"If so," Paddy grumbled, "the lad has yet to reveal his talents!"

"Now, Husband! Dune's magic will appear in its own good time. Birdie could na talk with the birds until he was twenty or twenty-one. And now, his magic has brought important news to the Matriarch."

Paddy mumbled something under his breath but dropped the

argument.

Dune let his father's comment bounce off his back. He'd heard it all before.

Maureen squeezed Dune's shoulder. "'Tis time for our guest to arrive. Would you go out and meet her?"

He grabbed his faded tweed jacket and bowler hat from the coatrack. "Meet who, exactly?"

"Mother Cass," Maureen said. "She'll be coming up from the harbor."

"What? She's coming here? Tonight?" Paddy stammered. He smoothed his hair and his vest. He gestured at Dune to hand him his jacket. "She dinna tell me she would be joining us for dinner!"

"She dinna tell me either," Maureen said. "Nonetheless, be here she will, and shortly at that."

"Wicked," Fionn said, nodding her head with approval.

"Don't forget your athame," Paddy called as Dune stepped outside.

"Got it, Da." Dune patted the side of his boot where the thin dagger hid.

Paddy pointed the ladle at Dune. "Keep it—and your senses—always at the ready. Let no harm come to the Matriarch."

Dune slipped out the door before Paddy could launch into more detailed instructions about handling knives and being constantly vigilant, subjects Dune had had drilled into him since he was a child. *Whoever decided Leprechauns were lucky gave us more trouble than any amount of luck is worth,* he thought as he ambled down the grassy lane.

Thinking of his father's words made him angry for another reason. Paddy obviously didn't think Dune could be trusted to keep the Matriarch safe. His words were a stinging vote of no confidence. Again. Although the night was mild, he shrugged himself deeper into his jacket.

The Claddagh

Bungalows like the one Dune and his family were staying in lined the lane, glowing in the light from the setting sun. Dune stopped at the point where the path forked. In the junction of the two forks, an outcropping of limestone, twice his height and shaped like an arrowhead, pointed skyward toward the North Star. The right fork led down to the beach. The whole area—the secret village of bungalows, the sandy path winding down the side of the cliff, and the beach, backshore, pastures, and sports fields below— were hidden by Mother Cass's cloak of magic. Only the cobblestone trail to the left could be seen by all—including Humans.

Dune tapped his fingers against his thighs. Should he wait here, or proceed on the path down toward the harbor? He gazed down the cobblestone path to the left that led inland. It was empty, quiet, obviously not a well-known or well-traveled route. *If Humans were coming up that trail, what would they see?*

With a deep breath, Dune strode past the limestone boulder onto the cobblestone path. He took a couple steps and turned around. Instead of the cottage-lined lane going up the hill on one side, the whole expanse beyond the limestone rock was a wild alder woodland with a thick understory of shrubs. The path leading down to the beach was obscured, with only the sheer cliff face visible, dropping off into the crashing waves far below.

Suddenly, Dune felt exposed and vulnerable. He looked around to ensure he was alone, then stepped forward and placed a hand on the limestone rock. "Echo of the Kelly clan, Echo in the son, a man. Let me pass, then close the door, hidden to the world once more."

The woods ahead of him remained unchanged.

Now he felt even more unprotected. *I know I said it right. Why canna I see the path?*

He took a few steps past the rock, and the woods melted away like fog carried away on a breeze. The bungalows reappeared, and the path to the shore became discernable once again. Dune exhaled a heavy sigh of relief.

Even if most of Rune Éire *is tall tales and blarney,* he thought, *"Entrances and Extrances" is a useful chapter.*

As Dune walked along the sandy path toward the harbor, he spied a pillar of stones stacked two meters high. He decided this was a good place to wait for the Matriarch.

Leaning against the pillar and staring at the star-speckled sky, Dune thought of Kyna.

"The paths we walk are on the same planet," he mused aloud, "but she might as well be in another galaxy."

"I think you are the one who is in another galaxy."

Dune leapt to attention and drew his blade from its sheath. The voice was close to him, practically at his elbow. A mistake like that could cost a Leprechaun his freedom, or worse.

Fortunately, the tiny old woman standing before him was no stranger. She was engulfed in a billowing black dress. A long black scarf was draped over her head and tied loosely under her chin. Dangling from a leather thong around her neck was a golden amulet. In one gnarled hand, she gripped an equally gnarly wooden walking stick with the visage of a bearded old man carved into it.

"Mother Cass! Do forgive me! I'm usually not so—I mean I'm usually more—I mean—"

"'Tis my own fault, Dune. Sneaking up on you like a ghost in the night." Mother Cass jiggled the necklace, making the amulet affixed to it bob up and down. "I was cloaked so as not to betray my presence to fellow residents of *this* galaxy."

Dune surveyed the area again, resolving to be especially vigilant while responsible for the Clan Matriarch's safety. He turned the knife in his hand, debating whether to re-sheath it inside his boot. Although he detected no danger, he was anxious to get home. He decided to tuck the athame in a loop on the side of his trousers where it would be more accessible.

He offered his arm to Mother Cass. "Shall we head home, then? My ma is expecting you. You must have sent her a message?"

"Not in so many words." The woman tucked her claw-like hand in the crook of Dune's elbow. Her touch was light as a feather.

She's two hundred years old, Dune thought. *'Tis a wonder she's not a ghost herself by now.*

"Late afternoon is my favorite time on Achill Island," Mother Cass said.

"But Mother Cass, 'tis night-time, and we're not on the island. We're in Doolin."

She continued as if she hadn't heard him. "'Tis the time when the sun casts its golden glow on the cabins of our kin. A beautiful sight, is it not?" She swept her cane in a wide arc from left to right, illuminating a panorama that Dune knew well—although it wasn't in Doolin.

A moment before, Dune and the Matriarch had been walking along the narrow lane above Doolin Harbor, bungalows on either side. Now they were walking on another lane lined with other tiny homes, most with gingerbread trimmings, all unmistakably part of his village overlooking the western coast of Achill Island.

"We're in Yulnear? How did we get here?"

"Nae, child, 'tis not Yulnear. 'Tis a vision that I am sharing with you."

"But why are you showing me this? I've lived here—there? I've lived in Yulnear my whole life. Aren't visions supposed to tell you something you dunna ken?"

"How closely have you ever looked at our village?" Mother Cass asked.

When he looked again, the vista was different somehow, as if a veil had been lifted, revealing details of his hometown that Dune had never noticed.

Warm, yellow auras radiated from the windows of the tiny cabins as lamps were lit and hearth fires were started in the little town below the ancient ruins of Slievemore. The late afternoon sky—for the vision conjured by Mother Cass replicated the precise time of day she most enjoyed—was bathed in paintbrush strokes of gold, deep purple, and pink. Even the ancient stones of Slievemore's desolate forts and walls seemed to glow as if from an inner flame.

"'Tis beautiful," Dune murmured.

"Yulnear is more than a collection of humble cottages," Mother Cass said. "These are the homes of our kith and our kin. Yours and mine. You owe them your respect and allegiance. Your name, don't forget, means *Protector*."

A shiver rushed from deep in Dune's chest to the tips of his fingers and toes. Even his scalp tingled. He pulled his jacket close to his chest. "Aye, ma'am. I know the name of every man who has a house in Yulnear."

"What of their wives?"

"Their wives, ma'am?"

"Aye, the women be the true heads of the family. Would you not agree?"

"I, well, I," he stuttered, unsure of how to respond until he saw a smile crease Mother Cass's time-etched face. He smiled too. "My ma would surely agree with you, ma'am."

That set Mother Cass into a loud, cackling fit of laughter. After a moment, she regained her self-control, wiping a tear from her eye. "'Tis a small detail, Dune, but ye'd do well to remember not only the men and women, but the children, too. And not just the mates on your football team."

"You know of my team?"

"Of course. Your skills are legendary."

Dune squared his shoulders, proud that the Matriarch knew

such personal details. Did it mean she had been investigating his qualifications? That he was being considered for Keeper of the Clover? *That* would show his father.

He badly wanted to ask her, but he couldn't ask outright. What if she laughed at the idea? It would be even more embarrassing than his father's derisions. No, he had to figure out a less obvious way to find out.

But before he could come up with an idea, Mother Cass was off on a different train of thought. "Now, Chriona. *There* was a born leader. Have you heard her name?"

"Aye, ma'am. The first Keeper of the Clover." Maybe this was a fruitful line of conversation after all.

"A darling girl she was," Mother Cass said with a sigh. "Not a true Kelly by birth, but as her name implied, a heart of gold. I could not ask for a more devoted daughter."

"Yes, ma'am."

"And she kept the Kelly Clover safe for the duration of her service. Ah, the Kelly Clover!"

Dune's ears pricked with interest. He needn't have worried about devising a way to talk about Mother Cass's intentions in naming a successor to Paddy: She was headed there herself.

"Some might think being Keeper of the Clover is merely an honorary title," Mother Cass said.

"Not I, ma'am. My da has often told us how important the Clover is to our family."

Mother Cass chuckled. "Knowing Paddy, he also impressed upon you his own stature, for being entrusted with such an important role."

"Aye. But 'tis true. You have chosen the Keepers for their loyalty to the Clan, their promise to protect and defend us all from harm."

"Quite so, Dune. There is more to being Keeper than

safeguarding a relic. Now, where was I? Ah yes."

They had continued their walk, and Dune noted that their progress had taken them north of Achill Island and east, as if they were walking through time-lapse photography. The wind rippled through field crops like waves on the ocean and snatched his hat from his head, sending it tumbling along the path. Dune clambered after it until he finally trapped it by trampling it with his boot.

As he punched the inside of the hat to reshape it, he looked up at the clouds scuttling across the sky, chasing the sun, which now hung low over the ocean behind them. As Dune watched, flowers which started out as tiny pastel nodes on the end of long stalks, bulged and grew to deeper shades of violet, orange, and magenta before bursting open and spreading their petals, all within moments. The rainbow garden seemed to hold every flower of every hue. Here a fox-and-cubs with its vibrant orange clusters like far-away galaxies; there the beautiful purple blossom of the common butterwort, waiting like a gargoyle for an insect to fly into the welcoming, carnivorous folds of its chartreuse leaves. They paused occasionally so Mother Cass could catch her breath. During these respites, the Matriarch was silent, and they simply witnessed together the ebb and flow of nature around them.

Finally, they were in an area Dune recognized as the outskirts of Sligo. Green fields of oats and potatoes spread out to the west, all the way to the monolithic Knocknarea hill in the distance. To the east, a few cottages huddled against the side of the road like a herd of cattle protecting themselves from the wind. Most of the cottages had smoke wafting from their chimneys, bearing the cozy scent of peat from their hearths.

Mother Cass pointed her walking stick toward one cottage, its windows dark and no smoke rising from its stone chimney.

"Do ye ken whose house that be?"

"Aye, 'tis the Greenapples' place."

"I wonder why they've not started their evening fire. No lamps are on, either."

"Are they na on their way to the Ceili? We ran into Birdie MacBressal on the way to Doolin, and he had a wild story about them being kidnapped. But that canna be true, can it?"

"Ah, yes. About that." Mother Cass bowed her head and shook it slowly.

Dune thought she was going to tell him more about the Greenapples' fate. He braced himself for the worst.

But when Mother Cass looked back up at him, she merely said, "Thank you for walking with me, Dune."

"'Tis my pleasure, ma'am. Were you going to say something about the Greenapples?"

The Matriarch waved the stick in an arc, this time from right to left, and the vision of Sligo faded away like a sandcastle in a rising tide. They were once again standing on the lane near Doolin Harbor. "Never doubt yourself, Dune. Nor my belief in you."

Mother Cass's crystal blue eyes bored into him. He felt he couldn't look away, a mouse hypnotized by a cat.

From across the beach, the wind rose up the face of the cliff and whistled by. The Matriarch closed her eyes and cupped a hand behind her ear. "Did you hear that? That wailing cry?"

"'Tis the wind," Dune said.

Mother Cass turned her attention to the intricate carving of a bearded old man on her walking stick. "You heard the Banshee, did ye not?" She paused for a moment as if listening to a reply from the carving. "Ah, you old buzzard. You never let me down."

"You've had that walking stick a long time, have you not?" Dune asked. "If I recall, it was a gift to you from the first Keeper of the Clover."

"You've been studying up, have you now?"

Dune beamed, his smile so wide it scrunched his freckles into solid, wiggly lines across the bridge of his nose.

"But you are mistaken."

His smile disappeared. "I am?"

"'Twas a gift from my goddaughter, Chriona."

Dune's eyebrows furrowed. "Aye, Chriona. The First Keeper."

"*But*—she gave it to me as a gift from daughter to mother. 'Twas *before* the presentation ceremony, so she was not yet the Keeper. 'Tis a small detail, but sometimes small details are very important."

"Yes, ma'am. I will remember." Apparently, he would have to wait even longer to find out the fate of the Greenapples.

Mother Cass squeezed his arm and nodded. "Let's rest a bit here." She gestured at a large root poking out of the ground like a bench provided by nature. A circle of mushrooms, luminous in the moonlight, ringed the protruding section of root.

Dune wondered if the root were another vision conjured by the Matriarch. After all, there were no trees about, other than the alder wood that was itself an illusion. So a big root seemed out of place. Nor did he remember it being there on his way out to meet Mother Cass. Possibly one of those small details she warned him not to overlook?

The old woman lifted her long skirts and stepped daintily over the ring of mushrooms. She settled onto the root like a hen on a nest and patted the spot next to her. "Sit with me, Dune."

"I'll stand, ma'am. I would na want anything to happen to you."

"The faerie ring will provide cover, even if the alder curtain fails."

"I have more faith in the curtain than in a bunch of mushrooms that happen to grow in a circle." He remained standing, just outside the ring of mushrooms. Realizing he sounded impudent, he added, "Beggin' your pardon, ma'am."

A shadow shifted in the twilight, a few meters away.

"Mother Cass, take cover!" Dune instantly drew the dagger and positioned himself between the Matriarch and the unknown threat.

Mother Cass jumped up, surprisingly spry for such an old, seemingly frail woman. She clung close to Dune, and he felt his heart swell with a new sensation: *I am protecting the leader of our Clan*.

Mother Cass relaxed her grip on his arm. "Rabbit," she said with a laugh. "'Tis you in the flesh!"

At her voice, the shadow revealed itself: Not a rabbit, but a sleek, black Manx cat. The animal twitched her bobbed tail and, purring loudly, padded softly to the Matriarch. She brushed against Mother Cass's skirts, then wound her lithe body between Dune's legs.

"Beggin' your pardon, ma'am. That is not a rabbit. 'Tis a cat."

"Ah, now *that* is the eye for detail I expect from the son of Paddy Kelly." Mother Cass bent to stroke the cat. "Her *name* is Rabbit."

Dune remembered rumors about Mother Cass changing a rabbit into a cat, or possibly turning a badger into a rabbit, or some such. Now he put together that Mother Cass had simply named a cat, "Rabbit."

The cat nudged Mother Cass's fingers with her forehead. Mother Cass picked Rabbit up and returned to her seat on the bench-like root. The cat purred loudly and kneaded her paws against Mother Cass's shoulder. She smiled at Dune. "Rabbit tells me she thinks you are an able protector."

Dune returned his knife to its sheath. "Ha, ha. Animals canna talk."

"Of course, they can talk." Mother Cass gently placed the cat on the ground at her feet and pointed at the circle of iridescent mushrooms. "Rabbit spoke to me just now. You could na hear because ye are na standing within the faerie ring."

"The mushrooms? I've heard of that, but never put much store by it. The only faerie ring that I believe in is the Great Faerie Ring.

The one made of stones, not—" Dune waved his hand to indicate the luminous mushrooms—"fungi. In fact, I've just been practicing the Entrance Rune for the Gatestone."

"A good skill, to be sure." As she stroked the cat's shiny black fur, Mother Cass hummed a lilting tune.

After a few minutes, Dune thought the old woman might have forgotten all about him.

"Beggin' your pardon, ma'am," he said again, "but I think my ma is holding dinner for us."

"Hmm? Oh, yes, of course. The hours fly by when you are two hundred years old. Or is it two hundred one? I lose track of time when talking to friends whom I haven't seen in a while."

Dune was not sure whether the Matriarch was referring to him or the cat. Probably the cat. Thinking of himself as the Matriarch's friend was more than a bit self-absorbed.

She placed Rabbit on the ground. Leaning heavily on her walking stick, she stood up and again took Dune's elbow.

The cat darted ahead, then turned and meowed plaintively.

"Farewell, Rabbit," Mother Cass said with a wave. "I shall see you again soon, I hope."

The cat loped away, her long back legs giving her a movement similar to that of, fittingly, a rabbit.

As they continued their walk toward Dune's family's bungalow, Mother Cass groaned and leaned more heavily on his arm. "My knees be the oldest part o' me," she apologized. "And my eyes be not far behind."

"Although I canna say about your knees, ma'am, even my eyes are straining to see the path. The night has gotten quite dark of a sudden."

"Mayhap I can help." Mother Cass pointed her walking stick at the road before them. "Guide us, Old Man of the Mountain."

A pin-prick of light appeared between the eyes of the face

carved in the walking stick. "Come now, Old Man. You can do better than that."

The tiny light grew larger and larger until the top third of the walking stick glowed like a lantern, lighting the path and bringing a chorus of crickets to life.

"We live in an enchanted world, Dune."

"Yes, ma'am."

"There are places in this world that have magic enough to protect Folk who know the right runes. You yourself mentioned the Faerie Ring."

"Aye, the great stone circle. In *Rune Éire*, it says it provides shelter and food for Leprechauns."

"Aye, lad, and 'tis every bit as real as the earth under your feet. What parts of *Rune Éire* are you familiar with?"

"I have been practicing the Gatestone rune for the competition."

"So you mentioned, and a wise choice it be, Dune. One day soon, you might need that very rune for more than a competition at the Ceili."

Without any indication from Dune, Mother Cass halted in front of the bungalow where Dune's family was staying. "Ah. This must be the one."

"How did you know?" Dune asked.

"Those stones," Mother Cass replied, pointing with her walking stick to indicate Maureen's stones encircling the bungalow. "Your mother's doing, are they not?"

"Aye, she placed them as soon as we arrived. They go all the way 'round the house. 'Tis her talisman, her way of protecting our family."

"Says Dune the Protector."

Dune smiled sheepishly. If Paddy had made the same comment, Dune would have known he was being sarcastic.

"I hope you are na teasing me. I would protect you with my life, ma'am."

"I would na tease about such a thing."

Mother Cass breathed in deeply. "Mmm, baby red potatoes, barley, cloves." Her cheeks poked out like hard baby apples as she chuckled. "Paddy's cookin' his famous vegetable stew. That was not in my vision; merely a fortuitous happenstance!"

"Your vision? The vision of Yulnear?"

Before Mother Cass could answer, Dune's father appeared at the bungalow door. He had donned an apron that read, "Kiss me— I'm Irish."

"By the stars, 'tis Cassiopeia Kelly," Paddy said. "Marnie told us ye'd be dropping by. I trust the boy was helpful to you."

"Indeed he was. And a more pleasant companion I could na ask for."

Dune's mother stepped up behind Paddy. "Please come in, Mother Cass." Maureen nudged her husband out of the doorway. "We've set a place for you for dinner."

"Children," Paddy called over his shoulder. "Wash up and get to the table. Our guest has arrived!"

Fionn had been curled up in the overstuffed chair by the fire, reading Dune's copy of *Rune Éire*. Her eyes opened wide when she spotted the Matriarch. "Eep! She's here!" She dashed to the dining nook, ducked behind a ladder-back chair, and peered out from between the rungs.

Mother Cass laughed and twiddled her fingers at Fionn in a quick hello.

Fionn poked her hand through the rungs and wiggled her fingers back at Mother Cass. In a flash the little girl was smiling and not a bit shy.

In a graceful way that mirrored their mother's movements, Ayne waltzed to Mother Cass's side. "Do come to the table, won't you, ma'am?"

"Your daughters are beauties, both," Mother Cass said. "They take after their lovely mother, the lucky darlings."

"I have to agree with you, there," Paddy beamed. He strode to the hearth. "But the boys will be taking after their da, they will. Strong, strapping lads, all three. Especially Dune."

The words caught Dune by surprise. He felt a glow on his cheeks as his chest swelled with pride. He drank in the rare compliment as if it were sweet honey mead.

"Travis, Gilroy. Come say hello to Mother Cass."

Travis propped his fiddle and bow against the wall and stood ramrod straight by his father. Gil stood at attention, imitating Travis' posture. Both boys' eyes were wide as saucers.

"Pleased to have you in our home," Travis said.

"Peas to have you in our loam," Gil said, blushing. "I mean," he stammered, "same what he said."

Dune took off his jacket and hat and secured them on the coatrack. He understood his brothers' nervousness. He felt the same way in the presence of the Matriarch.

But Mother Cass set them at ease as quickly as she had with Fionn. "Thank you for having me. I love peas, but I've not tried them in loam. I do hope there are lots of peas in your father's stew, though."

Gil blushed to a shade that matched his thicket of garnet-colored hair.

"To the table, boys," Paddy said. He wrapped a cloth around the cauldron's handle and struggled to remove the heavy pot from its hook.

"Let me help, da," Dune volunteered. He rolled his shirt sleeves above his elbows and pulled the cauldron out of the fire. With a great effort, he set it on the mosaic-tiled center of the dinner table, just to the side of a silver candelabrum.

With everyone gathered around the table, the cozy nook was

quite crowded. Fionn played peek-a-boo with Mother Cass around the candelabrum that spread its many branches like an ancient, miniature oak tree.

"I'll move that out of your way," Dune said, reaching for the candelabrum.

"Please leave it," Mother Cass said. "Else I would have no place to hide from Fionn."

Ayne glided to the fireplace where she took a long matchstick from a green glass vase on the mantel. She lit the tip of the match in the fire.

"Ma, I want to light the candles," Fionn whined.

"You and Ayne may both light three," Maureen decreed.

Fionn counted on her fingers. "That's just six. What about the seventh one?"

"Perhaps Mother Cass will light it for us."

"'Twould be my pleasure."

"Honored as we are to have you sup with us, Mother Cass," Paddy said, scooping ladles of stew into the china bowls, "I know the real reason for your visit is more than pleasant companionship and stew, no matter how enticing my cookin' may be."

"My turn." Fionn grabbed the matchstick from Ayne.

"Certainly the supping and companionship can come first," Maureen said. She had that wide-eyed look from when Dune asked her about Birdie.

"You must be careful," Ayne cautioned her sister. "'Tis dangerous."

"True enough," Mother Cass said. "One must be prepared for the task at hand, and how can one find the strength without nourishment for body and soul?"

Dune had trouble keeping track of the overlapping conversations —or was it all one and the same?

Fionn stood beside Mother Cass and lit three candles. She

handed the matchstick to the grandmotherly guest.

"Aah, thank you, little one." The Matriarch held the flame a few centimeters away from the last unlit wick. The flame jumped like a ballerina from the matchstick to the candle, simultaneously extinguishing itself from the match.

Dune reached for the spent matchstick. "I'll take that for you, Mother Cass."

"No need," Mother Cass smiled. With a twist of her wrist, the matchstick vanished.

"Will you say grace for us, Mother Cass?" Maureen asked.

"Oh, no, Marnie, dear. Grace is too large a matter for any but the man o' the house."

This should be good, Dune thought, suppressing a snicker. Paddy never said grace.

The family held hands, Dune taking Fionn's on one side and Gil's on the other. Dune closed his eyes but squinted one open so he could see his father squirm.

Paddy cleared his throat and took Maureen's and Mother Cass's hands. The others joined hands as well so they were all connected. After a deep breath, Paddy spoke with a low, reverent tone that Dune had rarely heard from his father.

"God shares Her bounty on heaven and earth. We share with others regardless of birth. For all are creatures in Her name, all are worthy just the same. May the blessings She shares with us today, be shared with others along our way."

"Amen," Mother Cass said. "Beautifully spoken."

"Amen," Dune said, incredulous at the poetry of his father's impromptu prayer.

As the family settled in to their tuck, Fionn announced out of the blue, "Mother won't let me have a pony."

Dune elbowed her. "Ara be whist!"

His littlest sister ignored him as usual. "But I'm old enough to take care of one all by myself. I would brush her, and braid her mane, and I would sing her to sleep," Fionn explained.

"And who would be feeding it and cleaning up after it, is what I want to know," Paddy said. "A pony is a lot of work."

"She's been campaigning us mercilessly for a pony," Maureen explained to Mother Cass.

"Merci-*fully*, her mother has not given in to her," Paddy added.

"Hmmph." Fionn dropped her spoon in her bowl with a splash and crossed her arms tightly across her chest. "Not fair."

"Do you ken the wee Manx called Rabbit who lives hereabouts?" Mother Cass asked Fionn. "Could she not be your friend instead of a pony?"

"I've tried to catch that cat, so I have. She's the one what told me I've a pony headed my way." Fionn blew at her bangs in frustration. "But she's too quick to catch. Is that why she's called Rabbit?"

"Mayhap, my dear. But here's a secret: You'll not catch her," Mother Cass said. "You must catch her *attention.*"

The Matriarch laughed at Fionn's quizzical expression. "You'll find a way, lass."

Fionn turned back to her dinner with a deep look of concentration in her eyes.

"I believe she's mulling over my advice," Mother Cass said. "So many of the younger folks today seem to think of me as a quaint and harmless relic to be tolerated but not taken seriously."

"Never!" Maureen said.

"Not under *my* roof," Paddy added emphatically.

Dune concentrated on his stew.

Gil piped up, "Dune says—Ow!"

Dune elbowed his brother sharply in the side. No telling what Gil might have repeated.

The younger children dominated the conversation, giving Dune no opportunity to find out more about the Greenapples. He thought the Matriarch must be bored to tears with Gil and Travis's rivalries and Fionn's preoccupation with animals. But Mother Cass seemed to soak it all in with relish.

At the end of the savory meal, Mother Cass rested her spoon upside down in her empty bowl.

"Paddy," she said, "You may think you ken why I am here tonight, but you are only half right. The main reason is because I am not long for this world."

"Mother Cass! Dunna talk that way!"

She raised her hand to silence Paddy's objection. "But before I depart for my next journey, I must ensure the safe return of Seamus and Agnes Greenapple and their children. And I'll be needing your family's help."

"You mean, what Birdie said is true?" Dune asked.

"Aye. They have been captured."

"Ayne, please take the children upstairs," Maureen said. For once, there were no arguments, and all three young ones allowed Ayne to shepherd them to their rooms without a word. When the children were gone, Maureen stood and indicated that Dune should take her place beside Mother Cass.

Paddy clasped the old woman's frail hand in both of his. "Mother Cass, you know we will help in any way we can. Only please reconsider the plan you spoke of to Birdie and me. 'Tis far too dangerous."

"Now, Paddy, neither you nor I can choose who goes on this mission. The mission will choose the man."

"But Dune is but a boy! Not a man!"

The Matriarch fixed Paddy with a stare that caused him to drop his eyes and curl his shoulders inward. Dune had never witnessed this degree of subservience in his father. But he had no time to ponder on it, because of the meaning he gleaned from the conversation.

"You think *I* should search for the Greenapples?" Dune's eyes widened in disbelief.

"As I just said, young man." Mother Cass locked eyes with Paddy. "The mission will choose who should undertake it. But to be clear, 'tis not simply a search mission; 'tis a *rescue* mission. The longer the Greenapples remain under the control of Humans, the less likely they are to survive."

Mother Cass stood, slowly but unaided. Paddy and Dune immediately stood as well. "Paddy, I wish to speak with the Council at once. In fact, not just the Council, but every member of the Clan over age fifteen, except those who must tend to the wains."

"Tonight?" Paddy asked.

"Aye, tonight. Please call them together. We meet on the beach in half an hour."

Chapter 3: Kyna's Journey Begins

Violet Springs was a tiny hamlet in the Blue Ridge Mountains of western North Carolina. Tucked away in a bend on the South Toe River, it was the only home Kyna had known since leaving Ireland as a five-year-old. In the following years, she had never left her home village, much less traveled across the ocean, until last year, the summer before she turned fifteen, when her adopted great-grandmother, Mother Cass, had sent word that she should return for the family reunion. Kyna's parents, fearing it might be the last time Kyna could see the elderly Matriarch, arranged for her to travel with an older cousin to serve as a chaperone. At Kyna's request, her friend Dearbhorgaill was allowed to come too.

On that trip, with each mile she put between herself and her adopted home town, she felt like she was being dragged away from everything she knew and loved. From the train ride across the hilly piedmont and the Carolina coastal plain, all the way down to the shore, her loneliness and homesickness ballooned until she felt suffocated by their weight.

Even Dearbhorgaill could not snap her out of her sorrowful mood. As Kyna stood next to Dearbhorgaill at the caboose rail, watching the soft, haze-blanketed horizon drift away, tears had welled in her eyes. "Ah, Gaill, I miss the mountains already."

Dearbhorgaill squeezed her arm. "Don't cry, Kee. I'm sure we'll have fun! I can't wait to see Ireland!"

After the train, they had boarded an ocean liner at the Port of

Charleston. Going up the gangplank, Kyna thought about dashing back, somehow finding her way home to her beloved Violet Springs. But Gaill and the other passengers were a moving wall, pushing her forward, ever forward. There was no going back.

Once she had boarded the ship that would take her across the ocean, Kyna had stood in the stern, as close to her mountain home as she could get—her adopted home that she had grown to love and feel even more connected to than the Emerald Isle of her birth. With Gaill holed up in their cabin, seasick throughout the voyage, Kyna had never felt more alone.

Even the wind whispered, *Away. Away.*

Her mood had changed when she arrived in Doolin. She was met at the dock by Mother Cass, the matriarch of the Kelly Clan, who had specifically invited Kyna to Ireland for the Ceili.

Despite her advanced age, Mother Cass seemed to Kyna to be acutely in tune with every generation of her extensive family, including Kyna. The Matriarch had done everything in her power to wash Kyna's homesickness away. Kyna was drawn to the old woman, and the pair had spent much of Kyna's visit wandering the paths of Doolin together.

Kyna was thrilled that she and the Matriarch had such a strong connection. One evening as they braided pine needles together in front of the elder woman's crackling fire, Kyna had closed her eyes and thought of her favorite dish—deep-fried mashed potato balls with centers of garlic, squash, and mushrooms. At that moment, Mother Cass mused, "'It has been a long time since I've had potato mashies. Do you like them, by any chance?"

Of course, the Matriarch had many duties to attend to: administration of the Ceili, visiting with family members who had come from far and wide to the annual reunion, and high-level discussions with the Council regarding shelter, health, safety, and other issues that impacted the Clan year-round. During these times,

Kyna and Gaill spent their time enjoying the multiple activities at the Ceili, which was like an expanded version of the crafts fair held each summer in Violet Springs. They browsed through the crafts tents, listened to dulcimer concerts, and strolled by the paddock where they petted the ponies and fed them pieces of carrots and apples.

One day, an electric current of excitement charged the atmosphere. The semi-final match of the Gaelic football tournament was being held. Gaill had a crush on one of the players and begged Kyna to go to the match. "Sports are boring," Kyna complained. "And football is downright barbaric."

"I cain't go by myself," Gail pleaded. "Don't you want me to be happy? I'm such a plain gal, yet he *smiled* at me. I *know* he likes me. Please, Kyna, if our friendship means anythin'."

"All right, I'll go, if you'll stop pestering me about it. I'll bring a book."

The girls laid a blanket on the ground alongside other spectators. The gentle hill provided a good view of the pitch for Gaill and a sunny spot for Kyna to enjoy her book.

"There he is!" Gaill pointed to a stocky young man in a burgundy jersey with a tan collar. "The midfielder for Killarney."

Although Kyna would never say so to her friend, her first impression of the object of Gaill's crush was not favorable. Built like a bear, the boy pushed his weight around, shoving, tripping, and laughing at anyone who got in his way. *I suppose it's part of the sport,* Kyna thought.

"Well, what do you think?" Gaill asked, elbowing her friend.

"Oh, uh-huh. Well, he's certainly, um, enthusiastic."

Kyna's gaze drifted away, disinterested in the brutish combat, until the spectators erupted in a roar. Kyna looked up to see what the commotion was about. Her eyes locked on the keeper for the team from Yulnear. Tall and muscular, the boy seemed to sense the direction of the ball before the player even kicked a shot on goal. Lithe as a cat, he defended the goal with a seeming disregard for any injuries he might suffer as a consequence. The crowd cheered again, even louder than before, yelling the keeper's name, "Dune! Dune! Dune!"

After the match, when everyone was gathered on the beach, she had wanted to speak to Dune, but every time she approached, he slipped away. Her attraction to him was uncharacteristic for her. An athlete! She hadn't an athletic bone in her body. Had never cared for sports. She was more attracted to storytellers like herself, musicians, poets. And yet, here she was, infatuated with an athlete. Dune, she was sure, was too involved with the football tournament to even know she was alive.

The last night of the gathering culminated with the Ceili, the traditional dance for which the reunion was named. The members of the clan mingled on the beach, waiting for music to start. Kyna strolled through the crowd, arm-in-arm with Gaill, trying to spot Dune.

"Your mind is somewhere else," Gaill said.

Kyna squeezed her friend's arm. "No, it's right here."

The band took the stage—a makeshift platform on the backshore—and began warming up. Soon a half-dozen young men approached them. One extended a hand to Gaill. "Hello, ma'am. Care to dance?"

Gaill blushed as she took the fellow's hand and strolled with him to the circle of people lining up for the first dance of the evening.

Kyna heard someone call her name, "Kyna, dance with me," and she too was pulled into the circle of merrymakers. One after another, hopeful dancing partners asked Kyna to dance with them. She scanned the faces of the revelers, but Dune wasn't among them.

Too soon, the reunion was over, and it was time to go home, back to America. Kyna hadn't had a chance to introduce herself to Dune, much less hold a conversation with him or find out anything about him—other than that he was apparently an excellent footballer, admired by his teammates and most everybody else in the Kelly Clan.

Mother Cass saw her off from the docks in Doolin. The grey skies and choppy waters that day matched her mood. She hugged the Matriarch in a tight embrace, not wanting to let go. "I—I feel like I'm leaving home instead of going home," Kyna said, her voice trembling.

"I've a going away present for you," the Matriarch said. She pulled away from the embrace and placed a delicate gold chain around Kyna's neck.

Kyna brushed her fingertips across the pendant, which was a familiar symbol. "The Claddagh. You know this was the first picture I ever conjured."

"Yes, dear. That is why I'm giving it to you. So you will remember where you came from, and to whence you shall one day return."

"You mean, I'll come back?" While the wind whipped Kyna's hair into a golden tangle, the elements seemed to detour around Mother Cass. The Matriarch's long grey hair cascaded like a waterfall over her shoulders and down to her waist, rippling calmly but otherwise unbothered by the weather.

"Why, of course, dear. You must come back for next year's Ceili. 'Twill be a special observance. My two hundredth birthday."

"Mother Cass, why did you invite me to the Ceili? After all the years I've been gone, why now?"

"'Twas time for you to reconnect with your heritage, my dear. To prepare for the future. Many things will change between now and next year."

"I wish I knew what my future held. Maybe I should have asked

95

for a reading of the runes while I was here."

Mother Cass chuckled kindheartedly. "The runes canna tell the future; only possibilities. But I need no runes to tell you that you *will* return."

The whole trip back to Violet Springs, Kyna longed for the island of her birth. The rocking of the ship sent Gaill belowdecks again, and again Kyna stood at the stern, gripping the railing, this time gazing east at the smudge of land on the horizon that slowly dissolved.

From the ship they boarded the train. As it trundled across the flatlands of coastal Carolina, Kyna looked at the pastures dotted with haybales and thought of the pony paddock. The flatlands gave way to the rolling hills of the piedmont; the hills grew into the well-named mountains of the Blue Ridge; and Kyna's journey back to Violet Springs was complete. With mixed emotions, she greeted her Appalachian friends and family, breathed in the aroma of the hemlocks and rhododendrons, and yearned for the day she would return to Ireland.

Over the next few months, Kyna's thoughts of Dune faded, only to be reawakened at unexpected times, mostly when she was around water, and mostly having to do with the image of a four-leaf clover. Last month, she got the official invitation from Mother Cass to join the Clan for the Ceili, and ever since, it seemed that neither the symbol of the four-leaf clover nor the image of Dune with his strawberry blonde curls, high cheekbones, and emerald eyes were ever far from her mind. She had simply to run her hand under a stream of water and the droplets would shimmer and move together into a glittering clover. And every time she saw the clover, she thought of Dune.

Now she was almost sixteen, and headed back to Ireland for the Matriarch's bicentennial birthday celebration. Gaill was with her again, but this time, she had convinced her parents that she didn't need a chaperone. She stood as far fore on the ocean liner as possible, right in the bow. The wind that whipped her long butter-blonde hair seemed to carry the smell of the grass of Ireland, the taste of the salt air of Doolin Harbor, and the music of the Ceili. Her senses were awash in memories and possibilities as she anticipated her return.

Kyna resolved to meet Dune this year, to introduce herself, to find out if her infatuation was just that—or if her interest would deepen after she met him and got to know him. Then, too, he might not be interested in her at all. He probably had a girlfriend. If either was the case, she would set him out of her mind. Hopefully it would be as simple to get him out of her head as he had entered it, if need be. And besides, other than once a year, they were separated by a vast ocean. How could that ever work?

"Pardon me, Miss."

Kyna jumped at the voice of a man standing close to her. This almost never happened to her—someone approaching her without her knowing or sensing their presence. Instinctively, she clutched the talisman that dangled from its chain around her neck.

The man chuckled. He was tall and trim and wore a long black overcoat with silk lapels. "I didn't mean to scare you."

"You didn't scare me. You startled me, is all."

"You were deep in thought, no?"

Kyna took a deep breath and released it. "Mmm. The water is … mesmerizing."

"Indeed." The man held out his gloved hand. "Baron Simon MacLean, at your service."

"How do you do?" She shook his hand.

His eyes immediately went to the charm swaying on her necklace, and his grip on her hand tightened.

She pulled free and buttoned her burgundy cloak at her neck, concealing the charm.

"Have you been to England before?" the Baron asked.

"Once, last year."

"And where did you stay?"

The hairs on the back of Kyna's neck tingled, and she reminded herself that she did not know this Human; that any information she shared could endanger not only herself, but her friend Gaill, and even her Clan in Ireland.

"Here and there. It was just a quick trip."

"I do hope you'll be staying longer this time. Far too much to see and do than a quick trip can allow. I'm bound for London and then down to Greenwich. Have you been to Greenwich? It's where time starts and ends."

"The Prime Meridian. I know. I'm afraid I will only be in London for a day. Then I'm off to, um —." She caught herself just in time. "Norway. To visit my grandparents."

"Yes, I could tell you were Scandinavian. I must say you are quite beautiful."

"Thank you so much. Oh, look! Is that a whale?"

As soon as Kyna mentioned a whale, and swept her hand toward the ocean, a large creature rose majestically from the waves in front of the ship, spouted, and sank once more into the sapphire blue water.

"Why, yes, I believe it was a humpback—"

But Kyna had dashed away without waiting to hear the rest of the Baron's response.

Safely back in her cabin, Kyna chastised herself. First for letting someone sneak up on her, and second for almost revealing potentially harmful information. In the safety of her small village, she had no need to guard her conversation or look over her shoulder. But once she traveled outside the shelter of Violet Springs, she knew the danger that could befall her if anyone learned who—or what—she was.

The Claddagh

In America, and even in Ireland where her people were more common, no-one outside her family and a few close friends like Gaill knew that she was a Leprechaun. The tiny tattoo on the left side of her neck, a claddagh that appeared when her magic first revealed itself, was easy to hide with her long hair or a high-collared blouse or the cloak that she preferred to a coat.

When her eyes adjusted to the darkness of her interior cabin, Kyna saw her roommate's lumpy form huddled under the covers of her bunk. "Gaill, are you awake?"

Kyna's friend grumbled and rolled from her side to her back. "I am now." Her heart-shaped face was pasty and slick with sweat. Her short, curly hair, usually a billowy halo, was clamped to her brow and cheeks.

"Do you feel any better?" Kyna sat on the edge of the bunk and stroked strands of hair from Gaill's feverish forehead.

"Do I look any better?"

Kyna reached into her dress pocket and pulled out a sprig of rosemary. "Put this in your mouth."

Gaill wrinkled her nose. "Ugh, no! I can't stand the smell of it."

Kyna twirled the stem between her thumb and forefinger, then put the sprig back in her pocket. "Is there anything I can do to help?"

"Show me a picture." Gaill rubbed her eyes with the fleshy parts of her palms. "Something still and tranquil."

Kyna looked around the cramped, windowless cabin. "I'll be right back."

She went into the head and ran water from the sink over her hands. Cupping her hands in front of her, she went back to the cabin and stood in front of Gaill's bunk. "Are you watching?"

Gaill opened her eyes a sliver. "Mm-hmm."

Kyna threw her hands up in the air, scattering droplets of water. The droplets hovered in mid-air and formed a picture of a weeping willow, its boughs swaying gently as if lifted by a feathery breeze.

"A tree? I wasn't thinking of a tree."

"Nor was I," Kyna said, shrugging. "But it is tranquil, isn't it?"

"Mm-hmm." Gaill pursed her lips and blew gently at the image. The long tendrils of the willow fluttered, then the tree fragmented into glittering water drops that sprinkled down, dusting Gaill's face with a fine mist that evaporated in an instant in the heat of the tiny cabin.

"Ahhh. Thank you, Kee." Gaill rolled back onto her side and snuggled more deeply into the covers. "I'm cold."

"Cold? It's an oven in here."

"Then the oven needs to be stoked."

"Gaill, there was a man—"

Gaill's gentle snoring meant the end to the conversation. In her condition, Gaill wouldn't likely be venturing above decks. Kyna would remind her to be careful when she woke up.

She returned to the head and soaked a washcloth under cool water from the faucet. She wrung out the cloth and went back to Gaill's side. Perched on the edge of the bed, she gently wiped her friend's face.

The heat of the tiny room pressed in on Kyna, giving her a sensation of claustrophobia. She decided to go back on deck and let the sea breeze refresh her. This time, though, she would be more on guard. She wanted no surprise company, titled or otherwise.

As she climbed the stairs, she became aware of a jumble of noises coming from the deck. Shouting, laughter, clapping, and music filled her ears. Through the crowd she could see a four-man band. They were playing a snappy song she recognized but couldn't recall the name of. The words were a mix of English and a foreign language. As she concentrated on the tune, another sound floated higher than the others. It was a baby crying.

Kyna jostled her way through the partying crowd, following

the pitiful cry to its source. A thin young woman sat on a bench near the stage where the band played. She held a squirmy child, maybe a year or eighteen months old. The baby's cheeks were red and streamed with tears, and his mouth was open wide to let out pitiful wails. The baby obviously wanted to be anywhere else but here. To Kyna, the young woman holding him looked as if she felt the same way.

"Hi," Kyna said to the woman. "Can I help?"

"Sure," the woman shouted over the band. "Would you mind holding the little prince while I jump overboard?"

"That's a bit drastic, but I could hold him while you take a break. Only if you promise not to jump overboard."

"I'm Liz." The woman ruffled the baby's curly black hair. "And this is young Master MacLean. Adam. I'm his nanny."

Why did that name sound familiar?

The little boy swatted at Liz's hand.

"I'm Kyna. Can I hold you, Adam?" The baby quit crying and scowled at Kyna. She held her arms out and the baby went to her without hesitation.

"That's the first time he's stopped crying all day," Liz said. "He's not normally fussy. I think he might be slightly seasick."

Kyna held the baby close to her chest and bobbed up and down in time to the music. "That's a sweet boy."

"You're much better with kids than I am," Liz said. "Are you a nanny, too? No, you're too young. You probably come from a large family."

"I do, yes. Lots of cousins." Kyna held Adam's pudgy pink hand and twirled, her long skirt flaring. "Do you like to dance, young man?"

The baby reared back his head and laughed. Then he looked earnestly at Kyna. "Gah!"

"He wants you to do it again," Liz explained.

"Ah, you speak Baby. That's a skill." Kyna indulged Adam by twirling and circling Liz.

"I might speak Baby, but you can do magic."

Kyna had to smile. *You're righter than you know,* she thought.

The music stopped and the revelers applauded.

"Well, well, what have we here."

For the second time that day, Kyna jumped at a voice so close to her. When she turned, she realized why the baby's last name sounded familiar.

"Baron MacLean. This must be your little boy?"

Adam reached for his father, who took the boy in a brief hug before thrusting him toward Liz. "Somebody is a bit stinky."

"Oh, dear me. I'm so sorry, Sir. I'll see to it immediately."

"Please do."

Liz scuttled away, holding the baby at arm's length. Peering over Liz's shoulder, Adam reached his pudgy fingers toward Kyna and cried. The Baron watched his nanny and his child until they rounded a corner out of view, then turned back to Kyna. "So. I don't believe I learned your name."

"No, I don't suppose so."

"Is it a state secret?"

She did not want to give this man any more information about herself than absolutely necessary, but could think of no way to avoid answering him. "It's Kyna."

"A beautiful name, but it doesn't sound Swedish."

"It's Irish," Kyna said without thinking. "Er, from the other side of the family."

"I see. Well, the two sides of your family certainly produced a beautiful result."

"Thank you, Baron."

"Please, call me Simon."

"Is there a Lady MacLean?"

"Unfortunately, no. She died in childbirth."

"Oh! I'm terribly sorry. I didn't mean to intrude."

"Indeed, I'm terribly offended. The only way you can make amends is to have dinner with me tonight."

"I'm afraid I have a dinner companion."

"Well, then. He must join us as well."

"It's a she."

The Baron's eyes lit up. "Even better!"

He blushed and cast his eyes downward, covering his face with his hand. "I do apologize. I didn't mean that the way it sounded. I only meant that I was relieved to hear you were not accompanied by a gentleman friend, for this means I might have a chance to, well, to learn more about you."

Kyna began to soften toward the Baron. He seemed harmless enough, and his inept advances were, she was sure, borne out of his loneliness after losing his wife.

"We'd be honored to sit with you at dinner."

"The honor will be mine."

"Until then."

As Kyna brushed by to take her leave, he grasped her upper arm. "Can you stay for a dance? The band is quite merry."

She stiffened as she looked at his hand on her arm.

He immediately withdrew it.

"I must go back and check on my friend. She's a bit seasick."

"I do hope she's feeling better by dinnertime." He touched his forehead and bowed briefly. "Until then, Kyna."

Chapter 8: The Council

The men and women of the Kelly Clan gathered around a low, crackling bonfire on the beach. Those who were members of the Clan Council wore long, Kelly green scarves draped around their shoulders. Each scarf bore the symbol of the clan—a golden four-leaf clover, embroidered on the left side, close to the Council members' hearts.

For the first time in his life, Dune was allowed to attend the Council meeting. Several of his teammates and cousins his age from other cities across Ireland were there as well. Instead of standing with his parents, Dune joined Brian and Kane and a few other of his mates from the Gaelic football league.

Mother Cass added a piece of driftwood to the fire, and luminous blue sparks swirled high into the air. This was a signal for the crowd to quiet. "By now, you have all heard Birdie MacBressal's account of the Greenapple tragedy," Mother Cass began, her hushed voice demanding attention. "Before I make my comments, are there any questions?"

Many had questions, which they asked all at once in a tumult of voices. The Matriarch quieted them so she could answer their questions one by one. She pointed at one man. "Yes, Martin?"

"Are you sure the Greenapples were captured?"

"Aye, Birdie's account is accurate. I have consulted Marnie Kelly. Her rune casting bears it out."

"Do we know if they're still alive?" a woman asked.

"Aye, although why their captors have na turned them to gold, or how much longer they will wait to do so, is anyone's guess."

"What can be done, Mother Cass?"

"Much," the Matriarch replied, looking directly at Dune. "By the right person."

Then Kane asked, "Is there a reward?"

Dune elbowed him. "What kinda question is that?"

"All questions are valid," Mother Cass said.

Dune's face flushed. "Sorry, ma'am. I just thought that bringing them home safe and sound would be its own reward."

"That is exactly correct. Kane has his answer. Do you have yours?"

Dune looked at his boots, scuffed one in an arc in the sand. "I— I dunna ken." He had not one question but many. *Why are you looking at me? Why is everyone looking at me? Why are you choosing me? Are you choosing me? Because it feels like you're choosing me.*

And another question niggled at his brain, one which he admitted to himself was just as wrong as Kane's question about a reward: *If I accept this rescue mission, and the Ceili goes on without me, will someone else be named Keeper?*

"Remember what I said earlier, Dune," Mother Cass continued. "Neither your father nor I nor anyone else can choose who goes on this mission. The right person must accept it for him- or herself."

Murmurs rose from the crowd. Someone asked, "Will the Ceili proceed as planned?"

So, Dune was not the only one wondering about the Ceili. The crowd quieted, waiting for the answer.

Mother Cass stared at Dune. They were suddenly alone on a deserted beach. The wind whistled in his ears and whipped his hair, stinging his eyes. Dune was not even sure it was the same beach where they had been standing a moment before. The stars in the sky seemed to swirl with the passage of time. A shooting star blazed a blue trail across the ebony heavens. The moon set and the sun rose. Clouds sped by and the sun made its trek from east to west as Dune waited for the Matriarch's answer. From the folds of her cloak, Mother Cass withdrew an object and held it out for Dune to see: a green apple.

Finally, Mother Cass tapped her walking stick on the hard-packed sand at her feet. The crowd reappeared. The bonfire crackled. The wind died to a gentle flutter.

"The Ceili will go on," Mother Cass announced. "'Tis powerful magic, and the Greenapples will be needing all we can generate."

Dune exhaled with a mixture of guilt and relief. He knew it was selfish to want the Ceili to commence as planned, and how could cancelling it help the Greenapples?

But something gnawed at the edge of his conscience; a half-formed thought that Dune didn't want to investigate for fear that it would turn into a barrier to his participation in the Ceili. Something Mother Cass had said when showing him her vision of Yulnear. And now, this second vision she had shared with him—*a green apple.* As his mates jostled around him, his gaze was focused on the Matriarch, and hers on him. The look in her eyes amplified his unease.

Mother Cass held her hand up, silencing the crowd. "Yet someone must rescue the Greenapples," she said, staring straight at Dune.

He knew what he would be giving up: His chance to excel at the Ceili, to impress Kyna.

To prove himself worthy of succeeding his father as Keeper of the Clover.

To prove it to the Matriarch, his father, himself.

Rescuing the Greenapples would prove all these things—if he was successful. But it felt like jumping straight from the beginning of class to the final exam. Surely someone more experienced would be a better choice for a rescue mission. Someone with the benefit of magic.

"What about your own magic, ma'am?" someone in the crowd asked, as if plucking the word from his thoughts. "Canna you wave your cane and bring them home?"

"Now, Colm, you know our magic does na work that way." Mother Cass's tone was gentle, but her gaze had not left Dune, and her steely grey eyes bored a hole straight through him.

In his heart, he knew the answers to all his questions.

***

After the Council meeting ended, Dune said good night to his friends and rejoined his parents.

Maureen gave Paddy a hug. "I shall return home and help Ayne with the wains. Will you be coming, too, Husband?"

"I'll have a word with Dune first. I'll be home anon."

Maureen squeezed Dune's arm and walked up the path toward the bungalow. Dune and Paddy strolled to the edge of the Bay and stood staring at the moon-frosted water. The only sound was the waves rhythmically lapping the shore.

After several minutes, Paddy broke the silence. "You dunna have to go, son."

"'Tis not my decision," Dune replied. "According to Mother Cass, the mission will choose its champion."

"I might not say it often, but your family needs you," Paddy said softly. "You will break your mother's heart if you go off and get yourself captured."

"I know, Da."

"You are a hero on the pitch. There, I've said it. That should be enough for you, and for Mother Cass."

"Is it enough for you, Da?"

Paddy exhaled heavily. "You will na do any of us any good if you are captured or killed." He turned and walked briskly away.

Alone on the beach, Dune put his hands on his hips and gazed out at the dark water. An eerie green line of bioluminescence wove through the waves where they curled and crashed ashore. Dune scanned the far horizon for—for what? Would guidance sweep across the bay like a sea breeze and whisper in his ear?

"I've always loved the ocean," a lilting voice said behind him.

Dune jumped and turned. His eyes widened.

Standing there, her golden hair streaming behind her in the gentle sea breeze, was a girl. And not just any girl.

Chapter 9: Kyna

"Kyna. I dinna ken you were there."

"Obviously. You were listening too hard to the sea. Did you hear it?"

"The sea?" Dune scuffed his boot in the sand.

Kyna slipped silently to his side. She nudged his arm until he turned back toward the waves kissing the shore.

"Don't pretend you don't know what I'm talking about." Her voice bore the soft inflections of a far-away land. "Did the sea give you an answer?"

"How would you ken what I ask of the sea? I mean, I dinna ask anything of the sea."

Kyna's silky, waist-length hair fluttered in the breeze. She stooped to pick up a long stick and began drawing doodles in the sand.

Her silence rattled him even more than her conversation. "Okay, then. If I've a question, tell me what you think it is, and I'll tell you if you are right."

She curved the pointy end of the stick back and forth in the sand. "You have yet to discover your magic. Your question of the sea is, where will you find it? At the Ceili, where your skills are sure to shine? Or on a rescue mission of impossibly long odds that you mightn't even survive, much less succeed at?"

Until Kyna put his thoughts into so many words, Dune could not have expressed the angst he felt. Instead of answering her, he folded his arms across his chest. He watched her draw arching lines and swirls in the sand.

He knew he should leave, find a quiet spot by himself to mull over his options. But he was mesmerized by the tilt of her slender wrist, the artistic sweeps of her hand, the intricate designs she drew in the sand. Being near her simultaneously lit off fireworks in his chest and sank him into the deep, muddy bog of self-doubt. "And what is your magic?" he asked. "Have you found it yet?"

"I reckon it found me, rather than the other way around." Kyna continued doodling in the sand. "Pictures, I guess you would say."

"Oh, you're an artist?"

"In a manner of speaking. For as long as I can remember, I've loved to draw. I draw with whatever I can get my hands on—a piece of chalk on a boulder, a pen and paper, a stick in the sand. I love to make pictures."

"You're saying then," Dune interrupted with a serious expression, "that this gift of yours, you were *drawn* to it."

Kyna looked bewildered until Dune could hold his thoughtful look no longer and broke into a guffaw of laughter.

"Oh, you grinnin' possum," Kyna said, shoving him gently.

Dune got serious again. "How did you realize it was more than talent? A lot of Folk are artists. How did you ken it was magic?"

"Oh, I can pinpoint the exact moment when I knew my magic went farther than just drawing pretty pictures."

"So, what was this remarkable moment?"

"It was before I left for America. I was four or five, and I was playing with my friends at Glencar Lake. You know the place?"

Dune nodded. "With the waterfall at one end?"

"That's right. We were splashing each other and having a grand time. I was so happy, I cupped my hands full of water and threw it in the air, purely for the joy of it. The water floated in the air, just for a few seconds, and the drops of water formed a picture in the air."

"What was the picture?" Dune said. His arms, neck, and scalp tingled with goosebumps. "Wait! Was it the Kelly Clover?"

"Nuh-uh." She shook her head and pointed to the picture she had drawn in the sand: a heart held in a pair of hands, topped by a crown. "It was that."

"The Claddagh?" Dune had long admired the simple elegance of Ireland's national symbol.

"Love, loyalty, and friendship," Kyna said. "Like the three legs of a milking stool, right?"

"You need all three legs or the stool will tip over."

Kyna pulled on her necklace, revealing the charm that had been hiding under her blouse. "Mother Cass gave this to me before I left for America. She wanted to remind me that my home was in Ireland. She said it meant that I would return one day."

"I'm glad you had something to bring you back. I—I wanted to see you again."

"I would have wanted to come back even without it."

"Oh? Why is that?"

"I have my reasons." Kyna grabbed his hand and pulled him away from the surf.

Waves lapped the shore where they had been standing and erased Kyna's design.

"Well, Dune?" Kyna dropped Dune's hand and stood with her hands on her hips. "Am I right?"

Dune shrugged. "I need time to think through my question before I ask the sea, or anyone else, for guidance."

Kyna nodded and backed away. "I'd like to know your decision. Will you tell me?"

Dune nodded. "Aye."

"You know where to find me when you have your answer."

"Well, not really."

"That's okay. I know where to find you."

As she turned to leave, Dune called, "Kyna?"

She looked at him over her shoulder. Her long hair glowed in the light of the near-full moon.

"Fair well with you."

Kyna smiled. "It's good to see you, too, Dune."

Chapter 10: The Decision

Dune slept fitfully, his dreams crowded with images of Kyna, Mother Cass, the Claddagh, and another symbol, sacred to his own family, the Kelly Clover. As if Dune's father had eavesdropped on his dreams, Paddy began lecturing Dune as soon as he went downstairs for breakfast the next morning.

"Dune, my boy. Finally you've graced us with your presence."

"'Tis barely five," Dune said.

"Even the wains are awake afore ye. I was just telling the wee lads about the Kelly Clover. Though no four-leaf clover is ever ordinary," Paddy droned on, "the Kelly Clover is even more special than any other ever known. Pure gold it be, grown in the magical cave-garden in Aillwee, cared for tenderly for a century until it reached its full perfection, then harvested by our own clan Matriarch."

Dune folded his lanky frame into the chair by the hearth, curling his feet underneath his legs and stretching his hands to the glowing warmth of the flames. "I know the legend, sir. You've told me about it since I was a wee lad, so you have."

"Is that right. Then mayhap you would like to tell the story to Gil and Travis."

Gil ambled casually to a spot on the floor in front of Dune and sat cross-legged. "Would you, Dune?"

"Tell us, Dune," Travis chimed in. "You are a far better storyteller than Pa."

"I am sitting right here," Paddy grumbled. "My hearing is clear."

Travis hunkered beside Gil and looked up at Dune expectantly.

Dune rolled his eyes. "Am I the only storyteller in this family?"

"Nae, but you're the best," Travis said.

"And the clan lore is what you want to hear at the crack o' dawn in the morning?"

The two boys nodded.

"Then I'd best start at the beginning."

Maureen brought him a cup of coffee, which he held in both hands, letting it warm him. After taking a sip, he put his feet on the floor and leaned forward. "The Harvesting was over a hundred years ago. Mother Cassiopeia Kelly was the Matriarch way back then, same as she is now." He shook his head at the thought of it. "What an ancient bird she is."

"You mustn't speak of her that way," Paddy said with a heavy sigh. "You're almost sixteen, the same age I was when Mother Cass designated me to be the Keeper of the Clover."

Paddy pulled a velvet pouch from his vest pocket and slid from it a golden shamrock. Dune's posture straightened and his eyes widened with sudden alertness as a hazy aura glowed around the object in Paddy's hands. Gil and Travis gasped.

"The Kelly Clover," Dune said in awe. The aura from the clover expanded and magnified in intensity until Paddy almost disappeared within its glare. The golden four-leaf clover shone luminously, casting a glow on the two little faces at Dune's feet. He felt the warmth of it on his own face as well.

Dune stared at the clover, hypnotized. "For all my life, you've been the Keeper," he said to his father. "Yet 'tis the first time you've ever let me lay my eyes on the Kelly Clover. 'Tis truly—" he reached for the appropriate word—"spectacular."

"'Tis more than a spectacular souvenir to gawk at, son. 'Tis the talisman of our Clan. The Kelly Clover holds mystic powers of protection far beyond what any of us may truly understand. Anyone but the Matriarch, that is."

Dune put his cup down and extended his hand. He longed to feel the clover in his own hands. His fingers fairly itched for want of touching it. To his amazement, his father gently laid the golden relic on his outstretched palms.

"How can you tell the whole story," Paddy asked gently, "if you've not even laid eyes on the thing itself?"

Dune briefly thought of all the stories he'd told about places and things that he'd never seen. Yet this was different. This relic was an essential element, like the earth itself.

Like air.

Holding the Kelly Clover, he felt connected to generations past and generations to come. Now he could tell the story with his whole heart and soul.

As he started to speak, images flooded his mind. He wasn't simply retelling the story; Dune felt he was living it.

The people of the Kelly Clan are gathered in a garden for a special harvest, one of food for their souls. They have gathered here in this magical garden for the harvesting of the Kelly Clover.

Mother Cass, the Clan Matriarch, leads the ceremony. She leans on her walking stick and smiles at the hopeful faces of the people of her Clan. She kneels in the dewy, fragrant patch of clover; before her: a glowing, golden shamrock. She pulls from her cloak an athame, a sharp dagger made of cold steel. Its handle is intricately braided in Celtic knots, its blade glints in the evening light. She holds the knife up to the sky, first facing East, then South, then West where the last glow of sun lights the horizon like a crown, then North, where the guiding star glimmers, and again to the East. She chants,

Echo, echo of our clan,
Echo of a son, a man.
Voices in the future night,
Fulfill the magic, true and right.

She kisses the cold steel blade, then holds the athame close to the stem of the golden shamrock and cups her hand opposite it. So strong is the magic of the garden, and of Mother Cass herself, that the cut is made without the blade ever touching the clover's stem.

She slips the athame back in its hiding place beneath her cloaks. Cradling the clover in one hand as delicately as if it were a baby bird, Mother Cass grasps her cane in her other hand for support and rises. Now she holds the clover to the sky as she had done with the dagger, first to the East, then to the South, the West, the North, and again to the East.

Mother Cass lifts her strong voice so all the kin may hear. "This clover was planted one hundred years and five days ago, on the first day of June, which was also the first full moon of June. Twenty-nine days later, on the Blue Moon, I was born."

"Happy birthday, Mother," calls a man at the front of the crowd. A pair of white doves perch on his head, blinking and cooing contentedly. "And may you see a hundred more."

"Who is that?" Mother Cass's eyes search the congregation.

"'Tis I, Ma'am." The man waves at Mother Cass. Disturbed by the motion, the doves flutter their wings and squawk their displeasure. They pluck at strands of the man's hair, then re-settle.

"Ah, Mack MacBressal. Is that a blessing or a curse?" Mother Cass chuckles.

As the congregation laughs quietly along with her, Mother Cass waves her cane in an arc. A rainbow contrail traces the cane's path and rises like a zephyr, hovering a few meters overhead.

The crowd oohs and aahs, then hushes as Mother Cass lowers the stick. The rainbow rises and spreads across the sky.

"Chriona, please come forward," Mother Cass says.

A willowy teenage girl with waist-length, flaxen hair steps forward, her eyes to the ground.

Her resemblance to Kyna is uncanny. Her appearance momentarily pulls Dune from the story, but he quickly regains composure and resumes where he left off.

Her gossamer cape flutters in the evening breeze like the translucent emerald wings of a butterfly.

"Chriona, child of my heart, I have known you all your life," Mother Cass says, beckoning the girl close. She props the cane in one elbow so she can grasp both the girl's hands in her own, transferring the newly harvested clover to Chriona's open palms.

"You have always behaved in a way to make your adopted Clan proud of you. Therefore, with the power vested in me as Clan Matriarch, I hereby appoint you the first Keeper of the Clover."

The crowd cheers and applauds.

"Under your care, and the care of future Keepers, the magic of this sacred shamrock will nourish and protect the Kelly Clan for many generations. But if the Keeper's protection should waver, the Clover's magic will wither, and with it, the fortunes of the Kelly Clan. Chriona, do you promise to keep and care for the clover as an eternal symbol of your Clan? Do you accept your appointment to be the Keeper of the Clover?"

Chriona looks up at the Matriarch, her adopted mother,

with wide open eyes and a dazzling smile. "Mother Cass, I accept this honor," she says. "And I promise you and all the Kelly Leprechauns, I will carry out my duties proudly and well."

"She ain't even a real Kelly," someone in the crowd shouts.

Mother Cass frowns, and the rainbow turns grey. "I have chosen," she says.

"Hooray for Chriona!" someone else in the crowd yells. The crowd erupts in applause once more. Amid loud cheers of "Hip-hip, hooray! Hip-hip, hooray," the rainbow's colors return.

The Leprechauns hug each other. The men slap each other's shoulders; the women rush forward to kiss Chriona's cheeks while the children dance and chase each other around the legs of the adults until Mother Cass sends everyone away.

"Are you coming?" Mother Cass asks Chriona.

"In a bit. I want to stay in the garden, breathe it all in."

Mother Cass kisses her protégé on the forehead and slowly walks away.

As the crowd disperses, Chriona is left alone in the garden. She kisses the golden relic, and its glow intensifies, washing her porcelain face in the color of sunshine. "They will not regret Mother Cass's choice. I will keep my promise made this day."

Dune's eyes fluttered and he realized his head was tilted back on the chair. "Did I fall asleep?" he asked. His hand was clenched at his chest. He spread his fingers to be sure the Kelly Clover was still there. It glowed reassuringly on his palm.

"Nae, you've just finished telling us the tale of the Kelly Clover," Gil said.

The Claddagh

"'Tis all history, not just a tale," Paddy said. "Except that part at the end about Chriona."

"That happened too, Da. All of it." Dune handed the clover back to Paddy, who slid it back in its pouch and tucked the pouch inside his vest.

Travis squinted at Dune. "If she was alone in the garden, how do you ken what she said?"

"I saw the whole thing," Dune said with a shrug. "Like I was standing right there at the ceremony." He rubbed the back of his neck. "I thought I was dreaming. But you say I was talking?"

"Best story you ever told," Gil said.

Maureen walked over from the kitchen, drying her hands on a dish towel. "You're a natural at history, son. I believe the Kelly Clover spoke through you."

"Nae, Marnie," Paddy said. "The Clover never 'spoke' to me, in all the years I've been the Keeper. You heard the boy. 'Twas a dream. How he was able to get it right while he was stone asleep, is a wonder."

"But Dune," Gil said, pulling Dune's sleeve. "You have na finished the story! How did Da become the Keeper?"

Paddy took over the history lesson. "When Chriona died twenty-five years after becoming Keeper, Mother Cass appointed her son, Will. They decided that twenty-five years was a good time to hand over the reins to the next Keeper. So twenty-five years after that, Mother Cass chose Will's son Cedric, and twenty-five years after *that*, she chose me. Now I've served my twenty-five years, and she'll choose someone else at the closing of this year's Ceili."

"I don't suppose you'd let me take the clover with me," Dune said. "For luck?"

"Take it with you where? In the football match?" Paddy guffawed loudly. "Not a chance!"

Maureen took hold of Paddy's forearm. "That is na what he

meant, Husband."

Paddy raised one scruffy auburn eyebrow. "Then what did you mean, lad?"

"I am going to find the Greenapples. I'm leaving tonight."

Chapter 11: Hunted

A slight movement on the sandbanks caught Dune's eye. He had been walking along the shore for about an hour; by now he was well beyond the protective curtain at the Hidden Harbor. Even though the night concealed him, the beach provided scant cover. To the left were the waves of the Atlantic; to the right, steep, sandy banks. The open stretch of beach was unbroken but for a boulder about the size of a sack of potatoes. He dove to the ground behind it and covered his head with his arms.

He felt ridiculous. Whatever was ahead would see his legs and bum—as well as most of his torso—sticking out. What was he? A wee wain who thinks no-one sees him when he shuts his eyes?

Dune peeked out from the side of the rock. A shadow slipped between the sandy banks, closer now. He ducked back down.

The pouch full of stones his mother had given him bumped against his thigh. With as precious little movement as possible, Dune untied the pouch from a loop on his right pants leg. He drew out a stone and placed it in front of his head, then another and another in a clockwise pattern around his body. He used his feet to push the stones into place around his legs. When the circle was completed, he whispered the rune his mother had taught him.

Echo, echo, hear my call.
Dim the lights and raise the wall.
Dark-on-dark the curtain rise

Conceal me from unfriendly eyes.

The moment of truth.

If the stones were not placed well enough, or if he had misspoken the rune in any way, he would be fully exposed.

He took a deep breath and exhaled it through pursed lips.

He stood up.

The beach was empty, the only sound the waves crashing ashore, the only light a faint glow cast by the stars on the white sand.

A shadow emerged from behind the sandbank where he had detected movement.

Dune held his breath.

A sleek black cat stepped out onto the beach. She blinked her eyes at Dune and twitched her bob tail. "Mow."

"Rabbit! 'Tis you!"

Then Dune heard a sound that curdled his blood.

Dogs. Hunting dogs, at full bay.

He leapt toward the cat and scooped her up under one arm like a furry football. With another leap, he was back inside the protective stone circle.

Then a dreadful thought struck him. The cat had seemed to see him, even though he was inside the circle. The dogs would see him, too! He must run for it!

But it was too late. A pair of Irish wolfhounds skidded down the sandbank onto the beach. Tall with shaggy, grayish brown coats, one with a black stripe down the middle of its face, they stopped directly in front of Dune, sniffing the air and the sand.

Dune stood as still as if he'd already been captured and turned into a statue of gold. There was no option to run. Either the stones would protect him, or not.

The beating of his heart pulsed, a cacophony of drums in his ears. Surely his own heart would give him away.

"Mow."

The hounds turned their muzzles left and right, then dropped their noses to the ground. They sniffed at the rock behind which Dune stood.

Dune held the cat tightly. She struggled in his arms, but he dared not let her go. If she leapt free and landed outside the circle, the dogs would rip her to shreds. And Dune didn't know if her body passing through the protective curtain would expose him as well, leading to the same fate. He hoped the curtain held, as it seemed to have done after he broke through — twice — to pull the cat into the circle of stones.

He stroked Rabbit between her ears, as Mother Cass had done.

The little cat stopped struggling and nudged her forehead against Dune's fingertips.

One dog went around the rock to the left, the other to the right.

Dune shifted his chin just enough to keep his eyes on the hunting dogs. Dogs that were hunting *him*. Had they heard the cat's cry? Perhaps, but it was obvious that they could not see either Dune or the cat.

The dogs snuffled the sand outside the protective barrier created by Maureen's stones, bumping heads at six o'clock, directly behind Dune. The hound with the black stripe down its muzzle snapped at the other one, which yelped and promptly rolled over on its back. The first hound growled with its muzzle millimeters from the other's throat.

"Mow."

Dune cupped his hand over Rabbit's mouth, but the cat struggled free of his arms and landed at his feet.

The wolfhound on the ground scrambled and stood up, slightly crouched as if ready to spring.

Afraid to move a muscle, Dune hovered over the cat, prepared to grab her if she stirred. Was he afraid for the cat's safety, or afraid she would break the curtain of invisibility if she stepped out of the circle, exposing not only herself but Dune as well?

He knew the true answer: He did not want to have to tell Mother Cass that her cat had been killed because of him. What kind of "Protector" was he if he couldn't even keep a wee cat safe?

His father would not understand such a decision—sacrificing his own safety for that of an animal. Paddy would only approve of such an action for the sake of a member of the family, or another Leprechaun. But as these thoughts rushed through his mind, Dune felt deeply that protecting the little Manx cat was every bit as important as protecting his own family. He knelt and stroked the cat, holding her in place with his touch.

Both dogs growled and paced, but neither broke through the invisible curtain demarked by the circle of stones. After a few tense moments that seemed to Dune to last for hours, the dogs trotted off in the direction Dune had come from, obviously following his path in reverse.

"I dunna ken how you could see me, Little Rabbit, but I am surely glad the stones protected us from those dogs." He stroked the cat's back from her shoulders to the knob of her tail, eliciting a loud, rumbling purr. He patted her side then began the task of retrieving the stones.

Rabbit meowed and stretched up on her back legs to rub her head against Dune's knee. "You'll not be going with me," Dune said. "You'd best be getting back to Mother Cass. And if you see my ma, tell her thanks for the stones. Or tell Fionn. She'll take the message to Ma."

The cat blinked at him and trotted obediently back down the road toward Doolin.

Ha! Dune shook his head. *I may be daft, but I'll be hanged if that cat didn't understand me.*

Gently returning the last of Maureen's rune stones to their leather pouch, Dune wondered how Rabbit saw him, even though the stones—and his reciting of the rune—apparently kept both him and the little cat safe from the hunting dogs. He thought of the day Birdie stumbled upon his family on the road to Doolin—was it really just two days ago? Birdie could see them through the protective veil. Dune thought it was his fault, that he had somehow banjaxed the rune. But now, he wondered. "Unfriendly eyes," he murmured. "That must be it. Only *friendly* eyes can see through the veil."

Dune hitched his coat collar up around his neck and rubbed his hands together. He decided to walk along the beach a bit farther, searching for a way to climb the bank and access the road.

As he walked, his thoughts returned to Kyna. He had told her he would let her know his decision, but had left without speaking to her again.

He remembered how she looked in the moonlight and starlight, her hair glowing like a halo. Her face and her hair seemed to collect each particle of light from the stars and the moon and radiate it like a candle.

A shadow shifted up ahead, barely discernible, but enough to rivet Dune's attention. He quietly drew his athame from his boot. He would stand and fight if need be, rather than risk botching a hastily recited rune. "Who goes there?" he demanded.

A ghostly figure, wrapped in a hooded cloak, stepped into view and walked silently toward Dune. When the figure was scant meters away, she dropped her hood.

"Kyna!"

"I thought you were going to tell me when you made your decision," she said.

"I know. I'm sorry. I had no time to spare." He looked around the beach to ensure they were alone. "How did you know where to find me?"

In answer, Kyna kneeled and picked up a handful of sand from the beach. She cast it into the air, where the wind immediately grasped it and swirled it this way and that. For a brief moment, the particles of sand formed a "W" before scattering in the wind. Kyna pointed overhead at the constellation Cassiopeia, an exact replica of the image she had just conjured. "I took a guess that you'd be headed north, toward Cassiopeia. That's the constellation Mother Cass was named for."

"I didn't know that," Dune said. "I just headed north because that's the direction the Greenapples would have been coming from to get to the Ceili."

"Then you've decided to accept Mother Cass's quest."

He remembered the vision of the Matriarch holding the apple at the council meeting. "Not sure I had much choice in the matter. Like Mother Cass said, it felt like the quest chose me."

"Then I'm sure your magic will steer you to success."

"My magic?" He couldn't tell Kyna that he hadn't found his magic yet. He changed the topic. "Why did you follow me? You know you canna come with me."

"Why can't I? I want to help."

"'Tis far too dangerous."

"I think we're safer together."

"Nae, 'tis not a good idea. You'll have to turn back."

"Dune, there are hunting dogs back there. I heard them. Surely you don't want me to face them alone."

Dune gritted his teeth. Knowing now that Kyna had been following him, he was relieved the dogs hadn't come upon her instead of him. His delay with the dogs must have given Kyna time to get ahead of him, yet she somehow knew or sensed where he'd be.

His thoughts swirled. He couldn't risk sending her back alone, unprotected. "I'll have to take you back."

"You said yourself you have no time to spare. Your priority must be the Greenapples."

"Won't you be missed? Won't they worry about you back at Doolin? The last thing we need is a search party coming after you, putting themselves in danger unnecessarily."

"I told Gaill I'd be with you. She'll tell the others."

"And how did you know you were going to be with me, might I ask?"

Kyna's cheeks grew pink in the glow of the moon. "I, well I, well, the truth of the matter is, if you must know, I dreamt about you last night."

"Did you now?" Dune felt his own cheeks flush. "And what might I have been doing in this dream of yours?"

"You were trying to catch a golden clover, but it was dancing like a butterfly, just out of your reach. Then I was standing next to you, and when we both reached for it, we caught it."

"I'm not chasing clovers, Kyna. I'm on a mission to rescue the Greenapples."

"And I'm here to help."

"I dinna ask for your help, nor do I need it," Dune growled.

"You might not think you need me, but you do," Kyna replied. "You need a friend or two."

"I have friends. A whole team of 'em."

"Then why aren't they helping you?"

"I canna have the whole Clan traipsing through the countryside. I need the elements of stealth and surprise. And I don't need to be worrying about you when I have to concentrate on the Greenapples."

"I think you'll find I can tend to myself. And if nothing else, I can be a second pair of eyes."

Dune wanted her to go back to Doolin, to be safe, but he knew that wasn't an option at this point. Besides, he wanted her to stay, too, more than he cared to admit to himself or to her. Despite what he said, he felt a need to have her with him on this journey.

Kyna fell silent, but when he glanced at her, he saw she was watching him with a small, pleasant smile on her lips.

Dune felt his cheeks burning again. *For the love o' Mike, I've never blushed so much in my life!* Again, he lowered his gaze to the rock-strewn shore.

"Well, if you're coming with me, we'd best get moving. We've wasted enough time as it is."

"Which way do we go?" Kyna asked.

"Good question. The Greenapples were travelling from Sligo, so north, to be sure. Other than that, I dunna ken. Say, can you conjure a map to guide us?"

"I can try." Kyna scooped another handful of sand and tossed it in the air. The granules twinkled and swirled, briefly forming the "W" again before being swept away on the wind. "That's not much help, is it?"

"I guess we'll follow the coast a bit farther, then turn inland where the forests will provide cover. We'll go up to Galway, then cut over toward Brownsgrove."

As they walked along the beach, the waves erased their footprints almost as soon as they stepped out of them. "Have you used your magic before? To help someone, I mean."

"Well, sure. That's what it's for, right?"

"But all you can give me is a star map to a place I'm already standing in."

"I don't always know what I'll conjure. Do you?"

Instead of admitting that he hadn't found his magic yet, he took a different tack.

"I dinna mean to offend you. Your star map guided you to me, after all. Tell me more about your magic. How have you used it?"

"Little ways, mostly. My friend Gaill gets terribly seasick, for instance. I make pictures to soothe her."

"I doubt that's a little thing to her."

"I reckon you're right. I can't always show her exactly what she wants to see, but the pictures do seem to help."

As they walked, the sand hills gave way to rocky cliffs. Dune pointed to a tumble of boulders that were jammed against the cliff face. "Let's rest here."

Kyna sat on the topmost boulder, and Dune climbed up beside her.

"You might not think it worthy of our magic, but I saved a family of badgers once."

"I suppose Mother Cass would say we should use our magic to help anyone in need, including animals." Maybe helping Rabbit was, in a way, Dune's magic, even though he was using his mother's rune stones to protect both the cat and himself.

Their perch on the pile of boulders gave Dune a good view of the beach in both directions, but he felt a little uneasy about the obstructed view of the cliffs. He hopped down so he could have a better view of the cliffs as they rested and he learned a little more about Kyna. "Tell me about the badgers."

"They were being rounded up by poachers. Three Humans, with clubs, beating the ground to scare them from their den. I gathered some dirt and threw it into the air, and it formed a pair of dragons."

"Dragons?" Dune shook his head in amazement. "And to protect badgers, no less."

"They were helpless. I had to do something. You would have, too. It's in your name."

"Aye, 'Dune' means protector. I know."

"You there!"

The man's voice took them both by surprise.

Standing on the rocks above the beach, not ten meters away, was a Human.

Chapter 12: The Faerie Ring

At the sound of the man's voice, Kyna jumped off the pile of boulders. Dune took her hand and pulled her behind himself, so that he was between her and the man, with the mound of rocks behind her.

"What're you doin' there?" the man said. His pale grey eyes glinted in the moonlight, which cast shadows on his craggy face. He wore red rubber clamdiggers and mud-splattered wading boots, and carried a wire basket and a clam rake. He crooked the rake in his elbow and pulled a torch out of the basket. As he walked closer, he turned the light on Dune's face.

"Nothin', sir." Dune squinted against the light and covered his eyes with one hand.

"He'll not bother us," Kyna whispered. "He's only coming down to the shore to dig for clams."

The man tilted his head to the side. "Who's that behind you?" he said, flashing the torch. "Get out here where I can see you."

Dune tried to keep Kyna behind him, but she stepped out to his side, tossing her wind-blown hair away from her face.

"What's that on your neck?"

Kyna slapped her hand to the side of her neck. "Wouldn't you like to know."

"I recognize it. It's some sort of tattoo for the magical people." Realization washed the man's face. "You're a Leprechaun!"

Kyna opened her mouth to reply, but before she could respond,

Dune said, "What would you be knowin' of Leprechauns? If there was anything rich or magical about this lass, other than the obvious, dunna you think I'd've found it by now?" He winked conspiratorially at the man.

"Then what're you doing off here by yourselves, eh?"

Dune leered suggestively at Kyna. She furrowed her brow and frowned at him but stayed quiet.

"What would you imagine we'd be doin'?" Dune grabbed Kyna's waist and pulled her roughly to his side. "I've been tryin' all week to get her to kiss me, and just when she was about to, you had to come along and ruin the mood! Since it seems this beach is a little crowded for my preference, we'll just be movin' along."

Dune clutched Kyna's hand and pulled her behind him.

She stumbled and he jerked her to her feet, snarling, "Wench, be careful you don't sprain that pretty ankle."

As they passed by the man, Dune could smell his dead-fish odor. The man ogled Kyna and put out his hand as if he were going to touch her neck, possibly to get a closer look at Kyna's tattoo. Kyna smacked him on the wrist.

"Ow! Tramp!" the man shouted.

"Ogre!" Kyna hissed back.

"Let's get out of here," Dune said.

When they had gotten far enough away to be out of earshot, Kyna said, "I thought you had to tell the truth when someone asks if you're a Leprechaun."

"He didn't ask if I was, and neither of us said you weren't."

Smiling, Kyna shifted her hand so that Dune's grip was less possessive, more intimate. She gave his hand a small squeeze. Dune squeezed back, astounded that he was even holding hands with her at all.

"You know, Kyna, there's a reason I'm not totally against you coming with me."

"I know." Kyna grinned. "You like me."

Dune scuffed at the gravel on the hard-packed sand. "It's not that. Of course, I like you. But that's na what I meant. You ken I dunna have the tattoo. I have na discovered my magic. You have yours. I hope it will help us on the journey."

"Ah, yes. The question you asked the sea." Kyna nodded. "What will your magic be, and where will you find it. Maybe the Greenapples will have the answer."

Dune nodded.

They continued up the beach until Dune spotted an ox trail winding up to the top of the cliffs. "This should take us right through the forest to a place where we can stop and rest and get a wee bite to eat."

"I was just about to say the same thing," Kyna replied. "It's called the Great Faerie Ring."

"You know it?" Dune asked.

"Well, I know *about* it," Kyna said. "Doesn't everyone?"

"Apparently so," Dune retorted. "If *you* know about it, obviously they let anybody in these days."

"I'll have you know—" Kyna pulled her hand from Dune's and placed her hands on her hips. Then she caught the mischievous look in his eye and laughed. "Oh, you dope. Give me another day or so and I'll recognize that possum grin straightaway."

As they climbed the trail off the beach, Kyna asked, "Do you believe in the power of the Great Faerie Ring?"

"I asked me da if there was any truth to it. He said that thousands of years ago, the Druids wanted to build a cathedral that would provide shelter to anyone in need. The Leprechauns helped, imbuing the structure with magical powers."

The first hints of dawn pinked the sky. "So, is it a shelter for Leprechauns or a cathedral for Druids?"

"My da thinks it belongs to the Leprechauns, because without our magical abilities, it would just be a regular temple or castle."

"Is that what you think?"

"Nae, I think 'tis for anyone who needs shelter, as the Druids intended. I think its magic lies in the cooperation between the Druids and the Leprechauns. They built the Faerie Ring together. Not the luck of the Leprechauns nor the religion of the Druids was strong enough to build it alone. They had to work together, and the result was both a magical shelter and a spiritual sanctuary."

"They forged a strong liaison between two different kinds of magic," Kyna said.

"Aye."

At the top of the cliffs, they entered a stand of weeping willows. As they walked along the winding path through the graceful trees, Kyna let the long, leafy tendrils caress her hand. "This reminds me of one of my favorite places in Violet Springs," she said. "By the creek behind my house."

Dune reached down and grabbed a limb that had fallen across the path. He pitched it to the side. "We have to be mindful from here on," he whispered. "With it being light out, and we're near the place—"

"Where the Greenapples were captured?"

"That was Birdie's information, aye." Dune stopped beside a thick-trunked willow just off the ox trail. Beyond the tree line, a lush green meadow spread across their vista toward a hardwood forest. "Can you imagine? A whole family of Leprechauns, captured by Humans."

Kyna shook her head slowly. "Humans claim not to even believe in Leprechauns."

"The ones who captured the Greenapples will be believers now," Dune said. "Mark my words. Rich believers."

He peered through the V in the willow's trunk, surveying the meadow and the dark smudge of forest at the far end. Rising above the distant wood, the jagged outline of a great stone structure jutted toward the sky. An undiscerning eye would think it was a stone mountain, but Dune knew they had found the special sanctuary for Leprechauns. "See those rocks in the middle of the forest?"

Kyna gasped. "The Great Faerie Ring itself!"

"There's no shelter once we leave these willows, but for that one tree in the meadow. We'll run there. Are you ready?"

"Ready."

"Stay with me and hold my hand so I don't lose you."

Hand-in-hand, Dune and Kyna bolted across the meadow. Both were out of breath when they reached the lone willow. They stopped within its canopy of boughs.

"Look," Kyna said, picking up an object from the grass near the base of the tree.

"I think that's Mr. Greenapple's telescope. That means he was here."

"So close to reaching safety," Kyna said.

"We have to be eye-wide. Hand me that, would you?"

Kyna gave Dune the telescope, and he climbed into the tree. Sweeping the telescope around in a full circle, Dune saw no signs of Humans. He hopped out of the tree. "I think the coast is clear. Are you ready to go on?"

"Ready when you are."

They ran to the shelter of the thick forest, not stopping as they entered but running deeper into the woods, dodging low-hanging limbs and jutting roots. In a moment they burst through the other side of the trees onto a narrow gravel path. They stared at the sight before them.

Skyscraping stone blocks butted up against each other, shoulder to shoulder like military guards. The monoliths, each thirty meters high and six meters wide, formed a circle, Dune knew, of twenty-four nearly identical gigantic boulders.

They had reached the legendary Great Faerie Ring.

Dune squeezed Kyna's hand and smiled. "We made it."

"We sure did," Kyna whispered. "It's more magnificent than I imagined."

"'Twill be even more magnificent once we're inside."

"How do we get in?"

"We have to find the Gatestone. 'Tis 'round this side." Dune led Kyna a quarter of the way counter-clockwise around the Ring.

"How do you know which way?"

"Trust me." Dune winked.

"I'll have to," Kyna said. "I've not studied the architecture of the Great Faerie Ring."

"*Do* ye trust me?" Dune cocked an eyebrow at her.

Without hesitation, Kyna replied, "Of course."

"Then I'll trust you with my secret." Dune looked around to be sure they were alone. "'Tis round," he said with a wink.

Kyna stared at him.

Dune exhaled. "Whichever way we go, we'll get to the Gatestone."

Kyna rolled her eyes. "Of course, but how will you *know* it's the Gatestone?"

To a regular person who happened to find the Faerie Ring, or even to a Leprechaun who didn't know what to look for, the Gatestone would look no different from any of the twenty-three other huge granite slabs.

But Dune had memorized the description of the Great Faerie Ring in *Rune Éire*. He had scoured the library in Yulnear for references to the legend. He had found maps, drawings, and more important, runes that would open the door. In fact, the only way to distinguish the Gatestone from the other stones was to rely on the runes.

"I'll know it when I see it. Just keep quiet and be watchful.

Humans have discovered the Faerie Ring and—"

"Some might still be prowling around," Kyna finished for Dune. "Hoping to capture a Leprechaun."

"Aye, either the ones that captured the Greenapples, looking to add to their fortune, or others chasing their own pot of gold."

As he led Kyna by the hand around the monolithic stones, Dune whispered, "Echo, echo."

"Echo, echo," Kyna whispered behind him.

"Ara be whist!" Dune scolded her.

"Did you just 'whist' me?" Kyna's eyes widened in affront. "I might be from North Carolina, but I'm not a baby!"

"Sorry, but you need to be quiet."

"I thought you wanted an echo."

"Nae, that's the way to identify the Gatestone, like following a divining rod to water. But I need you to be quiet so I can hear the response."

"Oh. Sorry," Kyna whispered. "But you still didn't have to whist me."

"Forgive me for that. 'Tis a habit. I spend my life babysitting my little brothers and sister."

"Forgiven. So, why did you say 'echo'?"

"The echo calls the Gatestone to appear."

Dune stood silent for a moment, rubbing his chin as an idea formed in his head.

"Um, is everything okay?" Kyna whispered.

"I've just had a thought. What if the echo is more than a password? What if the Gatestone truly needs an echo?"

"You mean our voices might be stronger, together?"

Dune shrugged. "The Great Faerie Ring was built on magic and cooperation."

"Let's try it, then." Kyna held out her hand and Dune clasped it, twining their fingers together.

"Echo, echo," Dune whispered, tiptoeing stealthily around the Great Faerie Ring.

"Echo, echo," Kyna repeated his words as she shadowed his every step.

One massive stone seemed to throb in rhythm to their calls, pulsing more strongly as they approached.

"This is it," Dune said.

"Jiminy crickets, I can see that," Kyna replied. "I've never heard of a rock with a heartbeat."

"Nor have I."

"I must tell you, Dune, your magic is clever as all get-out."

Dune beamed with pleasure at apparently making his own magic. "I may have a wee bit of it," he said. He didn't want her to see it was as much a revelation to him as it was to her.

When he raised his hand to touch the smooth black surface of the Gatestone, he realized that he still held Kyna's hand. "Er, 'twill be more powerful if we both put our hands on the Gatestone," he said quickly, as if he meant to do it. "Do you know the Rune of the Echo?"

Kyna shook her head.

"*Echo, echo, courage sent,*" Dune recited. "*Give us rest and nourishment.* We'll say it together, all right?"

Kyna nodded. They both placed their hands on the wall—each with the pinkies on one hand entwined—and whispered to the stone,

"*Echo, echo, courage sent*
Give us rest and nourishment."

Nothing happened, other than the huge stone's continued pulsing.

After a moment, Dune cleared his throat and started again, "*Echo—*"

The ground beneath their feet rumbled and shifted. The gravel at their feet danced as if being shaken through a sieve. Then the monolithic Gatestone slid forward, creating a slender opening. Dune slipped through, then beckoned Kyna.

As soon as they were inside the Faerie Ring, the Gatestone scraped back into place with a rumbling echo.

Inside the Faerie Ring, a meadow of luxuriant rye grass spanned an area of many acres, much larger than would seem possible from the exterior circumference of the Faerie Ring. This didn't surprise Dune, having experience with spaces that were deceptively small from the outside but, due to the ancient magic, were much more expansive on the inside.

For Kyna, however, the experience was a first. She gazed around in awe. "Heavens to Betsy! I never thought any place could be so, so ... breathtaking!"

A small spring bubbled into a stream that followed a winding path through the meadow to a stand of ancient oaks and graceful willows. Tuxedoed chickadees called *Visitor-visitor-visitor* as they flitted from tree to tree.

"Hah! I understood those birds clear as a bell," Dune said.

"Well, it is a faerie ring," Kyna said, still enraptured with the expansive beauty around her.

In the middle of the Ring, an ancient live oak tree spread her boughs invitingly over a wrought iron bench and a round, stone-topped table. Steam rose from a tray of food on the table and, beside it, a cast iron pot. Beads of condensation trickled down a glass pitcher of water.

"That must be the nourishment we requested," Kyna said.

"After you," Dune said. He bowed low, gesturing for Kyna to lead the way.

The snack tray overflowed with fresh grapes and cheese, a piping hot loaf of brown bread, and peeled carrots with their greens intact.

"Mmm, this bread is fresh baked," Kyna said, breathing in the aroma that drifted up when she broke the loaf into two thick portions.

Dune opened the lid on the pot. "And the colcannon is hot off the stove as well." He ladled the rich stew into two bowls, then tasted a large spoonful. "Mashed potatoes and cabbage, and soaking with butter."

"I won't even ask whose stove," Kyna laughed. "Their magic is too much for me!"

"'Twas our magic brought it, you silly lass."

"Yours and mine together," Kyna nodded. "Like the Leprechauns and the Druids."

After their meal, Dune stood and stretched, then leaned his back against the aged oak tree. "The Humans who caught Seamus Greenapple will be tempted to return to the Faerie Ring, in hopes of adding to their fortune," he said. "We'll have to be dog wide when we leave. We canna drop our vigilance for an instant."

Kyna looked at her hands, then took a deep breath and raised her eyes to Dune's. "Do you think the Greenapples are still alive?"

"The Matriarch says so, and her instincts about such things are strong."

"Why haven't the Humans turned them into gold yet?"

"It could be they dunna ken the code word." Dune had read about it in *Rune Éire*. He had also heard rumors about a Leprechaun who had met that most unfortunate fate. He didn't believe the rumors, instead considering them graphic warnings meant to impress upon children the danger of Humans. For according to the stories, if a Human caught a Leprechaun, it meant a greater prize than the mythical pot of gold; it meant that, by uttering the code word, the Human could turn a captured Leprechaun into solid gold.

"It's murder, pure and simple," Kyna said.

"Rare is the Human who would think of such an act as murder."

"Or maybe they think Seamus and his family are worth more to them alive." Kyna lowered her head. "Those poor children will be enslaved forever."

"Unless—"

"Unless what?"

Her face turned to him like a buttercup, beaming in the sun. Having her with him felt so right, as if she were as much a part of him as breathing. But he worried about what would happen if he failed. If he couldn't save the Greenapples, and lost Kyna in the attempt.

"Dune? Unless what?"

"Unless the Humans disclose that they've trapped a Leprechaun."

"Then their claim on the Leprechauns is broken?"

"Aye, but that's not the end of it."

Kyna stood up and leaned against the tree trunk next to him. "I can see why. The Human who finds out they have Leprechauns could then enslave them. Has that rule ever been invoked? Successfully?"

"Only once or twice in the known history of Leprechauns," Dune said. "The Humans of Ireland know that we Leprechauns are honor-bound to uphold the Code of Erin, telling anyone who asks that we are, indeed Leprechauns. For the sake of their greed, they are clever enough to hold their tongues. And to keep their captives out of sight somehow."

"Not just out of sight, for sure. Even a sound would give them away." Kyna drew in her breath as realization dawned on her. "Wouldn't it be easier just to turn them into gold?"

Dune shook his head. "That would be foolish. A bar of gold only goes so far, but a slave who not only waits on you hand and foot, but brings you good fortune? A clever Human would take the risk and reap the long-term rewards."

Kyna lowered her head. "They must have been clever indeed to capture a Leprechaun like Seamus Greenapple, and his family to boot."

"Clever *and* quick, for Seamus is known for his watchfulness. He must be dying inside a little more every day, knowing he let his family down."

"I'm sure he did all he could. That's the most anyone can ask for." Kyna traced a pattern on the wrought iron bench with her fingertip. "I think I'd rather be turned to gold right away than live a life of servitude, always under the threat, never knowing which dawn would be the day they decided to do it."

"I'd spit-shine their shoes for a hundred years if I had to, because the next dawn might be the day I escaped."

"I hope I never find out what I'd do. But isn't there any other possibility for escape?"

"Once a Leprechaun is captured, he's enslaved to the captors, and their heirs, till the day he dies."

"Does the Code of Erin say anything about how to free them?"

Dune turned his hat in his hands. "*Déanta na fírinne,* that is, to tell you the truth, I dunna ken how we're going to free them. Kyna, are you sure you want to do this? I can take you with me as far as Yulnear and you could stay there, be safe."

"You just said it yourself. *We're* going to free them. I'm in this for the long haul, Dune, right beside you. I'm certain this is where I'm meant to be. Just tell me what you need me to do."

Dune nodded briskly, working out a plan in his head. "First, we must find them. I was thinking, maybe, you could help with that."

"Help find them? But I've no idea where to look. Other than the vicinity of Brownsgrove, like you said. It's close-by, isn't it?"

"Aye." Dune clutched his hat in both hands. "But I thought you might be able to draw a map."

"I tried that already."

"You could try again. We're in the Great Faerie Ring. 'Tis sure to help."

"I suppose it's worth a try." Kyna looked around at the meadow and stood up. "Water will help."

Dune followed her to the little stream that curved through the meadow.

Kyna dropped to her knees and dipped her hands in the water. She cupped her hands, closed her eyes, and tossed the water in the air.

"Oh, now that's a surprise," Dune said.

Kyna opened her eyes and gazed at the water drops suspended over their heads. The image created by the shimmering droplets was a two-story building with a sign hanging over the front door. The sign had a wood-burned four-leaf clover and the words, *Lucky Lou's*. "Is it a house?"

"Nae, 'tis a pub. And I know that pub."

"Do you think that's where the Greenapples are?"

"'Tis at least closer to them than we are here."

"Can you get us there?"

"Aye. It's what we do once we get there that I haven't worked out yet."

As the water droplets dissipated, a red-winged blackbird sang, *Keep an EYE out! Keep an EYE out!*

"That bird is right," Dune said. "Once we leave the protection of the Great Faerie Ring, we need to be dog wide again. And fast."

"You already know I can run lickety-split. You lead the way, and I'll keep up with you."

"I canna say it will be easy. 'Twill take a clever soul to fool the Humans out of their treasure."

Kyna smiled. "Something tells me you're clever enough."

Chapter 13: The Leprechaun Hunters

From inside the Great Faerie Ring, the Gatestone was easily recognizable. Not only did a path lead up to it, but it had a message chiseled in the stone:

May the road rise up to meet you.
May the wind be always at your back.
May the sun shine warm upon your face,
The rains fall soft upon your fields,
And, until we meet again,
May the Divine Spirits keep you safe.

Dune and Kyna merely had to touch the Gatestone and it slid open for them. As soon as they were both outside, the massive stone slid closed with a *whoosh* followed by a rumble like the echo of distant thunder.

Dune was edgy in the daylight. He looked left and right, then peered into the dense, dark wood and up at the canopy of the trees. A bank of purple clouds swirled overhead, pushing a breeze that swished through the tree branches.

Kyna shivered and rubbed her arms. "Storm's brewing."

Dune eyed the heavy clouds that extended tentacles across the sky. "Storm or no, we need to watch for Leprechaun hunters."

With a bright flash like fireworks and a simultaneous *bang!*, a bolt of lightning struck the Great Faerie Ring within meters of where Dune and Kyna stood. They both ducked reflexively and clapped their hands over their ears.

Sparks drifted down from a sooty black spot near the top of one of the monolithic stones, marking where the lightning bolt struck.

Dune looked around again, at the woods, the sky. "Let's go," he whispered. Holding Kyna's hand, he darted into the woods.

No sooner had they stepped into the woods than they heard the unmistakable sounds of footsteps running on the gravel path behind them, a dog barking, and voices.

"They were right here, I swear it!" said a man's voice. "They must've fled back into the forest!"

"Leprechauns? You're sure?" a second man asked.

Dune and Kyna darted farther into the forest, going as quickly and soundlessly as possible, until they came upon a giant, pyramid-shaped boulder. Although Dune passed it without stopping, Kyna pulled his arm and motioned for him to follow her. They sank to the ground behind the rock with their backs against its cold, mossy side. Dune could clearly hear the voices, even over his pounding heart and rapid breathing.

"Maybe not both, but the lad, for sure," the first man said. "We can ask them when we catch them."

"What if they lie to us?"

"'Tis against their laws to lie, but they could try to hoodwink us with a convoluted bunch of blarney."

"What do we do then?"

"Some of them have a mark. A tattoo."

"A tattoo?"

"Aye. A symbol of some sort, like a four-leaf clover. We'll look for that."

Kyna silently placed her hand against her neck and searched Dune's eyes with her own.

"Anyone can get a tattoo."

"It's different from a regular tattoo. I canna explain it, but you'll know it when you see it."

The Humans continued plotting.

"But the entrance to the fort must be close by," the second man said. "Their fortune's bound to be inside."

"Let's split up, then. You try to find the entrance, and I'll follow the pair what runned away. They've probably run to a camp or some other hide-out."

"You say that like there may be more of 'em."

"There's always more of 'em, Danny-o. And the more there be, the bigger our fortune."

"All right then, Rafferty. You take Flynn. See if he's a better scent hunter than he is a setter."

Dune motioned to Kyna that they should flee.

Kyna shook her head.

"They'll find us for sure if we stay," Dune whispered.

Again Kyna shook her head. "Be still," she whispered.

"But they'll find—" Dune began, but stopped mid-sentence as he saw the look in Kyna's eyes. Without taking her eyes off him, Kyna swept up a handful of leaves and dirt from the ground where she knelt.

She has a plan. Dune felt a shiver of excitement mixed with fear, like when he was a lad playing hide and go seek. But this was no game. This was serious, life-or-death business.

The unmistakable thump-a-thump of paws running over the leafy path suddenly slowed and stopped. Dune could hear the dog's panting. It sounded like it was a mere two or three meters on the other side of the rock.

Before Dune could stop her, Kyna leapt to her feet and jumped directly into the path.

Without hesitation, Dune jumped to her side.

A flaming red Irish setter the size of a bear stood in the path, apparently stunned for a moment by the unexpected appearance of the two Leprechauns. Dune heard the crashing sound of one of the hunters approaching through the forest.

The dog bared its teeth and growled. The fur on its back stood up in a ridge. It lowered its head and took a step toward Dune and Kyna. As it charged, Kyna flung her handfuls of dirt and leaves into the air.

Dune gaped in awe at the apparition Kyna created: A huge, black dragon that seemed to melt the surrounding trees as it spewed out jets of fire from its crocodilian snout. The air was acrid with the burnt-match smell of the dragon's breath.

Through the thickening smoke, Dune saw the dog cower, its tail tucked between its legs. With a terrified whine, it turned and bolted away.

Dune could barely see one of the hunters, a fat, balding fellow carrying a shotgun, lumber up the path just in time to collide with the fleeing dog. The two tumbled in a knot on the ground, and Dune heard the man shout, "The devil's that? Let's get outta here!"

"Good advice, that," Dune said, grabbing Kyna's hand and escaping with her through the woods at a gallop.

Chapter 14: Friends and Foes

After walking throughout the day and a night, Cairdeen stopped at dawn at the top of a hill. She was not the least bit tired; in fact, she felt she could walk on forever. She whickered to herself, realizing that now she had the freedom to do just that if she wanted.

She bobbed her head down to the lush grass and nipped a mouthful, then panned her gaze across the landscape ahead of her. The rising sun behind her cast her shadow across a two-rut road that led down the hill to a cluster of thatched-roof cabins. Smoke drifted from most of the chimneys, and a low-lying fog blanketed the valley.

Here and there, Cairdeen saw movement in the little yards. Her inclination was to trot down the road through the middle of the village, and make new friends. She had been lonely for so long, and she could smell other horses, as well as goats and chickens.

But she also smelled Humans.

Cairdeen recalled Canavan's warning. *Not every face you meet will be a friendly one.* Cairdeen snorted, testing the air. *Would it be safe to walk right through town?* She took in the landscape—a shallow valley surrounded by rounded hills—and decided on a more circuitous route. She cut through a pasture behind the houses on the north side of the road, trotting down into the valley along a fence line that she could barely make out through the fog.

"You there, Filly." The voice, husky and quite close, startled her. She spooked a few feet away from the fence. Peering through the

low fog, she saw a figure emerging on the other side of the fence. The grey face, the same color as the fog, only became distinguishable as Cairdeen's eyes adjusted in the low morning light. The face belonged to a shaggy, grey-dun pony with shiny black eyes.

"*Who goes there?*" Cairdeen whispered.

"*The name's Jarmy Sean,*" the pony whickered. Cairdeen was thrilled yet again to have a conversation with another creature, although this was different somehow from when she was talking with Canavan. They were speaking, but not with voices.

"*I'm Cairdeen,*" she answered, bowing her head.

"*Daft mare. I know you're a friend,*" Jarmy Sean grumbled.

"*Beggin' your pardon, Jarmy Sean,*" Cairdeen said. "*I suppose I'm new at having polite conversation. What I meant was, 'tis my name. Cairdeen means 'friend,' but 'tis also my name.*"

"*Why dinna you say so,*" Jarmy Sean snorted. He narrowed his eyes as he looked at her. "*And where might you be off to, little friend, with nothin' but a rope around your neck, and nary even a Human on t'other end of it?*"

"*I dunna ken, to tell you true,*" Cairdeen replied. "*But this rope surely is a frightful nuisance.*"

A clanging metallic sound from somewhere behind Jarmy Sean made Cairdeen toss her head. Her ears pricked forward, toward the sound. She was at full alert, but Jarmy Sean merely cocked an ear toward the noise. "*Ahh, that would be me breakfast,*" he said.

A muffled light began to glow, and Cairdeen realized a door had been opened in a house, piercing a rectangular hole in the fog. The silhouette of a Human boy appeared in the doorway. He was scrawny with a shaggy forelock not unlike Jarmy Sean's, although the boy's hair was dark brown. He carried a pail that produced a wonderful sweet smell.

"*Time for me breakfast. 'Twas a pleasure to meet you, lass.*" Jarmy

Sean trotted over to the boy.

"Dunna be so greedy, there, ole fella," the boy said, pouring feed into a pan on the ground. Cairdeen had never heard such a tender tone in a Human voice, and it surprised her that the boy would speak with such affection to a pony.

The boy looked up and spotted Cairdeen. "And what's this? Do you have a girlfriend, then? Why, Jarmy Sean, you old dog!" The boy patted Jarmy Sean's neck, then grabbed a handful of the feed he had just dumped into the pan. He tossed the feed into the bucket and shook it. The sound triggered a memory from Cairdeen's past, when she was a yearling, before the Farmer took her away from her first home. The memory made her mouth water. It was the memory of being fed a hearty meal.

The boy moved toward the fence near where Cairdeen stood. He swept his hand inside the bucket, then extended his cupped hand toward her.

Instinctively she backed away a step, but she was intrigued by this Human—and attracted like a moth to a flame by the syrupy smell of the sweet feed in his hand.

"Would you like a wee bit of breakfast?" the boy asked. "I'm not going to hurt you."

Cairdeen tossed her head and snorted, but stayed her ground as the boy approached. She didn't understand his language, but the tone of his voice was soothing, friendly, and she knew he was offering her something to eat. Something that smelled delicious.

Step by step, she approached the boy until only the fence separated them. She leaned her muzzle over the top rail to gently lip at the sweet feed. When Cairdeen had licked the few nibbles of grain from his hand, the boy offered her the bucket. He slowly reached out his hand and touched Cairdeen's forelock. It was not an unpleasant touch, so she kept brushing her lips along the bottom of the bucket, tasting the sticky sweetness that clung there, and enjoying the few stray oats that she found.

The boy caressed her ears and the side of her neck. His gentle stroking was the first time in years that she had been touched with kindness by a Human, and it hypnotized her.

After a minute or two she realized the boy had hold of the rope. "Gotcha!" he said, dropping the bucket and grabbing the rope with both hands. He yelled over his shoulder, "Da, Da! Come quick! I caught me a pony!"

The boy had tricked her, tempting her close with the grain so he could catch her by the rope. Yet other than a small alarm at his sudden shout, she felt no fear of him the way she had felt fear of the Farmer. She nuzzled the tipped-over bucket, licking up the bits of sweet oats that had fallen on the ground around it.

Jarmy Sean ambled over beside the boy and stuck his head between the fence rails, trying to sneak some of the spilled grain for himself. *"This be my boy, Fergus,"* Jarmy Sean whickered to Cairdeen. *"And a good lad he be."*

Fergus's father appeared in the open barn doorway, wiping his hands on a rag. "Careful with that mare, Fergus," he said, trotting over to the boy. "She'll be bringing us a considerable reward, she will."

"I'm being gentle with her, Da," Fergus said, patting Cairdeen's withers. Then his eyebrows furrowed. "What do you mean, a reward? She's mine, I found her and I'm keeping her."

"If this pony belongs to who I think, you'd be a right better owner, though you are but a wee boy."

"Then why do we have to tell, Da? Why do we have to give her up? I just want to clean her up, brush her coat till it shines, and clean her hooves, and put a hackamore on her. I won't put a bit in her mouth nor a saddle on her back. I'll feed her and give her fresh water. You know I can do it. I take good care of Jarmy Sean, don't I?" The boy patted his pony's face and fingered a golden feather charm that was attached to his halter.

"That you do, Fergus. You take marvelous good care of the old boy. But 'tis costly to keep one pony, let alone two. And the reward for the mare will keep your old Jarmy Sean in sweet feed and sugar cubes all the rest of his days."

"I can teach her to pull the dray. She'll earn her keep by helping take our crops to market."

"Nae, the reward will be more profitable."

"I'll not let you do it, Da."

The father's back stiffened. "You'll be feeling the switch if you backtalk me, boy. You understand?"

Fergus's bottom lip trembled and he looked down at his shoes. "Aye, Sir. I'll not do it again."

"See that you don't," Fergus's father growled. He strode back into the house, barking over his shoulder, "I'll be callin' that farmer over to Seafield, so keep hold o' that mare and bring her into the paddock."

No sooner had the father closed the door, than Fergus slipped between the fence rails and set to work loosening the knot in Cairdeen's rope. "I mightn't be able to keep you myself, but I'll not be turning you over to some barnacle from Seafield," the boy said.

The boy's presence so close, without the fence as a barrier, worried Cairdeen. She thrashed her head, but the boy held tight to the rope.

"Whoa, there, lass. Whoa, there."

His calm voice reassured her and she stood still.

"You'll never outrun him or my father trailing this rope." His fingers deftly picked at the knot. "Aargh, 'tis bounded tight."

Fergus got a small knife out of his pocket. "Be still as you can, lass," he said. The knife was too small to cut through the rope, but working the point of the blade back and forth, Fergus was able to create enough slack to wrangle and wrench the knot free with his hands.

Sliding the rope off Cairdeen's neck, he noticed the raw patches where the rope had dug into her flesh. "You poor lass," he said. "I wish I had time to treat those wounds. But if you dunna leg it on outta here now, they'll catch you for sure."

Cairdeen looked from the boy to Jarmy Sean with confusion. *"Will he not be giving me any more feed, then?"*

"Sure and he would, but some danger must be heading this way for you," Jarmy Sean told her. *"You'd better do as he says and run, run now!"*

Cairdeen nudged her head against the boy's shoulder in thanks, then galloped across the field, away from the cottages and yards and sweet feed and kind voices and gentle hands.

"Goodbye, lassie!" Fergus yelled after her. "May the strength of three be in your journey!"

Cairdeen understood the concern and affection in his words, if not the words themselves. She cantered down the road, shaking her head for the joy of not having that rope around her neck. Part of her wanted to return to Jarmy Sean and his boy. After living so long with no sense of belonging, this feeling, this wanting to belong to someone, to have friends, to be part of a family, even, made her heart ache. The crushing pain of it, coupled with the exertion of running full bore and the lingering fog blanketing the ground, blinded her as if the sun had suddenly turned black.

She didn't see the jumble of barbed wire.

But she felt it bite into her legs and rip into the flesh just above the fetlock of her front right leg.

She tumbled to the ground. Her breath was knocked out of her. She coughed and wheezed, trying to pull air into her lungs.

She rolled to her side and, with great effort, rose to her feet. She stood on three trembling legs, feeling warm blood trickle down her injured leg. The rusty teeth of the barbed wire snagged at the hide on her right front leg, flaying it open and exposing bare flesh.

I canna stop running, she told herself. *The time and place for family is up ahead somewhere. I canna stop running until I get there.*

She tugged her leg against the grip of the barbed wire, but that only tightened the wire. The jagged points bit sharply into her leg, ripping hide and flesh.

Whickering in pain, Cairdeen continued pulling against the wire. Ignoring the searing pain, she struggled and pulled until her leg came free of the wire. She bolted across the field, trying not to think of the stab of pain each time the hoof of her injured leg touched the ground.

Chapter 15: Lucky Lou

The cobbled road bustled with evening activity: People walking, pushing carts loaded with wares, or riding bicycles. Horses pulling wagons piled high with vegetable crates. A young boy hawking newspapers.

Kyna and Dune stood in a dark niche between buildings across the street from the pub. Kyna recognized it from the image she had conjured. Dune knew it from past visits.

A dog chased a cat in front of a horse-drawn wagon loaded with produce. The horse whinnied and reared, toppling a crate of apples, and the driver yelled and lashed his animal with a long whip.

Kyna scowled. "I've half a mind to grab that whip and give that brute a dose of what-for."

"Or we could see what we can learn at Lucky Lou's."

"What's so special about this place?" Kyna asked. "Why would my magic show me a pub?"

"'Tis a safe house of sorts." Dune scanned the street for a way to get to the pub without attracting attention. "The owners owed a debt of some kind to Leprechauns for something that had happened a long time ago. Before I was born."

"So to repay their debt, they run a sanctuary for Leprechauns?"

"Nae, they run a pub. And they help Leprechauns in need."

"Like I said. A sanctuary for Leprechauns."

Dune decided not to waste time arguing. "Follow me. We'll go around back."

As they stole quietly down the narrow, dark corridor between rickety wooden buildings, a light rain began to fall. They emerged onto a dimly lit dirt alley. From there they hugged the shadows, dodging trash heaps and several feral cats that hunkered low and hissed at them. At the end of the alley, a tangled thicket of bushes grew. Dune ducked through a tunnel-like trail in the bushes, and Kyna followed. The trail led them back to the dead end of the road on which the pub stood. Here the street was deserted.

Dune stepped toward an opening in the brush. Kyna pulled him back.

"'Tis safe to cross here," Dune whispered.

"Wait." Kyna gathered a handful of fallen leaves that were only slightly damp from the rain, due to the canopy of brush. She slipped around Dune and threw the leaves into the air. The leaves swirled and multiplied, creating a curtain. "After you," Kyna said.

They crossed the street, hidden by the swirling leaves, and ducked down a path beside the last shop on the end of the row. They came out on another back alley and crept along it until they reached the back door of the pub. A wooden sign hung from chains over the door—the sign in Kyna's conjured image, bearing the name "Lucky Lou's" and a four-leaf clover. Below the sign, light glowed from a thick-paned window in the door. The glass was etched with a the clover surrounded by the words "Lucky Lou's Tavern."

Muted voices and music on the other side of the door became louder as they entered. They stepped into a hallway with scuffed, hardwood floors and three doors marked "Guyes," "Galles," and "Employees Only." The hallway opened on to a small pub filled with people laughing, drinking ale at crowded tables, and more people drinking at a long, polished wood bar. The pub was packed and loud, but none of the patrons seemed to take an interest in them.

As Dune gazed casually around the tavern, the bartender caught his eye and waved him to a pair of stools on the end of the bar. "Dune, isn't it? What brings you here?"

"Long story," Dune answered. He nodded to Kyna to take a seat at the bar, but stood beside her instead of taking the other stool.

"What can I get you?"

"A cup of hot tea, please," Kyna said.

"Pint of your finest for me," Dune said.

The bartender arched an eyebrow as he dried a mug. "I dunna think so."

Dune sighed. "Nae, I dinna think so, either. Cup of tea for me as well."

While the bartender went to get their drinks, Kyna asked, "He knows you?"

"Aye, that's Lou. He's the owner. I believe his father was the one helped by the, uh, family."

"And the pub is designated as a safe place for 'the family?'"

Dune nodded. He leaned his back against the bar, resting his elbows on the rim.

Lou returned with their drinks and a plate with slices of barmbrack and butter on the side. "Two Bewley's and a bit of tuck for you," he said.

"Thank you kindly," Kyna said. She blew on her cup of tea and sipped it.

"How's your da?" Lou asked Dune.

"Fine. Fine as silk." Dune cut a slice off the loaf of brack and slathered it with butter.

"Pardon me, Lucky Lou?" Kyna asked.

Lou gave Dune the raised-eyebrow look.

"She's okay. She's family. Sort of."

"Aye, lass?"

"Are we … safe … here?"

Lou nodded and flicked the bar rag over his shoulder. "The pub is protected by a rune, aye."

"So, Humans can't see it?"

"They can see the pub," Lou said slowly. He poured more hot water into both their cups. "They just don't notice that some of the patrons are, well, different."

Dune popped another bite of bread into his mouth, savoring the warmth and the sweetness of the raisins. Leaning in toward Lou, he spoke quietly. "Did you hear about the Greenapples?"

Lou wiped the rag across the bar. He dropped his head and looked up at Dune from beneath bushy grey eyebrows. "Aye. I heard."

"Have you seen them?"

Lou simply nodded.

Kyna inhaled sharply and squeezed Dune's hand.

"Do you know where they are? What can you tell us?"

Lou shook his head. He straightened his posture and threw the rag into a pan of soapy water behind the bar. He stared at a man who had just entered the pub.

Dune followed Lou's gaze. The man was tall with broad shoulders, dark, wavy hair, and a neatly clipped mustache. He brushed rain drops off his silk top hat with the back of his hand.

Dune realized that the man was staring at Kyna. "You know that guy?"

Kyna sipped her drink and looked over her shoulder. She choked on her drink as she turned back to the bar. "Oh my goodness gracious."

The man wove through the crowd to the bar and stood beside Kyna. He pointed for the bartender. "A pint."

Lou poured a glass of Guinness from the tap and set it on the bar in front of the man.

Kyna focused her attention on her drink. She held the cup with both hands and blew on the hot liquid.

The stranger put his fancy hat on the bar and took off his overcoat, shaking it by the shoulders, with his back turned to Kyna so raindrops would not splash her.

Kyna glanced up at Dune. He thought he saw something akin to fear in her eyes, but more like a warning. He glared at the man's back.

The stranger folded his overcoat over his arm and turned back to his beer. The foamy head had subsided, so he took a sip. As he put his glass down, he looked at Kyna and raised his eyebrows in mock surprise. "My word. It's you."

Kyna tipped her head at him. "Baron MacLean."

"No, no. It's Simon. Remember? And you're Kyna. You stood me up for dinner that night on the ship."

"My companion was ill. I stayed in the cabin with her and ordered room service."

"Yes, your *companion.*" MacLean arched an eyebrow at Dune. "I hope *she* is feeling better now."

"Much. Thank you."

"How amazing that I would find you here, in a pub, in Ireland. I thought you were going to Norway. Or was it Sweden? I don't think you were clear on that part of your plans."

"It was Norway."

"But it is still a mystery, is it not? That you wound up in Ireland?"

"Not such a mystery."

"Beg pardon," Dune interrupted, "but is there some reason the lady should have consulted you about her travel plans?"

"I don't believe we've met," the Baron said, straightening his shoulders and extending his hand.

Dune glared at the man's hand. "No, we have na." He slapped some coins on the bar. "Time to go, Kyna."

They left the way they had entered, through the back door, but when they got outside, they found Simon rushing toward them from the front of the building. "Kyna, wait!"

Dune pulled Kyna by the hand, but she resisted.

"I can handle him," she whispered. "We can't have him chasing us across the country."

Reluctantly, Dune released her hand. He stood close behind her, scowling.

"Kyna, please." Simon jogged to a stop in front of her. "I don't know what this—person—means to you. I only know that I can't get you out of my head. Ever since we met, I can think of no-one but you."

"Not even your son?"

"Of course, I think of him. That's not what I meant. There's something about you." Simon's eyes narrowed. Dune didn't like the way he looked at Kyna as if she were an object he wanted to possess. "I mean, you and I had a connection. I felt it. You did, too."

"Er-hem," Dune said, covering his mouth with his fist as he coughed loudly.

Kyna moved closer to Dune. "I'm sorry, Simon. I don't feel that way about you."

"You're not being honest with me," Simon insisted. "I'm not that much older than you. I could show you the world. And you, well, I have an idea that you would … enrich the relationship."

Dune stiffened. He grabbed Kyna's hand. She gripped his hand tightly but held her ground.

"Simon, this is Dune. He's the reason I came to Ireland."

"You're the reason *I* came to Ireland," Simon insisted. "I checked the ship's manifest, so I knew I'd find here. Somewhere. And I'll not leave until I know why you lied to me."

"I barely know you, so I don't owe you an explanation. But I don't lie, and I could spit nails that you'd suggest it."

"You didn't tell me the truth. Not the whole truth. There's something...magical about you. And I'm not trying to be romantic."

"Good, because I'm not attracted to you romantically, or otherwise."

Simon ignored her reproach. "And it has something to do with that charm you wear."

Kyna clutched her Claddagh necklace. Dune pulled her other elbow and she took a few stumbling steps toward him.

"Stop right there." Simon's voice pinned them in their tracks. "You'll tell me what's going on, and you'll tell me now."

Kyna's eyes were big and round as she looked at Dune, silently pleading for him to protect her.

Dune pulled Kyna behind him as he took a step toward Simon. "Where I come from, we dunna talk to ladies that way."

"And where *do* you come from, eh? This magical island? A place with faeries and ... leprechauns?"

"You there!" Lucky Lou charged out of the pub's back door, waving Simon's hat. "You forgot this!"

"Oh. Quite. Thank you." Simon took his hat and put it on his head. He turned back to Kyna, but Lou grabbed his sleeve.

"*And* you forgot to pay your bill."

"Did I?" Simon dug in his overcoat pockets, then his pants pockets, then patted his shirt. "I'm afraid my wallet's gone."

"Is it now? I've not heard that one since I was a wee lad in the turnip fields of Beagbealach. So when I say, I dinna fall off the turnip truck yesterday, you can believe it. Perhaps you left your wallet inside. Let's go take a look, shall we?"

"But, but," Simon protested as Lou steered him back toward the pub.

The Baron looked over his shoulder as he was led away, but Dune and Kyna had vanished.

For over an hour, Dune and Kyna half-walked, half-jogged

through the night. With no sign that MacLean had followed them, Dune searched for a place to rest. He pointed to a low cairn a few meters off the roadway. Kyna sat on the cairn, and Dune gave her his canteen.

"I think he really likes you," Dune grumbled.

"Simon? Well, sure, he does. In a 'she can make me rich and I'll never have to change a stinky diaper again' kind of way. Although he already has a nanny to keep him from having to attend to any distasteful child-rearing duties."

"What did you say to him? How did he guess that you're a Leprechaun? You certainly dunna look like the stereotype."

Kyna handed the canteen to Dune. "None of us do. We aren't ten millimeters tall, and we don't have pointy ears and green skin."

"But most of us have the tattoo."

Kyna pulled her long hair back from her neck to show Dune the tattoo below her left ear.

"The Kelly Clover? That's odd," Dune said. "You're only an honorary member of the Kelly clan, are ye not?"

"That's right." Kyna flashed Dune an irritated glare. "I'm not a *real* Kelly."

"Did he see your tattoo? Did you use your magic in front of him?"

"If *you* had magic, would you use it in such a careless way?"

Dune stiffened. "If I had magic? You say that as if I'll never have magic of my own."

Kyna's face softened and she held up her hand. "No, no, no. That's not what I meant."

"But 'tis true. I've no magic. None that will do me any good anywhere other than the football pitch."

"You see this amulet?" Kyna climbed down from the cairn. She drew the long chain into her hand and dangled the Claddagh charm a few centimeters from Dune's face. It glinted in the moonlight. "I wear this to remind me of my magic. Of my strength. You wear your strength like a challenge. A dare."

"What do ye ken of my strength?" Dune clasped the Claddagh in his fist to stop its swinging back and forth.

Immediately he was struck by an electric charge. Images flashed behind his eyelids. Not just a single story like when he held the Kelly Clover and channeled its history, but a series of rapid-fire images. Through chattering teeth, Dune described his visions. "Kyna, don't go to the door! A room. Cold, dark, clammy. Seamus is there, and the others. The Pooka! Kyna, be careful! Who's there? Kane, what are you—? A boy. Mother Cass—Oh!"

With a jolt, Dune was thrown off his feet by a surge of energy from the Claddagh. He landed on his back, his head hitting the ground.

Kyna knelt beside him, shook his shoulders, then felt his wrist for a pulse. "Dune! Can you hear me?"

"Uh, yeah. A bit stiff." Dune sat up and rubbed the back of his head and shoulder. Kyna's Claddagh charm was still in his hand, pieces of the thin gold chain dangling between his fingers. "Oh, Kyna, forgive me. I've broken your necklace."

"Don't worry about that. I can mend it." She took the necklace from his hand and tucked it in her skirt pocket. "Are you okay?"

Dune nodded and winced. He gripped the back of his neck. "What happened? I've a right headache. And my neck and shoulders are sore."

"You fell backwards. You hit your head on the ground."

Dune rubbed his eyes with the heels of his palms. "Uhh."

"Dune? You had a vision. Do you remember it?"

He opened his eyes wide, remembering. "Aye. But it dinna make any sense."

"Tell me what you saw." Kyna sat on the ground next to him and placed one hand on his thigh. She quickly jerked her hand away, blushing, but Dune reached for her hand and held it in both of his.

"I saw a boy. And a pony." He cut his eyes at Kyna, embarrassed. "I thought it was the Pooka."

"Why did you think it was the Pooka?"

"I recently told the story of the Pooka to my little brothers and sister. I suppose it was still on my mind. And I have a certain, er, lack of affection for horses and ponies in general."

"Not a fan of ponies?"

"Ha! That's an understatement. And by the way, with me and ponies? The feeling is mutual."

"Maybe this pony is different from the ones you've met. Maybe it needs a friend."

"If I see her, I'll be sure to ask if she's friendly or if she wants a bite of me like every other pony I've met."

"She? The pony's a mare?"

"I'd not thought about it, but yes."

"What color is she?"

"Dull sorrel. Matted coat. Long, tangled mane."

"And the boy? He was Human?"

Dune nodded. He looked around for his hat. He reached for it and winced.

"Here." Kyna handed it to him. He pushed it down on his head, wincing again when his fingers touched the tender spot where he had bumped his head on the road.

"Do you know who he is?"

"Never seen him. Maybe *you've* met him?"

"I've not met any Human boys in Ireland. What did he look like?"

"Scruffy brown hair, off the ears but long bangs in his eyes. His eyes…" Dune pictured the boy in his mind. "His eyes were different colors. One green, one brown."

"That should help us recognize him if we see him. Why do you think he was so important as to show up in your vision?"

"He must be connected to the Greenapples somehow."

"Why do you say that?"

"My one overarching—I dunna ken exactly, emotion, I suppose—during the whole vision was the Greenapples. Protecting the Greenapples. Kyna, we have to find them."

"We will, Dune. We will. What else did you see?"

He decided not to mention the brief inclusion of Mother Cass in his vision. "You. You were there. Strange."

"Really? I'm not too thrilled that you think I'm strange."

"Not you," Dune said softly. "I dunna think you're strange, except that you want to come off on a dangerous trek with the likes of me."

"Ah, Dune. Didn't you hear what I told Simon?"

He looked at her quizzically.

"The man at the pub?"

"Oh, that barmpot. I was a bit preoccupied trying to think of a way to escape him. What did you tell him?"

"I … I told him … you're the reason I came to Ireland." Kyna cast her eyes down.

"But you came for the Ceili."

"Mother Cass invited me to the Ceili, that's true. I would do anything Mother Cass asked me to do. But the truth is, I crossed the ocean for you, Dune."

"You did? For me?"

She nodded, keeping her eyes on Dune's hands, which enfolded her own.

"Kyna, look at me."

She raised her blue eyes to his green ones. In the moonlight, the Smoky Mountains met the Emerald Island.

"I would cross oceans for you, too."

"You would? For me?"

Dune nodded. He squeezed Kyna's hands and let out a breath. He felt like he had been holding his breath for weeks.

They grew quiet. The only sound was the song of crickets and nightbirds.

When Kyna shivered, Dune took off his coat and wrapped it across her shoulders.

She smiled her thanks and clutched the jacket close about her.

Dune stood and offered her his hand. He watched the road and the countryside, listening to the night sounds. Sometimes, he knew, the first sign of danger was a stillness of the creatures of the night.

"Do ye feel like moving on, then?" Dune asked.

"You're the one knocked your noggin on the ground. If you're up to it, I am."

Kyna buttoned Dune's jacket at her throat and they set out side by side.

"Back at the Faerie Ring, you conjured a dragon." Dune shuddered at the memory. "It was so ... real. How did you know to make a dragon?"

"I didn't ask for a dragon. I just thought, *scare the dog away,* and the dragon appeared."

"You told me about another time you conjured dragons. Do you often make pictures of dragons?"

Kyna shook her head. "Just those two times."

"Tell me what happened the first time. It had to do with badgers, aye?"

Kyna nodded. "Last year, when I was here for the Ceili, I went out to the countryside to visit a small spring that I remembered from my childhood."

"You went alone? Do ye ken how dangerous that was?"

"I do now. There were hunters."

"Kyna!"

Kyna held her hand up to stop Dune's protest. "I hid when I heard them. But I wasn't the one in danger. They were after a group of badgers. It wasn't a big colony. From what I could tell, it was a small family, a mated pair and their cubs. The hunters were yelling and striking the ground with wooden bats or clubs. When the cubs ran from the den, the hunters set about grabbing them and throwing them in wooden boxes. The cubs were crying in fear, trying to scramble out of the boxes, but they were just babies; they were too small to get out. The mama tried to save them, but one of the hunters—I can't even say it." She shook her head and shuddered.

"You dunna have to go on, if 'tis too painful for you to remember."

"No, I'm okay. But then, I was so scared! I wanted to help, but I didn't know how. I picked up fistfuls of debris—leaves, gravel, whatever I could gather—and flung it in the air. Water is better, but I hadn't time to look for it. I didn't ask for a dragon. I just wanted something to frighten the hunters away. I'd no idea what image I would conjure. I just knew I had to give the badgers a cover for their escape."

Kyna told Dune about the three dragons she had conjured. They were covered snout to tail with golden scales that glinted in the sun. Fire erupted from their mouths, and smoke billowed from their nostrils. The smoke spread across the ground and swirled with each step the dragons took.

"The hunters screamed in fear and ran away," she said.

"I canna say I blame them!"

Dune looked around at the empty fields on either side of the gravel road. All was bathed in moonlight. Nothing stirred other than the crickets singing their reassuring songs. He yawned and twisted his neck left and right.

"Tired?"

"Knackered, but we have to keep going," he replied. "What

happened to the badgers?"

"When the image of the dragons dissolved, the hunters were gone, along with the wooden box. I saw no sign of the adult badgers. The body of one baby lay on the ground. I thought it was dead, but it was still breathing, faintly. I took it to Mother Cass, and she promised to care for it and return it to its family when it was healed."

"She's always taking in animals, feeding them, nursing them back to health. My sister Fionn is that way, too. Cats, ponies—if it has four legs and fur, 'tis love at first sight."

Dune gazed at the sky, ribboned now with a sliver of pink in the east. "We need to get off the beaten path before it gets too light." He had been studying the terrain as they walked. He pointed to an outcropping of boulders a short way off the road, and they headed toward it.

Kyna stifled a yawn. "What about your vision? What else did you see? Everything is important." She gathered her hair into a loose braid as they walked.

"That's what's strange. I canna think how the boy and the pony could appear in a vision from your amulet unless one of us knew them. Unless—"

"Unless what?" Kyna stopped and turned to Dune, grabbing his shoulder and bringing him to a full stop. "Tell me, Dune."

"I think I might have been seeing things that haven't happened yet, or things that are happening now."

"What things?"

Dune continued walking toward the boulders. Kyna followed.

"I saw a room," Dune said. "It was dark, cold. Maybe a basement. I've not seen that room before, but the Greenapples were there, making shoes."

"Making shoes!" Kyna scoffed. "What do the Humans think we are, elves?"

"That room. I think 'tis where the Greenapples are being held. And…." He hesitated to tell her of the most disturbing image from his vision.

"You can tell me." She gave his arm a firm squeeze.

Dune shook his head. They had reached the formation of boulders, which appeared to have been dropped at the top of a low rise by giants playing some long-abandoned game. Dune unsheathed his athame. "Nae, I canna remember it now. Let's set up camp. 'Tis almost daybreak. We'll stay here until nightfall. Wait while I make sure 'tis safe."

"Why don't I go around one way and you go around the other?"

"I'd rather you stay here and let me do the protecting."

"We're in this together, Dune the Protector."

Dune realized that Kyna would not give in, and he was too tired to argue. "All right. You go 'round that way, and I'll go this way."

"Wait. I'll sew a veil for us both." Kyna looked around for a patch where the grass wasn't too thick. She swept her hand across the ground and collected a few grains of sand and a couple blades of dead grass. Morning dew clung to the grass.

"'Tis not a lot of fabric for a veil," Dune said.

"I've worked with less."

"Okay, then, give it a go."

Kyna shut her eyes and clasped her hands together. She took in a breath, made a shelf of her hands, and blew the grass and grit from her palms. The particles lifted and multiplied until they formed a cloud around both Kyna and Dune. As Dune watched in wonder, the cloud grew dark and billowy. Lightning flashed from its crown. Rain fell all around them, soaking the ground, yet they remained dry.

Kyna flicked her fingers at Dune, indicating for him to go around the right side of the boulders while she went to the left. As they parted, the cloud grew, covering them and the mound of boulders like an umbrella. Around them, rain bucketed from the cloud and ran in rivulets down the gentle hill. They met on the uphill side of the boulders. Kyna touched her fingertips to Dune's, and the cloud dispersed, leaving the grass glistening with raindrops that evaporated a moment later.

Dune stood in the shadow of the huge boulders and squinted at the sun, just peaking over the eastern horizon. "This side should give us shelter and shade until nightfall. Make yourself comfortable."

"Do you want me to sew another veil?" Kyna sat with her back against the boulder and her legs tucked to one side. "It won't last all day, but I could refresh it every hour or so."

Dune took his mother's velvet pouch of rune stones from his coat pocket. "Nae, I've something that lasts longer." He took two giant steps out from the boulders and began placing the stones on the ground, encircling the boulders.

Kyna walked along behind him. "Can I help with that?"

"Nae, just stay inside the circle." When he had placed all the stones except the pink quartz, he held this special talisman in his hand, slid his thumb over its smooth, translucent surface, then carefully positioned it under the stone that marked east. He stepped inside the circle and recited the rune that his mother had taught him.

> Echo, echo, hear my call.
> Dim the lights and raise the wall.
> Dark-on-dark the curtain rise,
> Conceal us from unfriendly eyes.

When he had completed the rune, Dune slouched back against the pile of boulders.

"Are you hungry?" Kyna asked.

"A bit. More tired than hungry, though."

"Here." Kyna reached inside her cloak and handed Dune a half loaf of bread.

"Where did you—?"

"The Great Faery Ring. I couldn't leave all that good food for the birds!"

Dune tore the loaf in two and gave half to Kyna. They shared sips of water from Dune's canteen.

"Do you think the boy from your vision is one of the hunters that captured the Greenapples?" Kyna asked.

"Nae, it dinna have that feel to it." Dune chewed a bite of bread. "I got the feeling the boy was on our side, a friend. The pony too. As bizarre as that sounds."

"You mentioned someone else. Keen? Or maybe you were saying 'Kyna.'"

Dune shook his head and rolled his eyes. "Kane. He's a fellow footballer. Plays for Killarney. I dunna ken what he could have to do with the Greenapples."

"How well do you know him?"

"He's a distant cousin. I see him at the Ceili every year, in addition to when our teams meet on the pitch, several times a year."

"Is he at the Ceili this year? Have you spoken to him?"

"Aye. He was on about having a job, making a lot of money, and impressing some lass. In fact, it was someone from the Appalachian clan." Dune thought a moment, trying to remember the name. "Deborah Something."

"Dearbhorgaill?"

"Aye, that's it. Do you know her?"

"She's my best friend. I call her Gaill." Kyna scrunched her eyebrows and shook her head. "And she's told me all about your friend Kane."

"Oh? What has she said?"

"At first she was flattered by his attention. But he's an ox. Sorry if you're friends, but that's what he is. He flashed some money at her and seemed to think she should swoon all over him."

"We're talking about the same Kane, then."

Kane was much more confident around women than Dune was, but completely oblivious to the way they perceived him. Women were a mystery, though, and there was no explaining who they were attracted to. Just look at Kyna. For some reason, she wanted to join him on this quest, despite the dangers involved. *She crossed an ocean for me!*

"What is that smile about?" Kyna asked.

Dune shrugged his shoulders in reply.

The sun was full in the sky now, and birdsong filled the air.

Kyna raised her face to the sun. "I wonder if the birds are talking about us." She leaned against Dune and rested her head on his shoulder.

"What would they be saying?" Dune asked, but Kyna was asleep.

He breathed in the scent of her hair, jasmine and something else, probably the fragrance of a flower that grew in her home in the mountains, an ocean away. She said she crossed an ocean for him, and he had told her he would do the same for her. But would he? Would he move to America to be with her?

He knew the answer. He would miss his homeland, but he would follow her anywhere, just as she was following him on this rescue mission.

The day grew warmer and Dune dozed off and on, waking intermittently to check for signs of danger—the sound of approaching footsteps or voices, a flash of movement—but nothing stirred. The birds chirped and sang as they flitted about, landing occasionally on the rocks above him. One blue-grey bird with a rusty breast and white bars on its wings lit on the ground just outside the circle of stones. It fluffed its feathers and opened its beak, releasing a powerful voice for such a small bird. After singing its brief song, it flew away.

Dune smiled. He was confident that the circle of Maureen's stones protected Kyna and himself. He drifted back to sleep.

As the sun hung low in the west, Dune awoke to notice Kyna watching him. "How long have you been awake?" he asked.

"Not long. You snore."

"I do not."

"Whatever you say." Kyna smiled, stood up, and stretched. "I'm hungry."

Dune stood as well. "Then let's move on." He retrieved the velvet pouch and began picking up the protective stones.

"Can I help?" Kyna reached for a stone.

"No! Don't touch that!"

Kyna jumped back in surprise, clutching her hand to her chest as if she had almost touched a venomous snake. "Sorry! Why can't I touch them?"

"You might ... contaminate them."

Kyna straightened her back and jutted out her chin. "I beg your pardon?"

Dune kept his eyes on the ground as he continued placing his mother's stones in their pouch. "I just ... canna take any chances. I was scared to touch them myself, the first time I helped my ma create the circle, for fear that I might banjax the rune."

Kyna exhaled and nodded. "I understand the importance of ritual, truly. But I don't think you're giving either of us our due."

"How do you mean?"

"Your mother trusted you, and she was right, wasn't she?"

"I suppose so...."

"And if she trusted you, and you trust me— Oh! You *do* trust me, don't you, Dune?"

"Of course, I do!"

"Then why won't you let me help you?"

"I've let you help in other ways, have I not?" He took in a breath and softened his tone. "And you *have* helped, Kyna. Very much."

"Well, thank you for that, at least. Go ahead and pick up your stones. And when you trust me enough, maybe you'll let me help with that as well." She turned her back on him and gazed at the setting sun.

Dune gathered the rest of the stones. He could tell Kyna wasn't happy with him, but he didn't know what to do to make things better. As he picked up the rose quartz stone, he squeezed it and felt it grow warm in his hand. "Kyna, come here."

Kyna looked over her shoulder at him. She jutted out her chin and looked away again. "Why?"

"Kyna, please. I've an idea." He slid the quartz into the velvet pouch, cinched the pull strings, and put the pouch in his jacket pocket. He stepped closer to her and when she turned around, he searched her eyes for … something. "Can I hold your Claddagh charm?"

She reached in her skirt pocket and handed him the charm on its broken chain.

This time, there was no jolt of electric current, just a soft vibration in his palm. Dune held the charm in his fist and clutched it to his chest. He closed his eyes. Images flashed in his mind. He saw Kyna as a little girl, playing near the waterfall in the lake at Glencar. He saw her again, still as a little girl, sitting on a chair in a farrier's shop, cradling her knees in her arms as she watched a man using a long-handled tool on a pony's hooves. He saw her a few years older, skipping barefoot down a mountain trail, her long hair streaming behind her like a flag. He saw her crossing the ocean, standing at the bow of the ship; a man approaching her—the man from the pub—and a huge whale breaching just off the bow. Finally, he saw an image of his mother, smiling.

He opened his eyes. Kyna was watching him quietly.

"Do you ken a farrier?" he asked.

She nodded. "My grandfather."

"Here in Ireland, or in your mountains?"

"Here. Over near Seafield. Did you see him?"

"Aye. He was trimming a pony's hooves. You were watching him. You were little, but I knew it was you."

Kyna smiled. "He died a long time ago, before I left Ireland."

"I'm sorry. About the runes...."

"Do you still think I would ruin the rune by helping you with the stones?"

"Nae. You are na a ruin runner. A run ruiner." He shook his head. "Gah!"

They both snorted with amusement. When he quit laughing, Dune handed the charm back to Kyna. "Nae, you would na ruin it. My mother approves. I saw her, too."

Kyna clasped Dune's hand in a handshake, the charm between their palms. "Then I hope I don't let either of you down."

I hope I dunna let you down. His eyes stung with the thought. *I've so many people I dunna want to let down.*

"Are you all right?"

Dune cleared his throat. "Yes, of course. I'm fine. Shall we find something to eat, then?"

Kyna slipped her hand around his elbow and they walked north, side by side, enjoying a sunset that flooded the western sky with shades from pink to purple. "Where are we headed?" Kyna asked.

"To Beagbealach, but we'll find something to eat before we get there."

"What's in Beagbealach?"

"The Greenapples."

"Was that in your vision, too?"

"Nae. Lucky Lou told us."

When she looked at him quizzically, Dune explained. "Lucky Lou was born and raised on the top floor of the building his pub is in. He knew we were looking for the Greenapples, so he dropped the name of the town where we should look."

"Quite clever," Kyna said, patting Dune on the back. "Now about those vittles…"

Now it was Dune's turn to look confused.

Kyna laughed her windchime laugh. "That's what we call food in Violet Springs."

Chapter 16: Beagbealach

The town of Beagbealach appeared as a single string of lights twinkling on the horizon.

"At least we'll not need weeks and weeks to search the town for the Greenapples," Dune said. "The whole of it's no bigger than a postage stamp."

Kyna asked. "Did Lucky Lou give you any details other than the name of the town?"

Dune shook his head. "We'll have to look around and see what strikes us as a place where someone would hide a family of Leprechauns."

"Where do you think we should start?"

Dune pointed to an abandoned shack on the edge of town. It was surrounded by oak trees and choked with vines that grew up the walls and through the open doorway and broken window. "There," he said. "We need to rest before we start searching."

He pulled vines out of the way, chopping the most obstinate ones with his athame, and stepped into a small, dark room. Dim moonlight shone through a dirty, cracked window. It was enough light to reveal silhouettes of a table with a chair, another chair tipped over on the floor, and another chair, this one missing a leg and propped in a corner. There was a stone fireplace with a ratty rug in front of it. Cobwebs draped the window, the corners of the ceiling, and the furniture. Despite the derelict state of the shack, there was a forgotten pile of wood stacked beside the hearth.

Kyna followed Dune inside and peered through a relatively grime-free corner of the window. "At least it'll be more comfortable than a pile of boulders. Do you think we'll be safe here?"

"Aye, after I arrange the rune stones for protection."

Kyna's lips tightened into a thin line.

Dune pointed at the fireplace. "It'd be a big help if you could build us a fire."

Kyna exhaled the breath she had been holding. She nodded and set to work arranging wood in the fireplace.

Dune went back outside and positioned the stones around the shack. As he chanted the incantation, he felt a chill course up and down his spine. He shook off the feeling of foreboding and went back inside.

Kyna had built a crackling fire. It illuminated and warmed the tiny room.

"I'm so tired," she said, sitting at the table. "I wish we had something to eat."

"I'll see if I can round us up some, um, fiddles?"

Kyna stifled a laugh and a yawn. She crossed her arms on the table, laid down her head, and closed her eyes. "The *vittles* can wait till morning."

"Okay, then." He righted the toppled chair, tested it for sturdiness, and sat beside Kyna. He rested his head on his arms on the table, his face a few centimeters from hers. He felt her breath, slow and deep, on his arm, and knew she was already asleep. He listened to her breathing, felt the warm exhales, and breathed in the jasmine fragrance of her hair until he fell asleep himself.

After a few brief hours of sleep, Dune awoke to birdsong. Dawn cast a soft grey light throughout their shelter. He stretched to dislodge the cramped-up feeling in his bones from sleeping sitting in a chair with his head bent over a table. Kyna was still asleep, her face veiled by her flaxen hair. As quietly as possible, Dune tiptoed to the door, cracked it open a skosh, and peered outside. A low fog lay over the scrubby yard, road, and pastureland in all directions.

He stepped quietly to Kyna and gently rested his hand on her back.

"Mmm, good morning," she said, yawning and stretching.

"Will you be ready for some vittles?" Dune asked.

Kyna's stomach growled in response.

"I'll take that as a 'yes.' I'll see what I can find."

"Be careful, Dune." She rose from her chair and gave him a quick kiss on the cheek.

Dune twisted his hat in his hands. He nodded and strode out the door, a mixture of exhilaration and anxiety coursing through his veins.

One side of the narrow road was a tangled mess of briars marching down a hill to the edge of the pavement. The terrain on the other side of the road was flatter, with a fringe of low bushes and weeds and pastureland beyond. Dune set off at a jog, glancing over his shoulder every few steps to ensure he would not be taken unawares by someone approaching from the west. He would have preferred to search under the cover of night, but both he and Kyna needed food.

As Dune approached the town, small stone-and-mortar homes lined one side of the road. With chimneys on either end and their yards guarded by spherical buxus hedges, the little houses were shoved right up next to the road, penned in by a continuous, low stone wall that ran as far as Dune could see.

On the other side of the road, several dozen black cattle grazed on late ryegrass. They stared at him with mild curiosity on their white faces, flicking their ears and chewing their cud.

Dune shoved his hat farther down on his brow and balled his fists inside his coat pockets. The fingers of his right hand found and grasped the velvet pouch, now empty because the stones protected the shack: a reminder to be even more vigilant.

He considered slipping around in back of the row of houses to check for any food that might have been left out. He thought about his mother's caramel apple pies, sitting on the pie rack to cool. He thought—

He thought he heard something. Without wasting a second, Dune leapt over the wobbly field fence and crouched behind a row of scraggly bushes. A foul odor engulfed him. He curled his upper lip, scrunched his brows, and looked at the ground beneath his feet. He had landed squarely in a fresh pile of cow manure. *Ugh, that's manky.*

He would have to deal with that later. The immediate need was to determine the source of the sound he heard, and create a plan of escape before he was spotted.

"You there!" A gravelly voice called from the road. "You behind the bushes!"

There went Dune's plan to escape undetected. He peeked through the branches. A skinny old man stood in the road beside a horse that was hitched to a cart. The cart was piled high with crates of vegetables.

"I canna see you, but I know where you are," the old man yelled. Holding the horse's harness for balance, he leaned forward and peered in Dune's general direction.

Dune remained motionless.

"Come now, lad. I know you're there! I'll not harm ye. In fact, you might be able to help an old man."

Dune drew in his breath and stood up. "Yes, sir. Here I am."

The old man straightened up. "Ah! You must be Lynch's new cowherd. I heard tell that Old Orin Lynch had come into an inheritance or some such and hired himself a hand to work the farm. Come over here to me."

Dune glanced up and down the road. When he was sure no-one

else was approaching, he shoved down the top of the field fence so he could climb over it.

"Are you good with horses, lad?" Before Dune could reply, the man looped the horse's reins over its head and took a few steps in the direction of Dune's voice. "Do me a favor. Grab these reins and convince Peppercorn—that would be this stubborn mule here—convince him to turn around. I've dropped a crate of apples a short ways back, and I canna get him to go back. 'Tis past his breakfast time, and he's keen on gettin' to the barn."

"I'm not very good with horses, sir, but I could run down the road and bring you back the crate."

The old man smiled and reached one hand toward Dune. He slapped Dune's chest and face before finding his shoulder, which he patted. He sniffed the air around Dune. "Aye, you're the cowherd all right."

The man looked up at Dune with milky blue eyes.

He's blind, Dune realized.

"Where do ye think ye lost the crate?"

"'Tis about 400 meters back."

"I'll find it and be back fairly lively."

Dune took off at a jog down the road until he saw the crate, upended in the grassy shoulder. He gathered a few of the apples that had fallen out and were strewn in the grass and on the road. *If I'd been just a half an hour later coming into town, I'd have found these apples and would have just taken them back to share with Kyna.*

Instead, he picked up the crate, heaved it up on one shoulder, and jogged back up the road to where the old man waited with his horse and cart.

"Here you are, sir." Dune lifted the apple crate to the top of the stack in the cart.

"I can see Lynch has found himself a right good hand. I'll tell him so the next time I see him. If he'll give me the time of day any more, that is. He seems to think he's a bit of all that, ever since he came into his good luck. That's just what he said it was, too. Good luck. Life is fickle, son. Best people I know dunna have two sticks to rub together, and here's Orin Lynch, treats his animals like rubbish. Never met a scheme he dinna like, that one, and him getting all the luck. If such a thing exists as the luck of the Irish, how come I've not found any of it meself?"

The old man shook his head. "Say, I should na be talking about your employer in such a way. Bring me one of those apples for Peppercorn, would you?" The man stroked the side of his horse's neck, running his fingers through its mane.

Dune plucked an apple off the top of the pile and bobbed it in his hand as he walked to the front of the cart. He tried to put it in the old man's hand, but the man waved him off. "No, no. You give it to him."

"Me?" Dune looked from the man to the horse and back again. "You want … me … to feed the apple to the … the horse?"

"Aye."

Dune gingerly poked the apple at the horse's mouth. The horse stretched his neck and pursed his lips. Dune held the apple by his fingertips and inched closer to the animal.

Peppercorn whinnied and stomped one hoof. Dune dropped the apple and backed away.

"Have you never fed a horse an apple?" the man asked.

Dune shook his head. Realizing the gesture was lost on the sightless man, he said, "Nae."

"Pick it up then, and try again. Hold it in the palm of your hand. Dunna be afraid."

Dune opened his hand with the apple on his palm. He stretched his arm out as far as it would go.

The horse took the apple in its teeth, lipping Dune's hand gently, and munched happily.

"I thank you kindly," the man said. "Sometimes he bites when he's past due for breakfast."

"Now you tell me!"

"Will you take a few apples for yourself in gratitude for your assistance? And some ears of corn if you like."

"Thank you. I will." Dune stepped away from the horse, eyeing him the whole time. He bumped into the old man, who pinwheeled his arms trying to keep his balance.

Dune steadied him by holding the man's arms just below the shoulders. He noticed how bony and frail the man was. "Is this your supper in your cart, then?"

"Aye, mine and the Missus, and Peppercorn's. I sell whatever is left over. Brings a few spondoolicks here and there."

Dune's stomach rumbled. "I'll just take two apples. That will be plenty for me and … that will be plenty." He turned to go, then thought of something. "By the way, do you ken where I can find Mr. Lynch? I—I'm supposed to check in with him, but I've lost the directions."

"You've just passed his place when you went to pick up the crate. From what I hear, it has a fancy door. Farewell with you."

"Farewell at you," Dune replied.

As Dune started down the road, the old man called out, "I'd clean up a bit before you meet Mr. Lynch."

"Thank you! I will!"

Dune jogged down the road with the two apples. Maybe he and Kyna would be able to find more food when they returned to explore the town for signs of the Greenapples. Starting with this fellow Lynch's house. Lynch. The name sounded familiar. It would come to him, he was sure.

Chapter 17: The Stake-Out

"Ugh, what's that smell?" Kyna wrinkled her nose as Dune opened the door of the little shack.

"My disguise. I'm posing as a cowhand."

"Your disguise is disgusting." Kyna barred him from entering. "Take your shoes off and leave them outside."

After removing his shoes, Dune sat on the hearth. The warmth of the fire felt good against his back. He tossed Kyna an apple. "'Tis all I could get my hands on. You can have the other one, too, if you'd like."

Kyna sat beside him and polished the apple on her sleeve. "This'll do. Thanks. Did you find out anything?"

"The man who gave me the apples mentioned—"

"Someone saw you? And you *talked* to him?" Kyna had opened her mouth to take a bite out of the apple, but her jaw dropped, as did the bite of apple, which landed on the floor. "Why weren't you more careful?"

"He dinna actually *see* me."

Kyna continued to eye Dune with alarm. "What in tarnation does that mean?"

"He's blind. Canna see the nose in front of his face. He mentioned someone named Lynch, who sounds like he might be the one who captured the Greenapples."

"Do you know how to find him?"

"Aye. His place is just down the road. We can hunker down in the field and scout it out."

"What's your plan, once we find them?" Kyna took a bite of apple.

Dune stood up and paced the floorboards. "From what I've seen of the area, 'tis slightly hilly with a few farm houses along the road and cow pastures on the other side."

"And the town itself?"

"I've not been there, but we might not have to go all the way to town. Lynch's place is just a kilometer from here."

"That close?" Kyna stood up and tossed the half-eaten apple into the fire. She looked around at the broken-down furniture in the dingy, abandoned house. "What if he finds us first?"

"No-one is going to come looking for us. They dunna ken we're here."

"Could they see the smoke from the fire? Do the rune stones conceal it?"

"I dunna ken. But 'tis chilly. Lots of people have fires going."

But he was worried, too. Before Kyna could say it, he added, "But not in abandoned shacks."

They both jumped up from the hearth.

"We should go," Kyna said. She grabbed an ash shovel and jabbed at the fire, separating the logs until the fire was almost out. She tamped the remaining embers with the back of the shovel.

Dune cracked open the door and grabbed his boots. He wrinkled his nose at the stench of cow manure. Finding a stick, he sat outside and cleaned his boots as best he could while Kyna closed the flue.

She joined him outside. "Ready?"

They darted along the side of the shack and ducked behind a boxwood hedge that ran behind the abandoned building's small yard. The hedge continued behind the other houses, running parallel to the road, with a pasture beyond.

"I think we'd be best hidden if we move along this hedgerow," Dune said. "Near the Lynch place, we'll place the stones in a circle and recite the Rune. We'll wait inside the circle until we're sure the coast is clear."

He slapped his hand against his forehead. "The stones! Help me gather them!"

They scurried back to the shack and picked up the stones like children scrambling to collect Easter eggs. They met at the front door where they dumped the stones into the velvet pouch.

A dog barked nearby.

"New plan," Dune said. "We'll wait in that pasture until dark."

"But we're so close!"

"Close only counts in horseshoes. We can't banjax this by being impatient."

Kyna nodded. "Then let's find a spot lickety-split and lay out the stones."

Dune climbed up the embankment and turned to lend Kyna a hand, but she was already climbing and was soon standing beside him. He pushed down the field fence for her to step over, and they slunk along behind the thin line of scrubby bushes until they came to a patch of pasture that was fairly flat and, Dune noted, free of cow dung.

"Hold out your hands," he said.

Kyna cupped her hands.

Dune selected six rune stones and placed them one by one in her hands. "I'll go left. You go right. Place the stones in an arc. We'll meet just this side of that big bush. The circle will have to be tight because we haven't much room."

Working silently, they placed the stones, meeting in front of the large bush Dune had indicated.

"I think you've forgotten something," Kyna whispered.

Dune looked at her quizzically for a moment until it struck him.

"The quartz! I'm glad you're here, or I would have banjaxed it, to be sure." He quickly retrieved the rose quartz from the velvet pouch. He held it to his lips, faced east, then turned to each of the four points of the compass as he had watched his mother do so many times. He tucked the smooth pink stone under the stone that marked east and led Kyna to the middle of the circle. Impulsively, he kissed her quickly on the cheek.

She smiled at him, touching her face where his lips had brushed her skin. "Now what?"

"Do you want to join me in the Rune?"

"What if I say it wrong?"

"You won't."

Together, they spoke the Protection Rune.

> *Echo, echo, hear my call.*
> *Dim the lights and raise the wall.*
> *Dark-on-dark the curtain rise,*
> *Conceal us from unfriendly eyes.*

Once the rune was completed, they sat in the grass, which was slightly damp from the morning dew. Light flooded through the windows at the house across the road from where they sat, and the tantalizing aroma of coffee brewing and bacon sizzling drifted toward them on the morning breeze.

Dune's stomach rumbled. He reached in his coat pocket and handed Kyna his apple. "Here. You must be leppin' with the hunger."

"We'll share it." Kyna took a big bite and handed the apple back to Dune.

As she munched, she pointed at the house across the street. "Is that Lynch's place?"

Dune shook his head and pointed at the next house. "The one there with the grand door."

The house was built from stone blocks like the others, squat and solid with vines growing up the walls and a slate roof that sagged in the middle. Smoke drifted from twin chimneys that jutted from either end of the roof. A rusty gate led from the road up a short walkway to the front door, at the top of three stone steps. The door, as Dune noted, was newer, fancier than the rest of the house, and more elegant by far than any of the other houses' doors. With a rounded top framed by red bricks, its knotty alder wood shone in the rays of the rising sun.

"Do you think that's where the Greenapples are being held?"

"'Tis very likely so. I'd wager that door is a piece of their handiwork."

"Now what?" Kyna peered at the house.

"Now, we wait. And watch."

Kyna sighed. "I hate the waiting. We're so close, I just want to go in and grab them and go."

"Listen at you! After bein' on *me* about bein' more careful!"

"I know, I know. I'm not saying we *should* do it. I'm just saying, it's hard knowing they're right there, and we have to wait." Kyna took a bite of the apple and handed it back to Dune.

"They might be there, but they might not. We have to wait for an opportunity to get inside undetected so we can find out." Dune pointed to the front window of the Lynch house. "'Tis hard to see with the glare from the sun, but someone is moving around in there. If we went in now, we'd be—well, we'd be in a lot of trouble. And no help to the Greenapples."

They sat silently, side-by-side in the grass inside the protective circle.

After several minutes, Dune whispered, "I think I saw something on the side of the house next door."

A lanky scarecrow of a man leading a brace of hounds stumbled around the corner of the house. He carried a shotgun in the crook of one arm as he guided the dogs along the hedgerow between the two houses.

"I recognize that gombeen," Dune snarled. "We ran across him and his dogs on our way to Doolin. There was another fellow with him. Maybe one of 'em is Lynch."

"He's looking this way." Kyna clutched Dune's sleeve above the elbow. "Are you sure the stones will hide us?"

"We'll find out soon enough."

The man approached Lynch's front door. His dogs pulled at their leads, wanting to cross the road in the direction of Dune and Kyna's hiding place. The man yanked the dogs' leashes. "Here to me, you eejits!"

The dogs cowered at his voice. They crept to him with their heads low, ears pinned back, and their tails wagging.

With his dogs' leashes in one hand and the gun cradled in his other arm, the man gave the door three swift kicks.

A woman with grey hair tied up in a scarf opened the door a crack, then opened it wider and stood with her hands on her hips. "Finbar, ye culchie, quit yer banging on my door!"

"Dunna eat my head off, Missus Lynch. I've no free hands to knock proper."

From inside the house a gruff voice called out, "Fin! Finbar! Where ya been?"

"I told you, Mr. Lynch. Me and the boys had to answer the call of nature."

"I hope they didn't piss on my gardenias," the woman said. "If those bushes die...."

"Canna you get new ones? You know, from your 'helpers'?"

"Ara be whist, you thick gobdaw," came the reply from the house. "Secure your hounds and get in here!"

"Sorry, Mr. Lynch!" Finbar looked up and down the street as he tied the dogs' leashes to a cast-iron boot scraper beside the door.

"No-one's about."

He clucked to his dogs and pointed at the ground. They immediately quieted, lying down and looking up at him with obvious adoration.

As the scarecrow man bent to pat his dogs' heads, the woman tugged his elbow so hard he practically stumbled into the house. "Get in here then." The woman glanced up and down the street with narrowed eyes, then followed the man inside and banged the door shut.

Dune and Kyna heard muffled conversation, and then all was silent.

They waited.

The dogs were curled in balls, sleeping, when the front door opened and Finbar walked out. They greeted their master with wiggles, wags, and whines as he stepped down the stairs.

"That one can't be all bad," Kyna whispered, "if animals like him."

"Dunna be so sure. He might be nothing more than a meal ticket for them."

"Like the Greenapples are for Lynch."

"Aye."

"Where to today, Mr. Lynch?" Finbar asked. He propped his gun against the side of the house while he untied the leashes from the boot scraper.

A short, round man emerged from the house, followed by the woman. She held up his hunting coat. Lynch juggled two rifles as he shrugged into his coat. "The boy said there was a big gathering of some sort down to Doolin. They sound like sitting ducks."

"Doolin? That's a far ways from here. Are you sure it's okay to leave the—" Finbar jerked his thumb back towards the house.

"Mrs. Lynch is here. She'll not let anything happen. They're more a help to her than I am. Aren't they, dear?"

"I suppose," the wife said. "But what about the gold? I thought the old fella was to show you a right good pot of gold."

"Aye, but there's only so much of that. He said so himself." Lynch set off down the road; Finbar and the dogs followed.

They were almost out of earshot when Finbar asked, "What happens when it runs out?"

Kyna and Dune strained to hear the response.

"There's more than one way to get gold from a Leprechaun."

Dune gulped and looked at Kyna. She looked back at him with terror in her eyes.

They waited several minutes after the pair of hunters and their dogs had disappeared down the road before either one said anything more or dared to move out of the circle of stones.

Finally, Dune drew in a breath and exhaled deeply. "It worked. Broad daylight, and they dinna see us."

"Do we pick up the stones now?"

"Nae, we'll be needing the circle again. If the Greenapples are in that house, we'll bring them here while we assess the situation."

"The situation?" Kyna asked. "I don't like the sound of that."

"We have to be prepared. They might be injured, shackled, too weary to get back to Doolin."

"Are you certain the circle will work again? Have you ever left the circle and returned to it?"

Dune nodded. "Aye. After my ma places the stones around our cottage in Doolin, we come and go without incident."

"But that was within the cloak that Mother Cass drew around the whole area. The Hidden Harbor."

Dune chewed his thumb nail as he considered their options. "We'll have to hope it works on its own."

"What if my taking part in the Rune botched it?"

"Kyna, don't ye remember? Our magic is stronger together."

She smiled tentatively. "Do you think there's only the one

Human now? The wife?"

"I think so, but I'd like to wait a while and watch to be sure."

"What if the hunters return?"

"They're headed to Doolin. They'll not be back today."

"I wish we could get a message to Mother Cass."

"We'll have to worry about that after we find the Greenapples."

Kyna stood up. "I've an idea. You wait here."

Chapter 18: The Rescue

Before Dune could protest, Kyna bolted from the protective circle and cleared the field fence like a deer. He scrambled to his feet and headed after her.

Kyna stopped in the road and motioned for him to stop. She walked up to the front door, raised her hand to knock. Pausing, she turned to Dune and pointed for him to go back to the circle of stones.

Every fiber of his body urged him to move forward, not backward. How could he protect her from the other side of the road?

Kyna obviously wasn't going to move until he was back inside the protective circle, so he backed up, not taking his eyes off her.

Kyna raised her fist and knocked three times.

Mrs. Lynch opened the door a crack. "Yes?"

"'Tis Mr. Lynch, ma'am. He said to come quickly, and bring a bucket of hot water."

"What's he need with hot water? Is he having a baby?"

"No, ma'am. He's injured."

"Injured! But he just left!"

"Did you not hear the shot? His helper—and the dogs—they all got tangled up in the leads, and the gun went off. Oh, mercy! The blood! You've no time to waste!"

The woman glanced around Kyna, straining her neck to see down the road. "And how would you ken this? Who are you?"

"I'm Kyna." She couldn't lie about her identity, but was free to weave a fiction. Blarney is a gift and it was her birthright to use it. "I'm staying down the road. I saw it happen! He told me to fetch you."

"Those damn beasts. Come in and help me get the water and some towels."

Kyna followed her inside.

Dune chewed his fingernails, wondering what they were saying to each other and whether Kyna was in danger. He paced the perimeter of the circle like a lion in a cage, took his athame from his boot and clutched it in his fist.

The door opened again, and Dune froze.

Kyna and the woman walked down the stairs. The woman carried a pail of water that sloshed with each step. A towel was draped across her shoulder.

Kyna pointed the woman in the direction Lynch and Finbar and the dogs had gone.

"Help me with this bucket, will you?"

Kyna put a hand to her forehead. "I canna go with you, ma'am. I'm faint from all the blood. If 'tis all right with you, I'll wait here until you return. Then I'll help you dress his wounds, if I'm able."

"Wait out here. Dunna go back inside. Orin would smack me if I let anyone in the house alone, be he injured or no."

"I promise not to go in alone," Kyna said.

It took Mrs. Lynch a long time to lug the bucket down the road. As soon as she was out of sight, Kyna waved for Dune to come to her.

"Did you see the Greenapples? Did she say anything about them?"

Kyna shook her head. "No, but she was very insistent that I stay where she could see me. And she closed the door to the bedroom straight away. I think she was trying to hide something—

or someone."

"Was anyone else in there? Other Humans, that is?"

Kyna shook her head again.

"Well, let's find out what she's hiding."

Dune turned the doorknob. "'Tis locked."

"Hmm, I wonder," Kyna said. She lifted up the doormat and found what she was looking for. "Aha!"

She handed the key to Dune. He unlocke the door and they ducked inside. The front room was a living area with an overstuffed couch and matching chair in front of the fireplace. A small, braided rug covered part of the hardwood floors, which were dulled and scratched by age, though spotless. Over the mantel, a stag's head glared at them with glassy marble eyes.

"The kitchen's back there, and the bedroom is through this door," Kyna said.

"Did you go in there? Or have a look?"

"No. She closed the door before I could see anything but the corner of the bed."

"How do you ken nobody's in there?"

"She said I couldn't wait inside the house because her husband didn't allow folks in here by themselves. I took that to mean that nobody else was home. No other Humans, at any rate."

"I guess we find out." Dune gripped his athame in one hand and the door knob in the other. He took a deep breath and exhaled, then opened the door and stepped in the room.

An ornate, four-poster bed with a lace canopy took up most of the space. A lamp on the bedside table cast a soft glow. A rug, this one quite new and luxuriously thick, covered the floor.

Kyna looked under the bed. She sighed as she stood up. "Nothing. Where else could they be? Are there any outbuildings in back?"

Dune stepped on the rug and shifted his weight from foot to

foot. "Hmm, I wonder." He knelt down and lifted a corner of the rug. He tapped several areas of the wooden floorboards with his knuckles. One spot rang hollow. He rolled the rug toward the bed, revealing a trap door.

Kyna knelt at his side. "Brilliant!"

"I dunna see a handle."

"Use your knife."

Dune stuck the blade of his athame in the space between the trap door and the floorboards and pried it back and forth until the door popped up a few millimeters. "Give me a hand."

He and Kyna clawed at the edge of the door until they got enough purchase to lift it. Below the floor, a narrow stairway led to a dark basement. "Wait here, and warn me if anyone approaches," Dune said.

"I want to go with you. What if it's a trap?"

"The trap would be if they come back and we're both down there. Stay up here so you can alert me if they return. Besides, I've got my athame."

As Kyna held the door open, Dune descended. He waited for his eyes to adjust to the darkness. On the far wall, a small, dingy window near the basement's ceiling let in a thin shaft of light.

As Dune felt his way down the stairs, something crashed. "Who's there? Show yourself," he called, his strong voice not giving away the lump in his throat.

He waited, but there was no response. "My eyes are not unfriendly."

From the darkness, a lone figure emerged. His hair was matted, his face smudged with soot, his clothes rumpled and dirty as if he'd slept in them in a dirty basement for days.

Dune gasped. "Mr. Greenapple!"

"Aye," the man said. He embraced Dune in a hug, patting Dune's back as they both laughed. "And you—you're Dune Kelly, are you not?"

"Yes, sir. Are you all right? And your family?"

Seamus lit a small lantern, illuminating the room. It was more a cell than a full basement, with a workbench and a sink. He was gaunt, his shoulders hunched. He pulled aside a curtain draped across the front of the workbench. "'Tis safe. You can come out."

One by one, his family emerged from under the bench. Mrs. Greenapple stood beside her husband, and the boys took their places beside her, rubbing their eyes.

"'Lo, Dune," the older boy said.

"Ard! Good to see you," The friends clasped arms.

"Oh, young man," Mrs. Greenapple cried. She rushed to Dune and smothered him in a motherly hug. "Have they captured you, too?"

"No, ma'am. I've actually come to rescue you."

At that, the family erupted in cheers as they encircled Dune.

"Shh," Dune warned. "They could return at any moment."

Seamus patted him on the back, while Ardeen squeezed his shoulder and Lucas elbowed his way in and hugged Dune around the waist with both arms.

"Is everyone all right?" Dune asked.

"We're alive," Seamus said. "We've not been harmed."

"Then shall we bid good riddance to this hole?"

"Aye, and not waste another moment doing it," Seamus said.

He helped Mrs. Greenapple up the stairs, but she stopped after a few steps. "There's someone up there."

"It's just me, ma'am," Kyna called down. "I've come with Dune."

Holding the trap door open with one hand, Kyna extended her other hand to Mrs. Greenapple. When they were all out of the basement, Dune shut the trapdoor and smoothed the rug over it.

"Good riddance," Lucas said. He stomped on the rug over the

trapdoor.

Dune explained the plan. "We've made a protective circle in the field across the road. I'll go first, to check that all is clear."

They followed Dune to the front door. He opened it a smidge and peeked out, then stealthily inched down the steps and along the walkway to the road. He hated to be out in broad daylight, but there was nothing he could do about it. He opened the gate and beckoned the others to cross. Kyna came first to lead the way. Seamus herded his family ahead of him.

Kyna directed them all into the circle of stones in the pasture, but Dune immediately set about picking up the stones and dropping them in the velvet pouch.

"What are you doing?" Kyna grabbed Dune's elbow.

He shook out of her grip. "Dinna ya hear what they said? They're headed to Doolin."

"But it's broad daylight! How can we follow them now?"

"We've no choice. I dunna ken how they know where to find the family, but if they get there before we do, we'll find naught but pennants and ponies."

"Mother Cass's veil will protect them."

"Until 'tis breached."

Kyna inhaled sharply. She picked up the nearest stone and handed it to Dune. "Then we've no time to lose."

As soon as all the stones were retrieved, Dune pointed down the road. "We've got to make it to Leacht Seoirse. We can rest safely there and have some supper. But we canna stop for long. We must keep going."

The town was small, and they were soon surrounded by wheat fields and pastures populated by cattle and cattle birds. They had walked for almost an hour without incident when they heard the dogs bay.

Chapter 19: The Protecting Fog

They all froze in their tracks.

Lucas, the smaller Greenapple boy, whimpered. "I dunna like dogs."

They'll be on us in a blink, Dune thought. Looking around, he realized with dismay that the landscape provided no place to hide. "We've no time! Kyna, find some dirt or gravel—something to hide us! Maybe another dragon to throw them off our tracks."

Kyna was already digging her hands into the weedy dirt on the side of the road. "I never know what I'm going to get."

She stood up and faced the direction of the baying dogs. Her tawny hair streamed out behind her, whipped by a sudden wind. She glanced at Dune, and a shiver ran down his spine as their eyes locked. She turned her back to the wind. "Everybody, come close beside me." The Greenapples huddled together behind her.

Dune stood beside her and looked over his shoulder. Two hounds appeared over a crest in the road. "Quickly, Kyna."

Kyna's shoulders arched as she inhaled and held her breath. She flung the sandy dirt into the air.

The dirt swirled and spun, tumbled and rose, until it had enveloped them all in a blanket of fog. It even felt damp like a normal fog.

Dune heard hoofbeats. "Listen," he said, grasping Kyna's shoulders and standing close beside her. "There! 'Tis a stag. You've done it, Kyna!"

"Are you sure it's a stag?" Kyna whispered. "Because I don't think it's a stag, and I didn't make it."

"What do you mean?" Dune said. He stared into the fog in the direction of the hoofbeats.

"Look for yourself," Kyna said.

A dark shape took form just outside the fog. Dune peered at it, trying to make out the figure. The fog shifted, and the figure became more distinct.

"The Pooka!" Dune shouted before he could stop himself. He threw his arms out as a barrier to protect Kyna and the Greenapples.

"Nonsense," Kyna whispered. She gently pushed his arm down. "And try not to yell."

Dune looked sheepishly at the Greenapples. Seamus and Agnes looked at him, looked at each other, and looked back at him with obvious concern.

Kyna moved toward the animal. "It's a pony."

The dusty-red pony, barely over a meter tall at the withers, stood before them, one foreleg raised. Blood trickled down the leg and pooled on the road.

"Your magic must have summoned her to distract the dogs," Dune said. "Shoo her away, and the dogs will follow her."

"I told you, I didn't make her. And she's hurt," Kyna said. "We must draw her into the protecting fog, not send her as bait."

Dune wanted to protest. He was sure the pony was part of the protective spell that Kyna had cast, but he thought she had been sent to lead the dogs and the hunters away. The pony's eyes were saucer-wide in fear.

"Wait a minute," Dune said. "I know this pony."

Struggling against his memory of bad encounters with ponies, including being bitten by that wretched pony in Doolin, and his fear of being seen by the hunters who would surely appear with their dogs at any moment, Dune stepped out of the fog and offered his hand to the mare. "Come here, girl," he whispered.

The pony's red hide, matted with lather, heaved in and out with her labored breathing. She had obviously been running hard, and for a long way, and was as terrified as they were.

"We won't hurt you," Dune said gently.

The pony cut her eyes left and right, looking from Dune to the road behind her where the baying hounds drew closer. On trembling legs, the pony limped toward him, bowed her head, and rested her face against his stomach.

He could feel her warm breath through his shirt. He had never been this close to a pony, not intentionally. He had fed an apple to Peppercorn, but the huge horse had only lipped the apple from his hand and turned away to eat it. This pony was purposely pressing her face to his chest, forcing him to accept her presence. She nibbled at his jacket, but Dune didn't flinch. Something about her was so child-like that Dune instinctively laid one hand on top of her head, between her tiny, triangular ears. He stroked away a twig that was tangled in her mane. "It's okay," he said, his voice barely a whisper. "We'll keep you safe, if we can trick these hunters into going away."

The fog spread, covering Dune and the pony. Kyna moved beside Dune and hooked her hand around his elbow. The pony looked at Kyna, and her fearful eyes grew calm. The long lashes drooped and the pony seemed to fall asleep on her feet. The heaving of her sides slowed and a quietness descended as Kyna's fog enveloped them all.

The fog billowed and swirled, grey upon grey. If Kyna and the pony had not been touching him, had he not smelled the pony's dusky scent and the sweet aroma of jasmine that wafted from Kyna's hair, he would not have known for sure that they were there. Even the Greenapples were but hazy outlines behind him now; Dune counted their blurry shapes. *One, two, three, four. All there.*

His vision may have been impaired by the fog, but his hearing worked fine. A rush of paws and panting grew loud and stopped as the dogs approached the fog. Would the hounds be able to hear and smell them?

Kyna squeezed his arm, and Dune knew she must be holding her breath, as he was. *If the pony makes a sound, if she neighs or stomps her foot,* he thought, *the hounds and hunters might hear her. They'll be on us like a hawk on a rabbit.*

But the pony, her head still pressed against Dune's body, seemed to sense the need for stillness. Dune couldn't even feel her breathing against his shirt anymore, and wondered if the pony was holding her breath, too.

Heavy footsteps told of the hunters' arrival. Peering through the fog, Dune saw two shapes—Lynch and his man, Finbar—standing mere meters away. Two other shapes—Finbar's dogs—paced back and forth but did not enter the fog.

"Gore, where'd all the fog come from?" Finbar said, wheezing as if he'd run hard.

"'Tis a low spot in the road, is all," Lynch responded. "Let's go on through."

"The dogs dunna want to go in, Mr. Lynch."

"They dinna want to go through that cloud-thing back in the wood, either, did they? And neither did you. Yet I went right through."

Dune heard a grumble that might have been one of the dogs or might have been Finbar's response.

Then, another shape joined the hunters.

"Are we going in or not?" Mrs. Lynch asked. "We've got to get back to the house. I tell you, that bird knew something she waren't telling me! Why else would she lie about you bein' hurt?"

"Go on, then, Mr. Lynch," Finbar said. "You first."

"Oh, no. You're the scout. I dunna need you and your dogs if all ye are is extra mouths to feed."

"Will you two culchies quit foostering about," Mrs. Lynch shouted.

"Watch your tone, woman!"

"Or what, old man?" She swatted him with the back of her hand. "Ye'll leave me? That ye might, but ye would na be leavin' your fortune. Hmph! Step aside. I'll go."

Dune clinched his teeth together. *The moment of truth.*

Mrs. Lynch passed within centimeters of the group of Leprechauns and the pony. Her skirt and apron brushed against Lucas's leg.

The boy drew in his breath.

The woman stopped.

Mrs. Greenapple grabbed Lucas around the shoulders and pulled him close against her, clamping a hand over his mouth.

"Hmph," Mrs. Lynch said. "Now that barmpot I'm married to and his eejit friend have *me* imagining ghosts in the fog."

She walked on, oblivious to the family and the pony standing as still as statues, centimeters away. Once she passed through the fog, she stood in the road with her hands on her hips, still holding the bucket she had left the house with. "I'm through the fog," she called back. "'Tis not far. Come on with ye!"

Lynch aimed his shotgun into the fog, then pointed it at the ground. "Makin' me look the fool," he grumbled. "Finbar, control those dogs and follow me."

The hunters and the dogs advanced into the fog, passing by so closely that Dune could smell the wet-dog smell of the hounds and the stale-pub-and-sweat smell of the hunters.

Once they too were on the other side of the fog, the dogs bayed and pulled at their leashes.

"Atta boy, Flynn!" Finbar called. He ran with his arm outstretched, trying to hold on to the leashes as the dogs bounded away. "This way, Mr. Lynch! Hurry! The dogs've picked up a scent!"

"Finbar! Come back!" Lynch ran after the hunter and his dogs. "We have to check on the, that is, we have to check on my house! And then we've that other business to attend to in Doolin!"

The baying grew fainter as Finbar and the dogs cut through a field, Lynch chasing after them.

"Damn those mongrels, and the dogs along with them," Mrs. Lynch mumbled. She chucked the pail to the side of the road, what remained of the water sloshing out as it tumbled end over end. "Once again, 'tis up to me to tend to business."

Dune watched as her shadowy figure lumbered back toward Beagbealach, finally disappearing from view.

A moment later, the fog cleared. Seamus Greenapple strode over to Dune, followed by his family. They all embraced him warmly. "That was close," Seamus said. "We owe you our lives, the second time in a day!"

Mrs. Greenapple squished Dune's cheeks between her palms, drawing his face close to hers, and planted a kiss on his forehead.

Ardeen punched Dune's shoulder lightly. "Your magic's pure bril, mate."

"'Twas Kyna's magic kept them from seeing us," Dune replied.

Seamus shook Kyna's hand with both of his. "Your fog screen worked, my dear!"

"And your pony was good as gold. She stayed completely quiet," Mrs. Greenapple added. "But when did you call her here?"

"I didn't bring her here," Kyna said. "I only just met her, myself."

"We all just met her," Dune said, stroking the pony's forelock. "But I *have* seen her before. In my vision, when I held Kyna's amulet."

"She's hurt her leg," Mrs. Greenapple said.

Lucas patted the pony's lathered neck. He pulled Cairdeen's mane aside to reveal the raw patches on her neck. "And her neck."

"Aye. Those look like rope burns. A bit of salve should take care of it." Dune bent to examine the mare's injured foreleg. "But these wounds are pretty bad."

The pony's leg bore several gashes below the knee where the skin was peeled back in ragged scraps.

"Dune," Kyna said, putting her hand on his shoulder. "If this is the sweet pony from your vision, then the boy might not be far behind."

"My thoughts exactly. We must be vigilant. We dunna ken for sure that the boy is a friend. And we still have to worry about those hunters coming back." Dune looked up at Kyna. "Can you help her? You said you've used your magic to help animals before."

"Aye, but you've seen my magic." Kyna dropped to her knees beside Dune and the pony. "It's all an illusion. Visual imagery."

The wounds need to be wrapped, to control the bleeding, Dune thought. He took off his jacket and handed it to Kyna. He removed his shirt and used his athame to rip off a strip of fabric along the bottom edge.

"But Dune, that's your team jersey," Ardeen said.

Dune poked his fingers through the hole in his jersey's elbow. "'Tis already been pony-bit." He wrapped the strip of cloth around the wounded area of the pony's leg, trying to be gentle but at the same time, wanting to get the makeshift bandage tight enough to stanch the flow of blood.

The pony flinched when he knotted the fabric ends together and pulled them taut. She whickered softly, the first sound she had made since Kyna cast the fog.

"Sorry, girl," he said. "Huh."

"What is it?"

"I never liked horses and ponies. A pony bit a chunk out of me not three days ago, don't you know. Yet here I am, feeding an apple to a horse in the mornin' and tending to this pony like a natural-born pony-doctor, not half a day later."

"It's what friends do," Kyna said. "They take care of each other."

Dune tied off the makeshift bandage. "That should keep her till we get back to Doolin. Then we'll find the pony vet straight-away."

"Will he be able to help her?" Lucas asked.

"More than we can." Dune put his jersey—now a few centimeters shorter—and jacket back on.

"Which way's Doolin from here," Seamus asked. He cut his eyes sheepishly at Dune. "My sense of direction's muddled after being imprisoned so long in that dreaded hole."

"This way." Dune pointed south. "And we'd best leg it. Did ye hear what Lynch said about Doolin? Somehow, they've learned about the Ceili. We must warn the others."

Chapter 20: Bait

The fog scared Cairdeen. It came up so suddenly. And then the lad appearing out of the fog scared her even more. Yet when he held out his hand to her, she felt pulled to him as surely as if she had a rope around her neck again, and him on the other end of it. She came to him and breathed in the earthy, grassy scent of him.

Had she not been following that scent for a fortnight?

She lipped his coat, realizing he was not food, at least not the kind for her physical hunger, yet unable to resist a kiss of that alluring sweetness. She noted without any fear that a lass stood beside him, a lass whose cream-colored, windblown mane evoked a strong memory in Cairdeen of her own palomino dam.

Then she felt the full force of her weariness descend upon her. She leaned her head against the lad's chest. She let his body take the weight off her injured leg. She fell into a trance of some sort, asleep yet aware of three things: Her own heartbeat, and the heartbeat of this fiery-headed lad, and the heartbeat of the lass with the golden mane. For the first time since she left her mother's side, she felt *safe*.

The fog enveloped her. Cairdeen was filled with a sudden and complete sense of belonging. These people, this lad and this lass, were different from anyone else she'd ever met. Different from the Farmer, most certainly. Yet different even from the boy, Fergus, who had helped her escape. These were more than friends. They were *her* people. As soon as she saw them, they belonged to her, and she to them.

On the edge of her awareness, she felt the presence of others passing by in the fog. People. Dogs. Their scents were pungent with the odor of danger. She held still, submerging deeper into her trance, sensing that the lad would protect her.

When the fog cleared, Cairdeen saw four more people. They did not smell of danger, and she was not scared of them. They drew close, and the woman spoke. As the woman ran her hand down Cairdeen's injured leg, the one that had been bitten by the tangle of wire, the pony leaned away. The lad put his face against hers and murmured, his lips so close that she felt his voice reverberate inside her head. A calmness settled over her. Her eyelids drooped and her breathing slowed.

Through her half-asleep state, Cairdeen heard the golden-maned lass speak. Her voice swirled in Cairdeen's head alongside the lad's and blended into a melody that Cairdeen understood on a deeper level than language. When the lass said "sweet pony," Cairdeen knew *she* was the sweet pony, and that being a sweet pony was much different from being an "old nag." She opened her eyes and looked at the lass. *My name is Cairdeen,* she whickered.

The lass smiled at her and stroked her cheek.

'Tis a beginning, Cairdeen thought. She would find a way to let her new friends know her name, and to learn theirs.

Friends, Cairdeen thought. *I have made so many friends in these few short days since I left the Farmer's field.*

There was Jarmy Sean, who shared his breakfast with her.

And Fergus, Jarmy Sean's lad, who freed her from the rope and stake.

She remembered Canavan's inky eyes and glossy, black-and-white face. *Not every face you meet will be a friendly one like mine,* Canavan had warned. But he had taught her something else as well: the secret of the faerie ring.

When standing in a faerie ring, be you beast or bird,
In the moonlight soft your voice, spoken will be heard.

Cairdeen whickered at the thought: *I'll find a faerie ring, and my new friends and I will introduce ourselves like proper folk.*

She nudged her lad—for from the moment she met him, Cairdeen thought of him as *her* lad, the same way Fergus was Jarmy Sean's lad. Despite the pain in her leg, she squealed with happiness like a young foal. The lad and lass laughed and patted her neck.

Cairdeen could tell that the other four members of the herd were a different family, although part of the same band. Their leader said something, and Cairdeen's lad stood up and pointed down the road as he replied.

When the lad moved in the direction he had pointed, Cairdeen followed, limping slightly with the throbbing in her injured leg. She and her new herd walked in silence but for the light scuffing of their feet and clip-clopping of Cairdeen's hooves on the hard-packed dirt road.

A twig snapped and they all stopped in their tracks. Cairdeen's ears pricked forward.

The lad said something that was obviously a command. He pushed the lass behind him, and the other members of their herd came to a standstill.

Cairdeen heard a voice in her head. *I've nothing to protect us.* It was the lad's voice, and she understood it. More, she felt his name: Dune. *Fortress. Protector.*

She looked at the lad and tried to send him a thought, *I will help.*

"But the pony," the lass said.

Cairdeen looked at her, knew she herself was "the pony," but more. She felt the lass's name: Kyna: *Beloved.*

Cairdeen put her neck out straight in line with her back. *I will see what's there.* She clenched her teeth, pinned her ears, and took a step forward.

Something was there that made her new family nervous. She could smell their fear. But she herself felt no fear. It was up to her to find out what was there. *'Tis what friends do,* she thought. *They look out for each other.*

She took another step, and another, and kept going.

Chapter 21: Fergus

At the snap of the twig, Dune stopped in his tracks. He put his arms out to his sides, signaling the others to stop. He heard a voice in the distance. "Someone's coming. Everyone, take cover."

The pony's head was erect, her ears pointed forward as she gazed at the road ahead.

Dune quickly took stock of the surroundings. The road was just a little lower than the fields to either side. Beyond a rickety wire fence supported by termite-eaten rails, tall grasses swayed across the fields to the wide-open horizon. Other than a small stone clearance cairn, which was not large enough to provide cover for six people and a pony, the nearest cover was a stand of trees, a half kilometer away. Too far. They would have to hide in the tall grass and hope for the best.

The Greenapples scrambled up the grassy embankment and ducked down.

"Kyna, let's go!" Dune grabbed her hand, but she jerked it free.

"The pony! We have to hide her, too!"

"Whist, lass!" Dune growled.

"Did you just whist me *again?*" Kyna asked indignantly.

"Please, Kyna! Get down and be quiet!"

"But the pony! You can't leave her out there, unprotected."

"She's willing to help. I feel it."

The pony walked forward.

"We canna do anything about her now. Please, Kyna."

"He's right, lass," Mrs. Greenapple whispered from her hiding place. "Do what he says. The pony's in no danger, but we are."

Kyna clambered over the embankment and tucked herself down beside Mrs. Greenapple. The boys hunkered on the other side of their mother, and Dune joined Mr. Greenapple on the other side of the boys.

The little mare stood like a warrior braced for battle. All of a sudden, her posture changed. She tossed her head and whickered. It sounded to Dune like she was laughing.

Dune heard the clip-clop of hoofbeats and raised his head barely above the top of the grassy embankment to peer down the road. Around the corner came a stocky gray pony, ridden by a little Human boy.

A boy with one green eye and one brown eye.

It was the boy from his vision.

Dune shivered as he realized how many elements of his vision had gathered on this lonely road.

"Would you look at that!" the boy cried happily. He pulled on the reins and patted his pony's neck. "'Tis your lady friend, Sean! Just who we were looking for."

The boy kicked his feet out of the stirrups and hopped off his pony. Leading Jarmy Sean by the reins, he walked up to the little red mare. "Looks like you've run into more trouble, girl," the boy said, observing Cairdeen's injured, field-bandaged leg. "But it also looks like you've found a friend."

The boy scanned the surroundings. Dune ducked as the boy's gaze panned their hiding place. "But where have they gone? Would friends just leave you alone in the middle of nowhere?"

When the boy looked down and began studying the dirt road, Dune knew he was reading their tracks. He couldn't risk the others being discovered. He stood up and leapt out into the road.

"Hey! That's *my* pony," Dune said.

The Human boy jumped, startled by Dune's sudden appearance. He regained his composure quickly though, Dune noticed, especially for such a young boy.

"I dunna think that's exactly right," the boy said. "Unless you're related to that barnacle from Seafield. And no offense, unless you are."

"I doubt it," Dune said. He made a decision and walked forward with his hand outstretched. "I'm Dune."

"Fergus," the boy said, shaking Dune's hand. "This here is my pony, Jarmy Sean. And this," he patted the mare's face, "is a runaway from over to Seafield. She's hurt."

"Aye. I dunna ken how it happened. Barbed wire by the look of it. I wrapped it up to staunch the bleeding."

"All right if I take a look?" Fergus asked.

Dune nodded. He furtively glanced around. A glint of light caught his eye, and he noticed it came from a feather made of gold, attached to the grey pony's bridle. Mesmerized, he reached out his hand. The second he touched the feather, a vision flashed before his eyes.

A Leprechaun boy sits cross-legged in the grass, surrounded by colorful feathers. Some of the feathers are made of gold. The boy's parents stand over him. "Explain yourself!" the boy's father demands.

"I called to Creidhne. 'Tis my gift. 'Tis our ancestry," the boy replies.

"What you've done is wrong," the father says.

The mother adds, "You know the Matriarch's rules."

"But I've hurt no-one," the boy cries. "I've collected these feathers from the ground."

"And what of these?" The father thrusts a fistful of golden feathers at the lad.

"They were on the ground, too."

"But you sold them! 'Tis strictly forbidden to profit off your

magic. You risked your own life, and the lives of your clan, with your carelessness! You must be punished so you'll not do anything like this again."

"Senan, wait," the mother says. "Look."

The boy and his father look up. Before them, the Matriarch stands with her walking stick in one hand and a small woven basket in the other. "Mother Cass," the father says, bowing. "Forgive us. Kane has disobeyed the Law. He must be punished."

"I will handle his punishment."

"What will you do to him?" the boy's mother asks.

"Kane will learn not to disobey our Laws. I will make him give away all the golden feathers — to Humans."

"Humans!" Kane's mother kneels behind her son and wraps her arms around him. "What if he is caught?"

"He'll not be harmed nor captured. I'll be there with him. He will be protected by my veil." The Matriarch gestures to Kane. "Gather up all the gold feathers and bring them here."

Kane scrambles to collect the feathers that he had turned to gold and, head bowed, brings them to Mother Cass.

"Put all but one in the basket. You may keep one feather as a reminder of this lesson."

The vision ended and Dune staggered backward.

"Are ye all right, Dune?" Fergus asked.

"Aye. Just got something in my eye. Where — where did you get that gold feather?"

"My da says it was left on our doorstep the night I was born. He gave it to me as a good-luck charm, and I gave it to Jarmy Sean, so we'd both have luck."

"Has it? Brought you luck?

Fergus knelt by the mare. "We're not rich. But we're happy."

The boy gently pulled the strips of cloth away from the pony's wound. He winced when he saw the wound. "She'll need stitches."

"I'm trying to get her to a vet I know."

"Then you better leg it out of here." Fergus replaced the makeshift bandaging and jerked it taut. Cairdeen bobbed her head but made no other protest. "My da's heading this way, along with the old barnacle I mentioned. There's a reward for the pony, and my da says we could really use it."

"Is that what you're after as well? A reward?"

Fergus frowned and shook his head. "You're dinkin' wrong if you think that! Now, are you going to get her to safety, or do I have to do it myself?"

Dune looked up the road, then surreptitiously scanned the heather where he hoped Kyna and the Greenapples would remain hidden.

"You're not alone, are you?" Fergus asked.

Dune gritted his teeth. "What makes you say that?" *I should na have looked off into the brush! I've given away my family's whereabouts.*

"The tracks." Fergus pointed to scuff marks on the dirt road. He scanned the field behind Dune—right where Kyna and the Greenapples were hiding. "Where are the others? Why dunna they show themselves—Yah!"

Dune closed his eyes, dropped his head and shook it back and forth. He knew before he looked what had surprised the boy. With dread, he opened his eyes and turned to see Kyna standing in the field. One by one, Mr. Greenapple, Mrs. Greenapple, Ardeen, and finally Lucas all stood.

"Who are all these people?"

"They're with me," Dune answered.

"Why are the lot of you hiding in the weeds when you *say* you're trying to help this pony?"

"We *are* trying to help her," Kyna said, slip-sliding down the embankment to the road. "We just didn't know who *you* were."

"You came up so fast, we dinna have time to hide the pony," Mrs. Greenapple added.

"Although I wanted to," Kyna noted with a cross look at Dune.

"So where are you taking the pony?"

"The vet over in Doolin."

Fergus nodded. "Must be Doc Bishop."

"Aye, that's him."

Fergus's eyes narrowed. "Doc Bishop is a *she*."

"Um, right. Didn't you say we need to shake a leg?" Kyna asked. "We've no time to waste if we don't want to be caught by the Humans."

As soon as the word was out of her mouth, Kyna realized her mistake.

"Humans? What do you mean by that?"

"She's not from around here," Dune explained.

"I could tell by her accent and…." Fergus's words trailed off as understanding washed across his face. His eyes grew wide. "You're, you're all Leprechauns, aren't you! Show me your marks."

"'Tis true," Dune said. The Code of Erin forbade him denying it.

Kyna lifted her hair away from her neck to reveal the clover tattoo below her left ear.

"I knew you'd figure it out if you discovered us," Dune said. "But I revealed myself anyway, because I could tell you'd want to help us. To help the pony."

Dune held his breath, waiting for the boy to reply.

"Aye," Fergus said. "You need not worry about me."

Dune exhaled with relief. Something about the boy made Dune feel he could be trusted. "Thank you, friend."

"But that old barnacle what's headed this way—he's a different story. And me da, too, for that matter. Sure, we're not rich folk. We could use a bit of luck. The measly reward for the pony ain't nothing compared to what a Leprechaun's worth."

A faraway voice called out. "Ferrr-gus!"

"'Tis me da." Fergus tugged at Dune's sleeve. "And the farmer from Seafield will be with him. He'll want to claim the mare."

The words speared Dune like a hot poker in the chest.

"If she is his pony, then I suppose he has a right to take her," he said. "As much as I'd like to keep her and get her wounds treated properly. You've earned the reward, as well."

"I dunna want the reward! That old barnacle doesn't love her the way we do. She'll die if he takes her."

Kyna touched Dune's arm. "Dune, we've not much time."

Dune nodded. "We have to hide before they get here."

"What about me?" Fergus asked.

"You must stay where your da can see you."

"And the mare?" The lad's eyes were wide with fear. Dune knew the lad was not afraid for his own safety, but for that of the Leprechauns and the sorrel pony.

"She must stay with you. Please, dunna give us away."

Fergus notched his shoulders back and knotted his hands into fists at his side. "I'll not give you away."

Dune smiled. "I know you'll not. I believe in you."

Dune took the velvet pouch from his pocket and poured a few stones into his trembling hand.

"Let me help," Kyna said. She cupped her hands so Dune could pour the stones into them and more easily sort out the ones he needed.

"Fergus! Do ye hear me?"

The voice was louder this time, closer, accompanied by hoofbeats approaching at a gallop.

"We've no time to prepare the circle." Dune quickly grasped the pink quartz stone from Kyna's hands and held the pouch open for her to pour the other stones back in. He squeezed the sliver of quartz tightly in his fist and thrust his arm up to the sky. Golden rays slipped through his fingers and radiated around the group of Leprechauns.

"Beauty!" Fergus exclaimed. "But 'tis supposed to hide you, is it not? I can see you clear as day."

Dune's thoughts raced wildly in his head. The answer spoke to him in Mother Cass's voice: *Friendly eyes.*

"You are a friend of our clan. But just in case, I'll need to make the magic stronger." He turned to Kyna. "Your Claddagh."

Kyna held the charm in her open palm.

Dune grasped her hand, entwining their fingers with the two talismans clutched in between their palms.

The golden rays shot through the spaces between their fingers, even stronger than before. With a blast of energy, a golden aura spread all around Kyna, Dune and the Greenapples, encasing them in a translucent dome.

The boy stood for a moment, staring at the shimmering golden bubble. He looked at Dune, questioning.

Dune nodded to him. Fergus nodded and turned to face whatever was to come.

Horse hooves clopped on the road and came to a stop. Two men dismounted their horses. One, a burly, bearded man with Fergus's curly black hair and long, thin nose, rushed to the boy and wrapped him in a bear hug.

"There you are, lad! What possessed you to run off like that?"

"I wanted to find the mare," Fergus said. "And there she is."

The second man, a tall, lanky fellow with a hollow face behind scruffy grey stubble, unbuckled a strap on his horse's saddle and pulled out a long stick. "Yes, there she is. That no-good, miserable nag."

Chapter 22: The Farmer

Cairdeen's ears pricked as she heard the voice. She pinned her ears as the man approached her.

Suddenly, the old man turned toward Fergus, jabbing his cane at the boy's chest.

"What have you done to her? Her leg's torn to bits."

"'Twould not have happened had I been able to keep her when I first found her," Fergus said.

"What did I tell you about sassing, boy?" The tender tone had gone from Fergus's father's voice.

"Snotty brat," the old curmudgeon added.

"Leave off talking that way to my boy," Fergus's father said. "And keep that stick to yourself."

The second man laughed, a harsh, cheerless, cackle that curdled Dune's blood. This was undoubtedly the Farmer. The image of Thurisaz, the rune of chaos, evil, and temptation, sprang to Dune's mind.

The Farmer limped to the mare's side and spat on the ground. "I should put you out of my misery here and now, ye worthless nag."

Dune's muscles were taut. He knew what was coming next, and what he would have to do. He slipped his hand from Kyna's, folding her fingers around the twin talismans. The bubble maintained its intensity.

When the Farmer raised his cane, Fergus dashed between him

and Cairdeen and held his arms out to fend off the Farmer's blow.

Dune's instincts drove him forward with a goalkeeper's lightning speed and agility. He leapt out of the protective bubble, positioning himself between Fergus and the Farmer. "Dunna touch them!"

"Dune, no!" Kyna gasped. She gripped the Claddagh charm and the rose quartz in her hands, held as if in prayer. Rays continued to pour from between her fingers and support the protective dome.

Dune wrestled the cane from the Farmer's fist. The Farmer stumbled backward as if struck in the chest.

"*Cad é an ifreann?*" Fergus's father asked with astonishment. He grabbed Fergus and pulled him away from the unknown danger he must have believed Dune posed.

"I'm not here to hurt you or the lad," Dune said. He threw the cane on the ground at the Farmer's feet.

"Who are you, then?" the Farmer asked. "Did you steal my pony?"

"No! I dinna steal her. I found her."

Cairdeen whickered.

The Farmer's eyes narrowed as he approached Dune. "Where'd you come from, anyway? You just appeared from nowhere, like magic."

Dune could tell the Farmer was about to make the connection. He had seen the same look on Fergus's face, but sensing the Farmer's imminent recognition filled him with dread like he had never known.

The Farmer wagged his finger at Dune and opened his mouth to speak.

"I recognize you," Fergus's father interrupted. "You're that large animal vet from, where is it again?"

"I'm from Yulnear, sir," Dune said, providing an honest

answer, if not a complete one. "I'd like to take the pony for care."

"And how much will that cost?" the Farmer asked with a snarl.

"I'll get her the care she needs for free if you let me have ownership."

"What are the chances she'll survive?" the Farmer asked.

Dune knelt by Cairdeen, examined her mauled leg. Tatters of his jersey, now soaked with blood, clung to the wounds. Dune stroked the mare's neck.

Cairdeen rested her head across Dune's shoulder. He felt her breaths against his back as she exhaled. He knew her wounds were not serious, but he also knew that the Farmer would not let him take the pony unless he convinced him otherwise.

"Fifty-fifty, at best. I hope she'll be able to keep the leg."

The Farmer stroked the stubble on his pointy chin. "I'm thinking I canna let you take her for free. How much is she worth to you?"

"I've no money," Dune said, his heart sinking. He had hoped the Farmer would simply let him have the pony to avoid the expense of veterinary care.

"What about the reward?" Fergus asked. "You owe him a reward for finding her!"

The Farmer shot Fergus a glance full of malice.

"That's right," Fergus's father said. "Why not keep the reward money and let the man take the pony? The vet bills will be as much as the reward, if not more."

"Aye, and she might not even make it," Dune said. "Let me have her, and you can keep the reward. We'll call it even."

Dune held his breath, waiting for the Farmer's reply.

Fergus turned to Jarmy Sean. He unclipped the golden feather from the bridle and held it out to the Farmer. "I'll throw this into the bargain. 'Tis yours, if you give up your rights to the pony."

The Farmer raised his eyebrows and stroked his scruffy chin.

"Well?" Fergus asked. He gave his father a sheepish look. "I mean, well, *sir?*"

"All right, fine." The Farmer snatched the golden feather from Fergus's hand and stuffed it in his vest pocket. "She's naught but trouble to me any way. Good riddance."

The Farmer picked up his cane and hobbled back to his horse. Grunting, he put his foot in the stirrup and grasped the saddle horn. Fergus's father boosted the Farmer's other leg over the horse's back.

"Come all this way, for naught!" the Farmer grumbled. "That nag never was worth the grain to feed her."

"Then 'tis your lucky day," Fergus's father said. "You'll not have to spend one more cent on her."

Dune's heart soared, then skipped a beat as the Farmer started to leave. He was headed straight past the spot where Kyna and the Greenapples stood within the golden bubble. If Dune had overestimated the combined power of the quartz rune stone and Kyna's clover charm, or if he had damaged the bubble by stepping through it, the Farmer would see them. They would all be caught.

The Farmer's horse shook her head and snorted. The Farmer pulled her to a stop. "Are ye comin', Dooley?"

"I'll catch up," Fergus's father said. "I'd like a word with the vet, here."

The Farmer clucked to his mare and, without waiting for her to respond, smacked her rump with his cane. The horse whinnied and broke into a trot.

When the Farmer was out of sight, Fergus's father turned to Dune. "I dunna really think you're a veterinarian, but I dunna care. I think you'll provide the little mare with the treatment she needs. More than that old barnacle ever would."

"Thank you, sir," Dune said, extending his hand. "I'm Dune. Dune Kelly."

"I'm Arliss Dooley. And this is my boy, Fergus."

"We've met." Dune shook Fergus's hand. The boy returned the shake with a firm grip. Dune winked at him, and Fergus smiled.

"How do you plan to get her to help? Yulnear's a far piece."

"I'm headed to—" Dune thought about lying, giving Arliss a false destination in case he realized Dune's true identity and decided to enrich himself by capturing a Leprechaun. "I've friends close by who will help."

"The boy and I'd be happy to assist as well."

"I canna trouble you."

"Nonsense. We've no place special to be."

"I appreciate the offer, Arliss, but I think you'd best get Fergus to a doctor. He suffered a wee fall and might have hurt his head." Dune shared a look with Fergus. It was a small lie, but necessary. *You canna see where I'm going,* Dune thought. *I hope you understand.*

"Oh, aye, sir," Fergus said, rubbing the back of his head. "I fell off Jarmy Sean."

Dune felt bad that he had led Fergus into a lie, but he had to be sure they wouldn't try to follow the Leprechauns to Doolin.

"What! You fell off Jarmy Sean?" Arliss felt the boy's head. "You've never fallen off a pony in your life. Are you hurt? Dizzy?"

"I feel fine," Fergus said. "But maybe Dune is right. Just to be on the safe side."

"Aye, your ma would whip me good if I dinna have you checked out proper."

Arliss shook Dune's hand again. "Could you write us a note and let the boy know how the pony fares? We're the Dooleys of Clover Road in Old Town, County Meath."

"Aye. I'll do that." Dune gave Fergus's shoulder a squeeze. "I canna thank you enough for giving up the reward."

"I dinna want to see the old barnacle take her," Arliss said with a shrug and a wink at Fergus. "And I dinna want him holding it over me that he'd given me money."

"I'll send you some cash for your troubles. No strings attached."

"Nae, lad. Just take care of the pony and let us know if she—Let us know when she's out of the woods."

"Thank you, sir. I will."

"Call on me and Jarmy Sean any time," Fergus said. "Cairdeen knows where our farm is."

"You've named her already, have you then?" Arliss said with a laugh. "'Tis as if you planned on keeping her for yourself all along."

"I'm no horse thief, da," Fergus said, bristling. "That *is* her name. Jarmy Sean told me."

"If you say so, son," Arliss replied with a laugh. "I've no doubt."

Cairdeen, aye, Dune thought. The image of Kyna drawing the Claddagh in the sand appeared in his mind. *'Tis her name, sure as mine's Dune and Kyna's is Kyna.*

Fergus adjusted Jarmy Sean's girth strap and leapt into the saddle.

His father mounted his horse and patted his neck. "Be careful, Dune. This area is full of desperate folk who might not look twice at an injured pony, but might be very interested in … strangers."

Dune nodded. "I shall. Farewell at you."

"Farewell with you!" Arliss clucked to his horse and applied a slight pressure with his heels. As he passed Kyna and the others, standing in the orb of light, he doffed his hat.

Stunned, Kyna nodded her head.

Arliss lifted his reins slightly, signaling his horse to gallop.

Fergus clucked to his pony, and Jarmy Sean responded immediately, breaking into a trot. Seconds later, Fergus pulled up on the reins and turned his pony around. He trotted back to Dune. "Will we see you again?"

"Aye. You're an honorary Kelly now, remember? Part of a proud clan."

Fergus grinned ear to ear. "Good luck to you, Dune." The lad tapped his index finger to his forehead and clucked to his pony. Jarmy Sean trotted a few paces, then broke into a gallop as they raced to catch up with Fergus's father.

In the distance, Jarmy Sean whinnied in farewell. Cairdeen whickered in response and dropped her head down, exhausted from effort and pain.

Chapter 23: The Parts of the Claddagh Are Three

When Arliss and Fergus had ridden out of sight, Dune nodded at Kyna. She spread her hands open, and with a breath of wind, the glow of the twin talismans, one rock, one metal, was extinguished. The golden dome evaporated.

Seamus let out a whoop of joy. He picked up his wife by her waist and twirled her in the air. He set her down and scruffed his boys' heads, then turned to Dune with his hand outstretched. "Ah, Dune! You've lived up to your name! Protected us all, so you have."

When Dune took his hand, Seamus pulled him into a tight hug.

"I've still got to get you back to Doolin safe and sound," Dune said.

Seamus patted Dune's shoulders. "And I've no doubt you shall."

"But first ..." Dune knelt beside Cairdeen.

"Do you really have friends nearby to help?" Seamus asked.

"As a matter of fact, you and your family, and of course, Kyna, are the friends I was referring to."

"Aha! Just tell us what to do."

They gathered around Cairdeen. Kyna stroked her long, cream-colored forelock, pulling out burrs and combing out the tangles with her fingers. "How are we going to get her to Doolin? She can't walk far on that leg."

Dune shook his head. "We'll have to mend it as best we can."

"She'll slow us down," Seamus said. "Canna we make her comfortable, and leave her here?"

"I canna leave her, any more than I could leave you."

Seamus nodded. "In that case, let's get to work."

"Kyna, will you help me set out my rune stones?" As Dune emptied the rune stones into Kyna's hands, he realized he had referred to them as *his*, not his mother's. When he returned, he would have to ask Maureen about getting his own set—not just the toys he practiced with.

After placing the stones in a circle large enough for the pony and the rest of the group, Dune chanted the protective rune that his mother had taught him. He and Seamus unwrapped the blood-soaked bandaging from Cairdeen's injured foreleg.

"We should wash the wound before re-dressing it," Kyna said.

Dune uncapped his canteen and splashed water over the wound.

The flesh and hide of Cairdeen's leg quivered as if shaking off a pesky fly, but the mare made no other complaint.

Agnes peered over Dune's shoulder. "Those wounds are quite deep. I'll stitch her up a bit."

"We've no needle or thread," Dune said.

From one of the pockets in her voluminous skirt, Agnes produced a tomato-shaped pin cushion, bristling with needles and pins, and a spool of thread.

Seamus hugged his wife tight and gave her a wet smooch on the cheek. "That's why I married you. You're so resourceful!"

"Ew," said Lucas.

Agnes selected a heavy needle and threaded it. "You'll need to calm her while I work. This will sting."

Dune stood in front of Cairdeen, and Kyna stood at her left shoulder. They both petted the pony and murmured to her reassuringly.

Agnes set about sewing up Cairdeen's wound with a precise line of stitches.

Cairdeen's hide flinched involuntarily. She raised her head and whickered. Dune pressed his cheek to hers and whispered soothingly. Cairdeen inhaled and exhaled deeply, then relaxed.

While Mrs. Greenapple worked, Kyna and Dune stroked the pony's neck and continued speaking to her in hushed voices.

"Fergus said her name is Cairdeen," Kyna said. "Did he just make that up?"

"I dunna ken, but it fits."

"How do you mean?"

"The third side of the Claddagh," Dune said.

Kyna waited for him to explain.

Dune cleared his throat. "'The parts of the Claddagh are three,'" he began.

Kyna finished for him: "'Friendship, Love, and Loyalty.'"

"Dune means 'protector,' but it also stands for loyalty," Seamus said.

"And Kyna means love," Lucas said and immediately blushed from his neck straight up to his scalp.

Dune cleared his throat. "Aye. And Cairdeen means friendship."

"Could you tear me another strip of cloth for your new friend's leg?" Mrs. Greenapple asked.

Dune removed his jacket and his jersey. He used his athame to cut another strip from his shirt.

Kyna, standing behind Dune, gasped. "Dune, your back."

"What is it?" He tried unsuccessfully to look over his shoulder.

"How long have you had that tattoo?"

"Tattoo? I've no tattoo. What is it?"

"'Tis a Claddagh," Ardeen said. At the top of Dune's spine, the unmistakable image of the Claddagh spread from shoulder blade to shoulder blade. "Are ye not supposed to get a clover tattoo, since you're a Kelly?"

Now it was Dune's turn to blush. "I've not found my magic yet," he admitted. "I've no clan tattoo."

"Dune, I think you're wrong," Kyna said. "I think you found your magic when you touched my Claddagh charm, and started having visions."

Mrs. Greenapple looked up at him. "Magic or no magic, you've earned your jewels in your crown in heaven." She finished re-wrapping the mare's leg with the clean strip of cloth. "There. That should keep down the bleeding."

"Thank you, Mrs. G.," Dune said.

He poured the last drops of water from his canteen into his hand and offered it to Cairdeen. The pony slurped the water then lipped his fingers.

The sun had sunk beneath the horizon, and a warm glow bathed the landscape. As Dune looked around at his little band, he realized that he and Kyna hadn't eaten all day. The Greenapples had probably been existing on starvation rations for a week. "I should hunt us up some tuck," he said.

"Lucas and I can help with that," Ardeen said.

Seamus stood between his two sons and patted their shoulders. "Aye, if not for these two, we'd be naught but skin and bones by now."

"The Humans barely gave us a slice of bread each day to share between the four of us," Agnes said. "The lads saved us, to be sure."

"All we need's a cooking pot," Ardeen said with a smile.

"And we can fill it with just about anything you'd care to eat," Lucas explained.

Dune scratched his chin. "Would a water bucket do for a cooking pot?"

"I think it would do the trick," Ardeen replied.

Dune jogged down the road and retrieved Mrs. Lynch's discarded water bucket. "Before you make dinner, could I bother you to conjure some more water for the pony?"

"No bother at all." Mrs. Greenapple waved her hand over the water bucket, filling it with cool, fresh spring water. Dune ladled some water in his hand and brought it to Cairdeen's lips. She drank it up, then stretched her neck to the bucket and gulped her fill.

"Is she finished?" Lucas asked. "I'm hungry."

Dune handed him the bucket. "Good luck to ye!"

"We're Leprechauns, mate," Ardeen said, chucking Dune lightly on his upper arm. "We've all the luck we need!"

Ardeen and Lucas sat on the ground facing each other, cross-legged with the bucket in between them.

"Ready?" Ardeen asked.

Lucas nodded.

They clasped hands and chanted together, "Echo, echo, prayers sent. Give us peace and nourishment."

The Rune of the Echo, but different, Dune thought.

But the boys continued with a verse that was unfamiliar to Dune. "Feed our hearts and feed our souls, warm our pot and fill our bowls."

As they spoke, smoke began to billow from under the pot. The pot itself filled with water that bubbled and steamed as it began to boil. The aroma of vegetables and herbs drifted through the air.

Dune closed his eyes and breathed in deeply. "Ahh, not even my own da's stew ever smelled that good."

"You've a knife?" Mrs. Greenapple asked Dune.

He unsheathed his athame and held it out to her, handle toward her and the spine of the blade resting between his thumb and index finger.

Instead of taking the knife, she reached once more into the pocket of her voluminous skirt produced a ball of twine. She unfurled a strand and held it out to Dune. "Cut this please. And here. And here."

Dune cut the twine as directed until Mrs. Greenapple held six, half-meter lengths.

"One more. A little longer though." she said. She measured a length of twine by holding one end up to her nose and extending her other arm straight out, spooling out string from the ball of twine. Dune cut the twine where Mrs. Greenapple indicated.

She laid each length of twine in a circle on the ground—six small circles and one larger one. She snapped her fingers and the circles of string swirled and transformed into wooden bowls, one larger than the others.

Lucas pointed at the family members, mouthing the numbers, "One, two, three…Why seven, Ma?"

"We canna eat without preparing dinner for the mare, can we?"

Lucas frowned. "I dunna think she'll eat vegetable stew."

"Right you are, my dear." Mrs. Greenapple snapped her fingers again, and the largest bowl was filled with grain and molasses.

Dune carried the bowl of sweet feed to the pony and placed it in front of her. Cairdeen whickered again, flaring her nostrils as she caught the scent. She dove her muzzle into the sweet feed and munched happily.

Mrs. Greenapple filled the other bowls with stew and passed them around.

When they had finished dinner, Seamus and the boys cleaned the bowls with leaves. Mrs. Greenapple snapped her fingers again, and all the bowls were changed back to lengths of twine, which Mrs. Greenapple twirled into a ball and slipped into a pocket.

"Right," Dune said. "Let's get the pony to the vet, and warn the others about Lynch."

Chapter 24: Return to Doolin

Travelling throughout the night, pausing when the pony's strength lagged, Dune and his group made it all the way to the outskirts of Galway before the sun rose. They gathered beside a public fountain where a marble statue of an angel smiled down at them.

Then they had a decision to make.

"Do we keep going in daylight?" Dune asked. He dipped his canteen into the water in the fountain.

"The lads are tired," Agnes said.

"Aye, we all are," Seamus agreed. "Dune, you and Kyna go on. We'll stay here with the pony until nightfall, and catch up."

Dune shook his head. "I'll not leave you behind. I'll not leave any of you behind. We either all keep going, or we all stay and rest."

"We can keep going," Ardeen said. He filled his canteen and motioned to his brother to do the same.

Lucas filled his canteen, then took a long swig as he nodded in agreement.

Cairdeen put her muzzle to the cool water in the fountain basin and drank deeply.

Mrs. Greenapple took her husband's hand. "If the lads can handle it, so can we."

"Then it's settled," Dune said. "We'll keep to the back roads as much as possible."

They trudged on for six hours, stopping in the heat of the day under a weeping willow. Dune and Kyna placed the rune stones in a circle for protection and they all rested. Lucas and Ardeen prepared a light snack that could be cleaned up quickly in case Humans approached.

Then they continued their trek. Hours later, dusk was upon them as they paused at the top of the cliff overlooking Doolin. The sapphire sea crashed against the cliffs far below, where the harbor lights twinkled. The sea breeze carried the bell-like chimes of the boats swaying in their moorings.

They cautiously made their way down the sandy trail to the large triangular boulder that marked the entrance to the Hidden Harbor. Beyond the boulder, the leaves of the thickly packed alder trees glowed red in the last rays of sunset.

Dune rubbed his hands together and breathed into them to warm his palms. He stepped forward and laid one hand on the limestone landmark. "Echo of the Kelly clan, Echo in the son, a man. Let us pass, then close the door, hidden to the world once more."

The alder wood stood just as before.

"Nothing happened," Lucas said. "I thought the arrow rock pointed the way."

Ardeen cleared his throat. "No offense, mate, but...." His look was a mixture of doubt and embarrassment.

"Go on, mate," Dune said. "Say what you need to say."

"Your tattoo is a Claddagh. 'Tisn't the Kelly Clover."

"And?" Dune stood to his full height, following Ardeen's train of thought, but enjoying his friend's confusion.

"Could you be blocked because, well, because the rock thinks you're an outsider?"

"Nae, mate." He stepped past the boulder. "Follow me."

As they passed the boulder one by one, the scenery shifted like glass melting. The magical curtain of alder trees and scrub dissolved, revealing twin paths, one lined with cottages climbing to the top of the cliff, the other winding its way down to the hidden shore, the site of the sporting events.

"You've done it!" Ardeen clapped Dune on his shoulder. "I've never doubted you on the pitch, and I'll not doubt you off it again!"

Dune thought fleetingly of the football tournament, wondering how his team had fared without him.

"Which way?" Seamus asked.

"Ardeen and I will take the pony down to the vet. You and the others go with Kyna to find Mother Cass."

Kyna placed her hand on Dune's arm. "Be careful, Dune. The Humans might already be here."

"How could they get past Mother Cass's cloak?" Seamus asked.

"I think they might have help."

"A Leprechaun, ye mean?" Agnes shook her head. "I canna believe it."

"I dunna ken, dear," Seamus said. "When the hunters found us, they said something ... strange. Something about getting information that only a Leprechaun would know."

Dune turned to Kyna. "You be careful as well. Dunna speak to anyone until you've found the Matriarch."

"Shouldn't I warn everyone?" Kyna asked.

Dune shook his head. "You could be telling the spy."

"But what if they want to talk with the Greenapples?"

"Just tell the truth. They've got to see Mother Cass before they speak to anyone."

Before they could go any farther, the Matriarch appeared on the path, accompanied by Kane.

Mother Cass held her arms wide and grasped Dune in a tight hug. "Dune! Welcome back! I see your mission was a success."

"Aye, Mother Cass, we found the Greenapples, but there is something you must know."

The Matriarch gripped his arm in her tiny, powerful hand,

234

cutting off his words. "I will hear it in a moment. First things first."

Leaning on her cane, she walked over to Mr. and Mrs. Greenapple, embracing them and gesturing to their boys to join in a joyous group hug. "Ardeen, Lucas. Were you terribly afraid?"

"No, ma'am. Not for a moment," Lucas said.

"But we were happy as larks to see Dune," Seamus said. "He and Kyna saved our lives, to be sure."

"I was petrified," Agnes admitted. "A mother is always worried when her children are in danger."

Mother Cass nodded. "I know exactly what you mean, my dear. As you know, I've birthed no children of my own, but the members of the Kelly clan are all my children. *I* was worried, I can assure you. Even knowing Dune would complete his quest. As you say, a mother always worries."

"Mother Cass, we must tell you—"

The Matriarch cut Dune off again. "One more thing first. You must all be hungry. Or have you boys already provided sustenance for yourselves and your family?"

"We did, ma'am," Ardeen said. "And 'twas our pleasure to help out."

"Maybe you could conjure a bite for Kane, then. I've only just now run into him, and I believe he has been on a mission of his own?"

"What kind of mission?" Dune asked.

"Well, I ..." Kane looked sheepishly at the Matriarch.

"Dunna be modest, lad. You've been protecting the Clan, have ye not? Patrolling the perimeter to ensure no breaches have occurred?"

"Oh, that. Why, yes! Yes!" Kane puffed out his chest in the self-confident manner Dune was familiar with. He had seen this posture when Kane had almost crippled an opponent on the football pitch, and again after that game, when he was chatting up several attractive female spectators. Instead of being horrified by the brutish display, the girls had seemingly been impressed with Kane's prowess.

Dune glanced at Kyna, expecting to see her similarly dazzled by Kane. Instead, he noted her narrowed eyes and a sneer playing on her lips. Dune wiped away his moment of jealousy. He shook his friend's hand. "I'm glad to hear it, for we are all in danger. Some Humans are on their way here. Hunters. Somehow, they've learned of our location."

Mother Cass sat on the bench-like root. She patted the pony's side but did not take her eyes off Dune. "Tell me what you know."

"'Tis the men who captured the Greenapples. They said they were headed here."

"They told you this?"

"No, ma'am. They dinna ken we were there. We were hidden by the rune stone circle."

"Ah, Marnie has taught you well."

"Mother Cass, there's more," Agnes said. "Tell him what they said, Seamus. When they captured us."

"We had almost made it to the Great Faery Ring when they surrounded us."

"With dogs," Lucas said with a shudder.

"Aye, the two hunters and their dogs," Seamus continued. "Lynch, the leader, said he knew where to look because someone told him where we'd be."

"Only a Leprechaun would ken that," Dune said.

"And only a Kelly Leprechaun would know where the Ceili was being held," Kyna added.

Mother Cass bowed her head and shook it slowly. "That means that one of our own family has betrayed us."

Ba-rooooh! A dog's baying howl echoed through the cliffs.

"They're here," Dune said. "Will they be able to come through the curtain?"

"Not without an accomplice," Mother Cass said. She looked around at the group. "Which apparently they have."

Finbar's Irish wolfhounds, dragging their owner on the end of their leashes, burst through the brush and leapt onto the path on the other side of the limestone boulder. A moment later, Lynch stumbled up behind them and bent over, hands on his knees, gasping for air. As the dogs sniffed around the path and the boulder, Lynch regained his breath. He slung his rifle from his back and cocked it. "We're close."

"Not these spanners again," Mr. Greenapple moaned.

Dune put a finger to his lips, warning everyone to stay quiet.

Kane jumped past him, beyond the curtain. "Mr. Lynch! This way!"

Dune's jaw dropped. "Are ye coddin' me?"

Finbar pulled his dogs in and grabbed them by their collars. The snarling animals struggled to get to Kane, snapping and pawing the air with their front paws.

Lynch walked up to Kane and slapped him on the back. "Good work, Kane! Where are they?"

From the way Lynch looked around, it was obvious the curtain still held.

Kane placed his hands on the limestone rock and chanted, "Drop the curtain, open the door. Make me rich forever more!"

"No, you mustn't!" Dune tackled Kane, driving him to the ground.

But it was too late. From the other side of the boulder, Dune saw the alder wood mirage disintegrate and fall to the ground like pieces of a shattered mirror.

"What have we here," Lynch gloated. He strode past Kane and Dune to where the others stood. "Good work, Kane. There'll be a hefty bonus for recapturing this lot, more than the first time."

Dune scrambled to his feet, attracting the dogs' attention. They growled and slobbered through clenched fangs and strained at their leashes.

"Kane! So, it was you," Dune snarled. "You gave up the Greenapples. And now, you've sold us all out. The 'consulting position' you boasted about is betraying your kin for a bounty."

"Betraying them? What have any of them ever done for me? Or you yourself, even? This one job will bring me more money than I could otherwise hope to see in my lifetime."

Kyna pushed past the others and slapped Kane in the face. "I doubt it will get you many lasses, once they find out how you've earned your wealth."

"Shows what you know," Kane sneered at her. "I flashed a fistful of money at your friend Dearbhorgaill, and I could barely keep her off me."

"You're delusional. For your information, Gaill doesn't give a possum's patoot about money. She saw something in you, although I can't imagine what. I doubt she'll give you the time of day after she learns of your traitorous actions."

"Enough talk," Lynch said. He poked Dune in the chest. "You think you could steal my treasure away from me so easily? Well, I've caught them again, and now you and the lass are mine as well."

"I think not," Dune said.

"You've not much say in the matter," Lynch sneered. "We have the weapons and the dogs, and I know the Code of Erin."

"I know the Code well," Dune said. "But I know something that you do not."

"Talk, then," Lynch growled. "Why should I not turn you all into gold, here and now?

Dune thrust his hands into his coat pockets. "Do ye ken the story of the Pooka?"

"What have legends like the Pooka to do with aught?"

"For one thing, this." Dune took his fist out of his pocket and spread his fingers to reveal an item his father had given him after all, when Dune announced his intentions to find the Greenapples. "I trust you with this," Paddy had said. "But you must promise me you'll bring it home, safe and sound."

Lynch's eyes sparkled. "Is that gold?" He reached his fingers toward the golden four-leaf clover in Dune's hand.

Dune snapped his fist shut and held his hand over his shoulder, out of Lynch's reach. "Aye, 'tis gold," he said. "A present from the Pooka, and there's so much more where that came from."

Kane pushed forward. "Hey, that dinna come from a Pooka! That's the Kelly Clover."

"Get back and be whist, Kane," Dune cautioned.

"Let him speak," Lynch said. "This one, I can trust not to fill me with a load of blarney."

"Kane, remember who your family is," Mother Class said.

Kane turned on her, his face red as tears streamed down his cheeks. "'Tis *your* fault more than anyone's! Everyone can use their magic except me! How is that supposed to make me feel? I could have changed all the leaves and rocks to gold. I could have paved all the streets in all the Leprechaun towns from Sligo to Shanagarry with gold. And yet, what have I got to show for it?" He pulled a gold chain from under his shirt. A golden feather dangled from the chain. "This one golden feather I turned to gold when I was a wain. You *graciously* allowed me to keep it."

"Dear lad," Mother Cass said, shaking her head sadly, "you could have used your magic for so, so much more."

"What do you mean, Kane?" Lynch grabbed Kane by the suspenders. "You were holding out on me! Instead of wasting my time with a family of shoemakers and carpenters, I could have just taken you!"

Kane looked around at his family. "No, my magic is na as

powerful as she makes it sound."

"That old harpy? Nae, *you* are the one boasting about your magic. You should have told me about this when I first laid eyes on ye. Instead, you sold out your family. I own you now. I'll not forget how you tried to fool me, and I'll not be satisfied with some small feather made of gold."

With Lynch preoccupied with Kane, Dune took his other hand out of his pocket. There he held the rose quartz rune stone. He raised his fist to the sky and yelled, "In the name of the Danu and the Kelly Clover, protect us!"

Golden rays shot out from the spaces between his fingers. A golden dome formed like an umbrella over the small group. Only Kane was outside its protection.

Mother Cass stepped toward Kane with her hand outstretched. "Please, lad. Please come back to your family. All will be forgiven."

As Mother Cass stepped outside the protective dome, the two wolfhounds lunged forward, pulling the leashes out of Finbar's hands. In an instant they were on the Matriarch, knocking her to the ground and snapping at her as she flailed her arms wildly, trying to fend them off.

Watching from behind Kyna and the Greenapples, Cairdeen reared up on her back legs. With a whinny, she charged toward the dogs. Her ears pinned back against her head, Cairdeen kicked and stomped at the dogs and bit at them, a ferocious protector of her new-found family.

With the dogs' attention turned toward the pony, Seamus and Ardeen rushed to the Matriarch and pulled her out of the way, back to the shelter of the golden dome.

The larger dog looked up at Cairdeen and bared his teeth. The hackles rose across his shoulders as he advanced, growling menacingly.

The second dog looked scared and confused but joined its furry partner. The pair advanced on Cairdeen, snarling.

Suddenly, Cairdeen charged the larger dog, her head low like a bull's. The dog's growl turned to a whine of pain as the mare knocked him onto his side.

The second dog moved in, clamping its jaws around Cairdeen's injured leg.

The mare screamed in pain. She sunk her teeth into the back of the dog's neck. It was the dog's turn to howl. Although the dog was nearly as tall as Cairdeen, the mare picked him up by the scruff of his neck and wrung her head from side to side, then tossed him into the limestone boulder.

The first dog was back on his feet. In a flash, he snapped at the pony's flank, but instead, Cairdeen's hooves connected with his side.

The dog yelped as he rolled with the impact. He stood and shook off the sting. Now both dogs advanced. The larger dog lunged at the mare's withers, knocking her to the ground. The second dog moved in, latching its jaws on Cairdeen's injured leg. Both dogs seemed to realize it was her weakness.

Dune handed the rose quartz to Kyna. As soon as he was sure the dome would remain intact, he ran to assist Cairdeen. He brandished his athame, but with all the thrashing about of the pony, he dared not try to stab the dogs for fear of wounding the mare. All he could do was yell to Kyna, "Can you help?"

Kyna stood like a warrior, spreading her arms wide with clenched fists. Holding the rose quartz tight in her right hand, she thrust her left hand open, revealing the Claddagh charm with its broken chain wrapped around her fingers. As she swung the charm in an arc over her head, it emitted a plume of jet-black smoke that swirled in the air.

The ground shook below their feet.

The cloud from Kyna's Claddagh charm expanded and

changed shape until it formed a huge black dragon.

It was the same dragon Kyna had conjured in the forest by the Great Faerie Ring, but this time, Dune saw it from the front. It made his blood run cold. Its face was like a horse's face, except that it had long, sharp fangs and coal-red eyes. It opened its mouth and roared.

"'Tis the Pooka!" Finbar cried. "'Tis going to eat us!"

The dogs looked up in alarm at the apparition. They released Cairdeen from their jaws. Whimpering, they tucked their tails and ran off, disappearing down the dirt path without a backward glance.

"Run for your life, Mr. Lynch!" Without waiting for his boss, Finbar took his own advice and fled behind his dogs.

The pooka/dragon blew one last blast of fire after them and dissipated into thin air.

Kyna's hands trembled, but she held firm to the rose quartz, and the dome held. "Come back inside the shelter," she called.

Dune knelt by Cairdeen while Kane backed away from Lynch.

"You think we're through here?" Lynch jabbed his rifle at Kane. "We've still a score to settle."

"Nay, I'm through with you." Kane grabbed Lynch's rifle. "Goibniu of the Iron Mountain, I call on you!"

Sparks flew from Kane's hand where he held the rifle. The sparks ran up the length of the rifle, shocking Lynch on the other end. The weapon turned to solid lead and dropped to the ground with a thud.

"You thick gobdaw." Lynch flexed his hands, forming fists then claws. "You dinna even turn it to gold."

"I dinna call to Creidhne, the goldsmith. I called to his brother, who is equally talented but would give me lead. I dinna want to provide you anything of value."

"You still have value to me."

Dune realized what Lynch was up to. He scrambled to his feet and ran to the dome. "Kane! Get inside the dome!"

Kane suddenly knew Lynch's intentions as well. He ran toward Dune.

Before Kane could reach the protection of the dome, Lynch bellowed, "Shillelagh!"

Kane's feet were frozen in place as if stuck in a muddy bog. With his eyes wide with horror, he saw his feet turn to gold. The transmogrification seeped up his legs. "Dune! Mother Cass! I'm sorry! I should never have betrayed my family. Please forgive me!" He ripped the gold chain from around his neck and threw it to Dune. "For Dearbhorgaill!"

Dune caught it in his fist. The golden feather tingled in his palm.

"Tell her she's beautiful," Kane screamed, his voice full of agony as the transmogrification seeped farther up his body. "Tell her she's worth all the gold at the end of the rainbow. Tell her I—" In the next moment, Kane's transformation was complete. From tip to toe, he was solid gold, an expression of sadness mixed with terror permanently etched on his face.

"No! No," Lucas sobbed. He pushed his face into his mother's side. Agnes wrapped him in her arms.

Lynch kicked the golden statue of Kane and it tipped over. When the statue came to rest on the dirt path, Lynch put his foot on it and laughed. "That's more like it."

Lucas sobbed uncontrollably, clinging to his mother.

Agnes smoothed his hair. "Shhh, laddy, shhh."

Lynch looked up. His eyes narrowed as he considered the group of Leprechauns within the golden bubble.

Dune kept the bubble intact with the rose quartz stone and Kane's golden feather gripped tightly in one fist, the Kelly Clover in the other.

"Ye can't stay there forever," Lynch said. He sat on the root near the limestone rock. "I think I'll just wait right here until your magic crumbles."

Dune and Kyna exchanged a glance. Dune knew they could take turns holding the bubble in place, but sooner or later, someone would come looking for Mother Cass, and they would meet the same fate as Kane. And if no-one came, they would have to go in search of medical assistance for the injured old woman.

"Mow." A little black Manx cat appeared on the path, blinking her eyes.

"Rabbit," Dune said. "Be careful."

Mother Cass, lying on the ground inside the protective bubble, raised her cane and groaned.

"Be still, Mother," Kyna said. "Please don't try to get up."

"Help me, dear. 'Tis important."

Kyna helped the Matriarch to her feet. The old woman, frail and weak from being pushed to the ground and mauled by the dogs, leaned against Kyna. "Rabbit," she whispered.

"'Tis not a rabbit, you daft old harpy." Lynch said. "'Tis a cat. But you're right—it had better be careful that I don't kick it right off this cliff."

"'Tis not a rabbit, true," Mother Cass said, her voice faint. "But 'tis not a cat, either. And you're the one best be careful."

With huge effort, Mother Cass raised her cane and swept it in an arc over her head. A brilliant rainbow formed, piercing the golden bubble and streaking toward the little cat. When the end of the rainbow touched Rabbit, she was transformed into a black cauldron full of gold coins.

An image of the Pooka turning into a pot of gold flashed across Dune's mind.

Lynch's eyes grew wide. A craggy grin spread across his face. "Gold," he muttered, reaching for the pot. As soon as his hands touched the metal, the pot transformed again; this time, into a

244

snarling badger.

Lynch jerked away.

The badger advanced on Lynch, growling, snapping her jaws, and throwing her front paws forward, slicing at Lynch with razor-sharp claws.

Lynch was at the edge of the cliff. He took one more step backward, and the ground crumbled under him. "Nooooooo!" he yelled as he plummeted into the sea far below.

Chapter 25: Rabbit

"Rabbit? Rabbit! Rabbit!" Mother Cass called, her voice weaker and weaker.

The badger sniffed the air, sniffed the statue that had been Kane, and blinked at the Leprechauns. Cautiously, she stepped into their midst, following the Matriarch's voice. They backed away to give her room.

Rabbit had a feeling that she knew the lass who supported Mother Cass's head in her lap. Behind them, a pony lay on her side, wheezing with every faint breath.

Rabbit laid her head in the young woman's lap and nuzzled the Matriarch's cheek.

"There you are, little one," Mother Cass said, her voice barely audible.

Rabbit lifted her ears. She could understand the words.

"I canna see too well," Mother Cass said. "But I feel an energy around us."

"Aye," Kyna said, noticing a luminescent circle of mushrooms. "A faerie ring surrounds us."

"Rabbit," Mother Cass said, "you have retaken your given form."

"Aye, ma'am," Rabbit said. She gasped at the sound of her own voice. "You have taken good care of me. Thank you for returning me to my true body."

"You must be the wee badger cub I rescued last year," the

blonde woman said. "You've grown up! And you're prettier'n a spckled pup. Are you all healed now?"

"Aye," Rabbit said. "I always hoped I'd see you again, so I could thank you for your help."

"I only wish I could have saved the rest of your family. I'm so sorry."

"You did what you could, and I am most grateful. You were a friendly face when I needed one. I shall be a friend to you as well, as long as I live."

Behind them, the pony whickered. "Friendly face?"

One of the Leprechauns—Rabbit had met him and knew his name was Dune—knelt by the pony. "Aye, pony, we are all friends here. Tell me, was Fergus right? Is your name Cairdeen?"

"Aye. And you are Dune, and the lass is Kyna. I have felt your names. They sound like … home." Cairdeen nudged Dune's hand. "The badger. Can she hear me?"

Rabbit crept closer to the pony and sniffed her muzzle. "Aye. My name is Rabbit. I can hear you."

"Rabbit, when you lost your family, were there dragons? And hunters who—did terrible things?"

Tears welled in Rabbit's shiny black eyes. "Aye," she whispered.

"I'm sorry to make you think of it," Cairdeen said softly.

Rabbit shook her head. "I think of it every day. 'Twas the day I became an orphan."

"Rabbit, is your father's name Canavan?"

The badger took in her breath. It was the first time she had heard that name in over a year. "You knew him?"

"I *know* him. You are not an orphan." The pony paused to catch her breath. "He is alive, and has been searching for you ever since that day."

Rabbit bounced on her front paws. "He's alive! Thank Danu,

my father's alive! Where is he? Can you take me to him?"

The pony whickered happily. "Perhaps not today." With another whicker, she dropped her head to the ground, exhausted.

"We have to get her wounds treated first," Dune said.

Rabbit ceased her happy dancing. "Yes, of course. And Mother Cass as well."

"'Tis too late for me," Mother Cass said, her voice a raspy whisper. "The Banshee is calling my name."

Chapter 26: The Journey

Dune smoothed his hand across the pony's muzzle, then rose and walked to the Matriarch. He took a knee next to her and gently placed her hand in his. *So small, so frail,* he thought. "Can you hear me, Mother Cass?"

The Matriarch opened her eyes. They were glassy and so pale blue that they were almost invisible. "I heard the Banshee, crying for me."

"Nae, 'twas not the Banshee," Dune said quietly. "'Twas a dragon Kyna conjured."

In the fading twilight, Dune could almost see the old woman's heartbeat fading, her spirit fighting to break free of its mortal cage and fly away like a bird. "Forgive me, Mother Cass. I've banjaxed everything."

"Nae, lad," Mother Cass said, her voice fading. "You have acted in a good and honorable way today. You've completed your quest. You've taken on a great responsibility, a man's work. A leader's work."

"But, Mother Cass, I could na protect Kane. Because of me, he has been turned…turned to—" Dune's voice trailed off, unable to put the horrible truth into words.

"You are a good and honorable person," Mother Cass continued. "Because of your kindness to Kane, his heart was changed. His soul was saved. Rest assured, 'tis not locked in that golden sculpture."

"But because of me, here you are in this grave condition."

"I am but at the end of one journey, the beginning of another." Mother Cass's voice was as quiet and soft as a butterfly's wing. "A new journey awaits you, too, Dune."

Dune shook his head. He wiped the back of his hand across his face, not caring if anyone noticed the wetness on his cheeks. "I'd rather take a journey to anywhere in the world than have to tell my da I've let him down, that I've let you down, let down the whole Clan."

Mother Cass lifted herself into a sitting position, still leaning against Kyna. "You saved your Clan with your quick thinking and powerful magic. You should be proud of who you are. *I* am proud of you." A smile played on her lips. She looked like she would laugh if she had the strength. "Ah, Dune, you dunna understand 'journey' any more than your father does."

"What kind of journey do you mean, Mother Cass?"

"'Tis your life journey, Dune. 'Tis a man you are now, and bringing the Greenapples home safely is just one page in your life's story. Are you ready for the next page?"

He wasn't at all sure what she meant. "The next page, ma'am?"

The old woman looked around, but Dune thought her sight must have already failed her. Her strength and, indeed, her life might not be far behind. "Kyna? Where is Kyna?"

"I'm here, Mother Cass." Kyna squeezed the old woman's shoulders.

"Ah, yes. Of course. Is everyone within the Faerie Ring?"

"All except the Greenapples."

"Then they've not been able to hear the badger and the pony. They are surely wondering what is going on. Seamus?"

"Yes, Mother?" He stepped forward.

"Seamus, listen to my words. Listen carefully, so you may tell the rest of the Clan what I am about to say."

"Yes, Mother Cass."

"Kyna, heart of my heart's heart, granddaughter of my dear Chriona, your journey begins today as well. Are you ready?"

"I am ready, Mother." Tears streamed down Kyna's cheeks.

"Ready for what?" Dune asked.

"And Cairdeen? Can she come before me?"

"She's down," Dune said. "She's badly injured."

"Whistle her up," Mother Cass told him. "She'll come to you."

Dune walked to the pony and rested his hand on her side. "Come on, girl. Try to get up."

The pony cocked her head at the sound of Dune's voice. Her tiny, triangular ears stood up alertly.

The pony heaved up on her left front knee, then straightened her back legs, and finally rose, quivering from the effort. She held her right front leg so the hoof did not touch the ground. Leaning against Dune for support, the mare hobbled to Mother Cass.

Mother Cass drew a rasping breath, obviously in pain. "Dear friend Cairdeen," she said.

"Aye, Grandmother," the pony said, a soft lilt in her voice that spoke of her days as a foal in Seafield.

Seamus, now standing within the faerie ring, looked surprised that he could understand her. "Tap me with a crayon and call me a rainbow," he said. "I've witnessed the power of the Great Faerie Ring. My family and I've received its gifts, to be sure. But magic in a circle of mushrooms? I always thought that was, well, a faerie tale."

"Like Leprechauns?" Cairdeen said with a whicker.

Mother Cass chuckled. "You might not even yet realize what fate brought you to this spot, Cairdeen, to this high meadow, to me. Fate it was that brought you to Dune and Kyna, and 'tis your fate to stay with them, to help them as much as you can, and mostly, to be their friend and companion."

"You dinna have to tell me, Grandmother. I feel it in the wind in my mane and ... deeper. The very bones in my body tell me that I was meant to be with them."

"Let me feel your breath on my hand, Cairdeen."

The pony stretched her neck low and brushed her velvety muzzle against Mother Cass's hand.

"Are you ready, my friend?"

"I—I dunna ken, Grandmother. I've come up lame from the biting wire and from fighting the dogs."

Mother Cass turned her head so it rested on Kyna's shoulder. "Do you see my walking stick, dear?"

Kyna found the stick on the ground and handed it to the Matriarch.

Cairdeen shied at the sight of the stick. Her hide twitched across her withers.

"Now, now, lass. I'll not hurt you. This cane has only ever been used for the good of the Clan. Dune and Kyna will get you to the help you need, but first I must impart the blessings of the Clan."

"I understand, Grandmother."

"Come close."

Cairdeen took a wobbly step and leaned her head forward.

Mother Cass gently held the walking stick against the pony's neck. She closed her eyes and chanted,

> *The parts of the Claddagh are three:*
> *Friendship, love, and loyalty.*
> *You are the one we shall call Friend*
> *The one on whom the Clan can depend*
> *To always be there, come what may*
> *To lead, to follow, to find the way.*

Mother Cass opened her eyes and smiled at Cairdeen. "Just two more blessings."

With Dune's help, Cairdeen backed away.

"Kyna," the Matriarch said, "come 'round in front of me."

Kyna shook her head.

"Kyna," Mother Cass said again.

"I'll support the Matriarch," Seamus said. He took Kyna's hand and helped her rise. "You do as she wants."

Kyna stood before the old woman, clutching her Claddagh charm in trembling hands. "I'm here, Mother. You should rest. Don't try to talk."

The old woman shook her head. "I've not finished what I need to say."

"You're not going to die." Kyna shook her head. "You're not."

"Yes, child, I am. Now give me your hands."

Kyna dropped to her knees in front of the Matriarch and bowed her head. Waterfalls coursed from her mountain-blue eyes, but she held out her hands as the Matriarch instructed, palms cupped. The Claddagh charm rested there, its broken chain wrapped around Kyna's fingers.

Mother Cass grasped Kyna's hands. She rubbed the Claddagh charm with her thumbs and smiled. "Ah, my dearest. You are more ready than you know." The old woman took a deep, rattling breath. In a reedy voice, she chanted,

> As the wind blows, as the cow lows, my heart knows, 'tis time to go.
> The sunset fades, the egret wades, the purest of maids, makes my heart glow.
> Be true to your heart, follow its spark, make a fresh start, as the new Matriarch.

Kyna's eyes widened. "The new Matriarch? Are—are you sure?"

Mother Cass patted Kyna's hands. "Very sure."

Kyna choked back her tears and took a deep breath. "I will proudly serve and honor you, Mother Cass."

"When I have gone, take my cane," Mother Cass continued. "'Twill serve you as it has served me."

Kyna nodded and kissed Mother Cass's hands.

"And now, Dune," Mother Cass whispered. "The final blessing."

Kyna stepped back and Dune took her place before the woman who had led the clan for over one hundred years.

"Ma'am." He knelt, bowed his head, and scrunched his hat in his hands.

Mother Cass placed her feather-light hand on his head. In a thin voice like the song of the wind being carried across the rugged Irish cliffs and out to sea, she chanted,

> *Echo of the Kelly clan,*
> *Echo in the son, a man.*
> *Guard your kin, protect the gold,*
> *Fulfill the promise long foretold.*
> *Leader and protector, true,*
> *Long is the journey ahead of you.*
> *Keep the Relic close at hand.*
> *Use it as you lead your Clan.*

She dropped her hand, exhausted. Her eyelids drooped and her chest fluttered as faintly as a dying bird's.

Dune pondered her words. *Relic*, she had said. Not *Clover*. "Mother Cass, did you—did you just name me Keeper of the Clover?"

"Nae, Dune." She shook her head without opening her eyes. "You dinna listen."

"Oh." Dune sighed. His shortcomings had cost him the chance to stand as a partner with Kyna in the leadership of the Clan. "I'm sorry, Ma'am. I understand."

"Nae, Dune, you do not understand. Your job is Keeper of the *Clan*. 'Tis far more responsibility than just looking after a relic."

"Ma'am?"

"When you travel with your family, where do you stand?"

"We walk in a line, single file."

"Are you at the front of the line? In the middle?"

"No, ma'am. I always take up the rear. My da is in front. He is the leader."

"Is he?" The old woman raised her head to look at Dune. Her eyes, though clouded with age, injury, and the effort of bestowing blessings, nonetheless twinkled.

Dune stared at her, not knowing how to respond.

"And when you were returning to Doolin with the Greenapples," Mother Cass paused for a deep, rasping breath. "Where were you then?"

"Sometimes in the front, sometimes in the back. Wherever I felt I was most needed."

"Have you seen shepherds with their flocks?"

"Aye."

"Sometimes, the shepherd walks in front, to forge the way for the flock." Mother Cass's eyes were piercingly clear. "Sometimes, the shepherd moves his flock from the rear—."

The old woman broke into a spell of coughing and wheezing.

Seamus placed a hand on her back, but the Matriarch waved off the assistance.

"Paddy needs you last in line to protect your family from the rear. Do you not realize your father puts you there because he kens he can depend on you?"

Dune's eyebrows shot up and his eyes widened. "My da? He

depends on *me?*"

Mother Cass chuckled. "Aye, Dune. Everyone knows it but you."

Dune exchanged a glance with Kyna. She was crying silently, letting the tears flow in rivers down her cheeks and dribble off her chin. He took her hand and squeezed it.

Cairdeen stepped between them and nudged their hands. They both laughed and stroked her mane and neck.

"Dune, this day you become not only the Keeper of the Clan's relic, which your father will present to you before the new day dawns."

"Ma'am, I have it already. 'Tis what helped me defeat Lynch."

"Ah, yes! Paddy made the right choice by entrusting it in you. After the official ceremony, where he passes it to you officially, it will change form. Just as I soon will. When the time comes, many years from now, you will bestow responsibility for the Clan's relic upon someone else. But from this day forward, until you yourself change form into stardust, you will be the Keeper of the Clan."

She closed her eyes and took several shallow breaths, then opened her eyes again and looked at the three faces before her — Dune, Kyna, and Cairdeen. "You three, you are the Claddagh. *Cairdeas, Grá, Dílseacht.* Friendship, Love, Loyalty."

Mother Cass fell silent yet again, exhausted. "Remember," she continued, struggling with every word, "and I say this to all of you gathered here as well as the rest of our family. My essence, my soul, my love will be with you always, even when I have left this vessel. It is time."

She patted her hollow chest, leaned back against Seamus, and sighed.

All was silent except for the night birds, calling as they winged their way through the air.

Mother Cass's head drooped, her eyes closed. One hand rested in her lap, and the other hand fell to her side, dropping the walking stick. The carving of the old man closed its eyes and the glow ebbed until it was little more than the last ember of a dying fire.

"Grandmother is gone," Cairdeen said.

"Oh, no! No!" Kyna fell to the ground beside Mother Cass's body. She wept silently, her back racked with her sobs.

Dune stepped to her side and stroked her back. "Kyna, please dunna cry. Mother Cass has finished one journey and started her next."

He helped Kyna get to her feet, and she buried her head in his chest, weeping.

He spoke gently, his lips a breath away from her hair. "This is our next journey, too. We must be strong. 'Tis our promise to Mother Cass, and our responsibility to the Clan."

Kyna pulled away, wiping the tears off her face. "Yes. Yes, of course." She looked around at the small group: Mrs. Greenapple, her boys huddled close to her. The pony, injured but standing bravely. Dune, claiming both his strength and his sorrow. And Mr. Greenapple, cradling the body of Mother Cass. Kyna leaned down and picked up the Matriarch's staff—hers, now. As she curled her fingers around the wood, a bright glow spread from her hand to both ends of the cane. The visage of the old man opened his eyes and smiled at her.

"Lay her down, please, Mr. Greenapple."

Seamus did as Kyna asked, gently laying the body on the ground and placing the woman's hands upon her shallow chest, then joining Agnes and the boys.

Kyna kissed the wooden visage of the old man. The staff's glow became even brighter, bathing them all in a golden light. Kyna waved the staff over Mother Cass's body. The wind swirled and the glow spread, enveloping the body in a dazzling aura. A column of golden light rose from Mother Cass's chest, swirling as it ascended and transforming into a sparkling, golden four-leaf clover.

"The Kelly Clover," Seamus Greenapple whispered in awe.

"'Tis beautiful!" Lucas said.

Slowly, the image rose, higher and higher, until it disappeared into the sky like a star at dawn. "Her essence, her soul, her love," Kyna said quietly.

"Have left her body, but are still with us," Dune said.

Chapter 27: Endings and Beginnings

Dune called the Kelly Clan together to share the good news that the Greenapples had been rescued, and the sad news that Mother Cass and Kane had died in the fight with the hunters. Dune had first spoken with Kane's parents, sharing with them that their son, although he had made a horrible mistake in betraying the Clan to the hunters, had been brave and honorable at the end.

Kyna asked if she could be the one to give the golden feather to Gaill, and Dune agreed. He knew it would be more meaningful for Gaill's dearest friend to bestow Kane's gift—and relate the message, Kane's last words.

As the members of the Kelly Clan grieved Mother Cass, they also celebrated, telling tales of how much she had meant to them. They listened with rapt attention as Seamus Greenapple described his family's ordeal. They cheered when Seamus recounted the daring rescue.

Then it was time to share the Matriarch's final instructions.

"Before she passed, Mother Cass gave three blessings," Dune said. "She made our new friend, the Connemara pony Cairdeen, an official member of the Kelly Clan. She will be a steadfast friend to us all."

Fionn edged her way to the front of the crowd. "You have a pony?" she asked. "Where is she?"

"She was hurt helping save Mother Cass," Dune said. "But Doc Montgomery is taking care of her."

"What were the other blessings?" someone called from the crowd.

"Next Mother Cass passed the title of Matriarch to Kyna. She bequeathed her the staff that was a gift from her goddaughter, Kyna's great-grandmother. And she made me Keeper of the Clan."

"Dunna ye mean Keeper of the *Clover?*" Kane's father, Senan, demanded.

"Nae, sir. She was quite adamant that I was to do more than guard a relic." He noticed Paddy's eyebrows furrow. "Not that guarding a sacred relic is a minor responsibility," he added quickly. "She told me recently that the Keeper of the Clover is a very important role. I only meant that times are changing. Our world is changing. The leadership of the Clan is changing."

A voice in the crowd called out. "And you are that leader? We appreciate all you've done, Dune, but how do we ken Mother Cass wanted you to be our new leader?"

"I was there," Seamus said. "Mother Cass told me to listen to what she said, so I could bear witness."

Senan pushed through the crowd. "How can we believe *you?* Who knows what deal you and Dune have agreed to? After all, you let my lad be turned to gold, right in front of you!"

"Sir, I tried to help him, but he—" Dune's voice cracked. His heart broke for Kane and his family, even though Kane had turned traitor on the entire clan. Dune had forgiven Kane, but Senan was in pain, lashing out in an attempt to reconcile his son's death.

Agnes Greenapple stood toe to toe with Senan. Her whole body shook with anger as she poked Senan in the chest, punctuating her words. "If not for Dune, the lot of us would have suffered the same fate. Not just my family and me. All of us here." She swept her hand in a broad gesture encompassing every member of the Kelly Clan gathered on the beach at the Hidden Harbor.

Dune touched her shoulder. "'Tis okay, Mrs. Greenapple. Mother Cass said there would be a sign. The Kelly Clover would take on a new form." He turned to his father. "Sir, would you please place it in my hands?"

Paddy reached into his vest pocket to retrieve the golden relic. Before all the members of the Kelly Clan who had gathered on the beach, the Kelly Clover glowed with an intensity never before seen. Paddy passed the relic, and the responsibility it represented, to his son. As he dropped the golden shamrock into Dune's hands, the aura exploded in a wave of energy.

When the flash subsided, there in Dune's hands lay the transmogrified relic. He held it high so all could see. "The Kelly Claddagh. Our clan's new symbol, signifying our three values, and the vow Kyna, Cairdeen, and I make to you all: The parts of the Claddagh are three: Friendship, Love, and Loyalty."

The crowd erupted in cheers and applause. Gaill rushed to Kyna and embraced her in a warm hug. When she stepped away, Kane's golden feather, hanging from a gold chain around Gaill's neck, glinted in the sun.

"Tonight, we celebrate," Dune said. "The first Ceili of the Claddagh will be held!"

***

"Are ye ready to go, Son?" Paddy asked. He held his chin up so Maureen could straighten his bow tie. She patted his shoulders and turned him around to face the mirror. He buttoned his vest and gave the points a tug.

Dune locked eyes with his father's reflection. He had never seen Paddy look so … relaxed. It wasn't his spiffy attire, or the new haircut Ayne had given him earlier. It was more like relief. Dune realized that he would surely be inheriting his father's worries along with his new role of protecting the Clan, but for tonight, he felt only happiness. "You go on," he replied. "I've got a stop to make on the way."

Fionn, whose hair was being braided by Ayne, pulled away and rushed up to Dune. "You're going to the vet's, aren't you? Can I come with you? I want to see the pony. Please?"

Dune bent down on his haunches, eye to eye with Fionn. "Not tonight, little one. But I'll tell her you said hello."

"And give her this for me." Fionn wrapped her arms around Dune's neck in a tight hug.

"I will that."

Dune found the vet in the barn by the pony paddack. He was in one of the box stalls, kneeling beside Cairdeen, listening to the pony's breathing and heartbeat through a stethoscope. As Dune approached, he heard a soft snort from the corner of the stall. Rabbit, now in her true form, wriggled her nose at Dune.

The vet looked up, smiling when he saw Dune. He removed the stethoscope's ear pieces and hung the instrument around his neck.

"Should you na be at the Ceili, then, Dune?" the vet asked.

"I needed to stop by to check on her first. How is she?"

"Sleeping soundly. The surgery went well."

Dune stared at Cairdeen's right front leg. It was shaved from the shoulder to just above the knee. Thick bandaging hid the leg from the knee down. He took a step toward her, then dropped to his knees. "What a brave little pony." When he looked up at the vet, his eyes were glossy. "Can I touch her? I will na wake her, will I?"

"You can touch her, but not her leg. She's sedated, so you will na disturb her."

Dune put his hand on the pony's sorrel flank. He felt her breathe in and out. "My friend," he whispered, "I'll be waiting for you when you wake up." He lingered at Cairdeen's side for several minutes, watching her long auburn lashes flutter in her sleep.

Then, he knew, he had to leave. Kyna and the rest of the Clan would be worried. He stood and shook the vet's hand. "I'll be back in the morning. Will you send word if she wakes before I get here?"

"Of course. And Dune, she's not the only one who's brave."

Dune nodded briskly, unaccustomed to accepting compliments, at least outside the football pitch.

He strode down to the beach, guided by the light of a dozen bonfires and the jaunty notes of fiddles and flutes. Dozens of his kinfolk twirled and laughed, while others watched the dance, clapping in time with the music.

He spotted Brian, his football team's captain, standing with several of his other teammates by one of the bonfires, and went to join them.

Brian clapped him on the back. "I guess you heard the final ended in a draw," Brian said.

"I'm sorry I could na be there to help out."

"You dolt," Brian said, not unkindly. "'Tis only a game! What you did, well, that was life-changing!"

"To be honest, I'm still trying to wrap my head around it all. Say, who'd you get for keeper?"

"Benji here did the honors."

"Got quite a knock on my head, too, thank you very much," Benji said. He rubbed the back of his head and immediately winced.

"So, you'll not be wanting the job permanently?" Dune asked.

Benji laughed. "Not a chance."

Brian narrowed his eyes at Dune. "You're not thinking of giving up the game, with your new responsibilities and whatnot. Are you?"

"I could never quit the team," Dune assured his mates.

The music stopped and the dancers clapped with appreciation for the band.

A breeze picked up, carrying the salty aroma of the surf, and another fragrance Dune recognized. A mixture of jasmine and some other aroma. He turned and saw Kyna walking toward him.

"Hello," he managed to say before a huge smile spread across his face, stemming the flow of words.

"Hey," Kyna replied. "I love this next song. Come dance with me."

"But they've not started playing another song. Is this another bit of your magic?"

Kyna laughed. "Much as I'd like to think so, no. I just asked the band to play it."

She pulled Dune to the beach where they joined the other revelers as the band started playing "The Crawdad Song."

"I'm not a great dancer," Dune apologized.

"Just pretend you're on the football pitch, where it's well known your feet are magic!"

Holding hands with each other and the dancers next to them, they formed a large ring that undulated like waves, swooping in toward a bonfire, then skipping back out, all the while bobbing up and down and circling round and round. After several passes, Kyna pulled Dune out of the dance and they walked together in the wet, hard-packed sand at the water's edge. Soon the merry voices of the Ceili drifted away, and the only sounds were the waves lapping the shore, the bells chiming on the boats moored in the harbor, and an occasional trill from a nightbird flying past.

"Where did you learn to Irish dance?" Dune asked.

"That? That's Appalachian clog dancing," Kyna replied. After a moment, she asked, "How is she?"

Dune knew who Kyna meant. "Resting. Doc Montgomery says she'll be fine. Kyna, I—I could na have rescued the Greenapples without you. I want you to know I was wrong to try to go it alone."

"Neither one of us could have done it alone. Or without Cairdeen." Kyna squeezed Dune's hand. "You know we're in this together now, right?"

"This?"

"This life. This family. The future."

"I could na ask for a better team." Before she could object to his sports reference, Dune held her tight and kissed her.

"Nor could I, Dune," she said when their lips parted. "Nor could I."

***

Two days later, Dune and Kyna stood at the edge of the cliff overlooking the sparkling sea. Beneath their toes, the sheer grey stone dropped two hundred meters to the beach and the rounded waves of Doolin Bay. The boats tied up at their moorings bobbed and rolled on the gentle tide. A smattering of wispy white clouds glowed against the robins-egg sky.

Beside them, Cairdeen stood on her three natural legs and the steel prosthesis that had replaced her right front hoof and foreleg. The damage was too great, and Doc Montgomery had not been able to save the leg. But with a medicinal poultice Ayne prepared, the pony's injuries healed quickly.

The wind at their backs tried to steal Dune's derby hat. He clamped the hat snugly on his head.

Kyna stood so close her hair swirled in his face and her jasmine fragrance whispered around him.

"Mother Cass loved days like this," Kyna said. She held a lidded clay jug, undecorated except for a small Claddagh inlaid in gold on one side and an intricate web of black-cord netting—Mrs. Greenapple's work—wrapped around the jug from bottom to top.

Cairdeen whickered.

It was time.

Dune held the jug while Kyna untied the cord and took off the lid. Inside, Mother Cass's ashes were grey and white and soft to the touch as they both took a handful from the jug.

As soon as Dune let go of his hat to scoop up the handful of ashes, the wind seized it and sent it tumbling and dancing out, out, and away. With the jug in one hand and ashes in the other, Dune had to just let it go. "Cursed hat, I hope you're happy wherever you may land, far out to sea for all I care."

Kyna giggled and when Dune looked at her, he couldn't help laughing along with her. He thought how lucky he was to be standing here next to her.

In unspoken harmony, they flung their handfuls of ashes into the air. The particles drifted together and for a brief moment formed a golden shamrock. As quickly as the image had formed, it dissolved, and the ashes were blown away by the sea breeze.

"The Kelly Clover," Dune said. "That was Mother Cass's emblem. Our Clan's relic for two hundred years."

"I wonder how long the new symbol will stand for our Clan," Kyna said.

Again, Cairdeen whickered.

"Of course, my friend," Kyna said. She took the urn from Dune, knelt at the edge of the cliff, and shook the rest of the ashes onto the ground.

Cairdeen stepped forward, a bit wobbly on her new limb. Kyna helped the mare press her prosthetic hoof into the mound of ashes, leaving an unmistakable impression. For Dune had asked the silversmith in Doolin to embed a special image in the bottom of Cairdeen's prosthesis. As the pony lifted her hoof and stepped back, she left a perfect imprint of a heart, cradled in a pair of hands and topped with a crown. From now on, every fourth step Cairdeen took would leave the imprint of the Kelly Claddagh. Magic would shield it from unfriendly eyes.

The wind swirled and lifted the ashes in a grey cloud that drifted far out over the sea. Dune, Kyna, and Cairdeen watched until the ashes had dispersed beyond their vision.

"Ready?" Dune asked.

Kyna nodded and tucked her hair behind her ears. "That I am."

As they turned into the wind, Cairdeen nuzzled Dune's elbow, urging him to wrap his arm around her neck. She pawed the ground with her new prosthetic hoof, stamping the Claddagh in the rich soil at the top of the cliff.

Kyna stroked Cairdeen's neck. Together, the three began the long walk home.

Glossary

Ara be whist; houl yer whist. Be quiet.

Banjax. To ruin or mess up.

Barmbrack. Bread with raisins and grapes.

Cad é an ifreann? (KAHD-eh-an IF-ren). What the heck?

Cad é an scéal? (KAHD-eh-AN-schkayl). How's it going?
(Literally, What's the story?)

Ceili (KAY-lee). A festive celebration with dancing.

Claddagh (KLAH-dah). An Irish symbol consisting of a heart
cupped in a pair of hands and topped with a crown. It stands
for friendship (hands), love (heart), and loyalty (crown).

Cairdeas, Grá, Dílseacht (Care-DEE-us, Graw, DEAL-shocked").
The Gaelic words for Friendship, Love, and Loyalty.

Codding (KAHD-eeng). Kidding.

Culchie, Gobdaw, Gombeen, Spanner. Unflattering ways to call
someone an idiot.

Dog wide. Cautious.

Foostering. Wasting time, especially bickering.

Leppin' with the hunger. Hungry.

Rune (ROON). A magic spell, an ancient symbol used in spells, or
a stone or other object on which such a symbol is etched.
Runes include Ehwaz (AY-wahz), the rune of teamwork, trust,
and loyalty; Hagalaz (HAG-uh-lahz), the rune of disruption;
Ingwaz (EENG-wahz), the rune of love, harmony, and peace;
Raido (RAY-doh), the traveler's rune; and Thurisaz (THUR-ih-
sahz), the rune of chaos and conflict.

Rune Éire (Roon AIR or Roon AIR-uh). A book of Irish lore.

Spondoolicks (SPAHN-duh-lix). Slang for money or cash.

Tuatha Dé Danann (TOO-ath day DAH-nan). An ancient, magical
people in Irish mythology.

Wains. Children, especially small children.

About the Author

M.R. Street is a native Floridian who, as she writes this note, is looking out her sliding glass doors at the paradise known as Ochlockonee Bay. She loves nature and magic and found these two elements connecting in surprising and serendipitous ways while she was writing *The Claddagh*. For example, when  Kyna drew the Claddagh in the sand, Dune could see it, but Kyna waited several months to show it to M.R. The moment M.R. saw the Claddagh charm on a friend's bracelet, she knew not only the title of the story, but why it was so important to have three friends on this hero's quest. In addition to writing and publishing, M.R. enjoys being on the water, listening to the rushing creek she visits in North Carolina, reading, and doing art projects. She lives in Tallahassee and Ochlockonee Bay, Florida, with her husband, Phil, and their dog, Pilot. Her two adult children live nearby.

Acknowledgments

Every book I write holds a special place in my heart, as do the people who helped it become a reality. Always at the top of the list are my family, whose support, love, and encouragement are steadfast: Phil (even when he's snarky), Allison (who is also an artist with amazing talent, as shown in the cover art), Derek (a talented artist and musician), Jane (twin brain), and Wes (little bro). My critique group, The Cove Critters, have provided high-caliber read-throughs and feedback for more than two decades: Jan Annino, Ann Morrow, and Debra Katz. I am inspired by the members of Tallahassee Writers Association and the authors and illustrators I publish with Turtle Cove Press: Thank you all!

Other Books for Young Readers
published by Turtle Cove Press
may be found at https://www.turtlecovepress.com

*The Adventures of Surf Dude: The Dog of Ochlockonee Bay,** by Zelle
Andrews

*Betsy and Bernie: Eco-Guardians,** by Abby Hugill, illustrated by
Cody Paddack

Dahlia in Bloom,‡* by Susan Koehler

*Charlie's Song,** by Susan Koehler

*Nobody Kills Uncle Buster and Gets Away with It,** by Susan Koehler

*Queen of the Clouds: Joan Merriam Smith and Jerrie Mock's Epic Quest
to Become the First Woman to Fly Solo Around the World,** by
Taylor C. Phillips

*Blue Rock Rescue,** by M.R. Street

*The Werewolf's Daughter,** by M.R. Street

The Hunter's Moon, by M.R. Street

*So Many Animals! A Child's Book of Poetry,** Anthology by 16
authors, illustrated by Barbara Psimas

Coming soon:

The Claddagh – Book Two: The Love of the Leprechauns
The Claddagh – Book Three: The Friendship of the Leprechauns

*Award-winning books
‡Starred review, *Kirkus Reviews*

Made in the USA
Columbia, SC
23 January 2024

30057762R00157